play

for

me

Praise for Céline Keating's fiction

Play for Me is a serious, moving, and utterly delightful portrait of a woman wavering between the bonds of fidelity and the pull of desire. Céline Keating knows as much about the world of folk/rock music as she does about the workings of the he rt.

—**Hilma Wolitzer**, author of *The Doctor's Daughter*
and *An Available Man*

What draws people to music and musicians? The answer speaks to the transformative power of music and art—that which makes the difference between mere existence and a life fully savored. In *Play for Me*, Céline Keating has woven together the story of a late-life journey to explore one's authentic self. For her character Lily, music and beauty as redemptive forces prevail, despite heart-wrenching ups and downs. You need not be a music aficionado to be riveted by this eloquent tale.

—**Alan Fark**, editor of minor7th.com

In Céline Keating's auspicious debut, *Layla*, the political and the emotional collide as one generation's raison d'être—the radical politics of the '60s—becomes their offspring's burden. What results is a wrenching look at the human costs of activism and the resiliency of love.

—**Helen Schulman**, author of *A Day at the Beach*
and *This Beautiful Life*

Céline Keating's first novel, *Layla*, takes a vivid and rueful look backward from the viewpoint of the daughter of a '60s activist couple. Layla's ambivalence toward her parents and their idealism is evoked in beautiful prose and telling details. The novel brings to life the complexity of family dynamics, with all its conflicts, dangers, and rewards. The reader travels with Layla as she searches to understand her past and present and comes out of the journey wiser.

—**Nahid Rachlin**, author of the memoir *Persian Girls*
and the novels *Foreigner* and *Jumping Over Fire*

Céline Keating's deftly plotted novel takes readers on a gripping journey along the underground railroad of post-'60s radicalism. I fully empathized with Layla and her search for a father lost in history. Every adult has to reinterpret the story of her childhood. Keating beautifully demonstrates the courage it takes for each of us to face that bittersweet truth.

—**Larry Dark**, director of *The Story Prize*

In *Layla*, Celine Keating has produced a fast-moving story of family secrets, political intrigue, and a young woman's coming of age. *Layla* is a rare combination of a novel that is both suspenseful and insightful, narrated by a character who is charming, intelligent, appealing, and most importantly, honest. Her search for the truth about her father and for meaning in her own life is a gripping tale and a memorable read.

—**Con Lehane**, author of *Death at the Old Hotel*

As the Great American Nostalgia Machine works to convert the idealism and anger and, yes, the naiveté of the '60s into a cartoon of funny hair and flowery shirts, Céline Keating's novel, *Layla,* provides a strong antidote by sending her eponymous heroine on the road in quest of the realities of her parents' past. Keating keeps the pace fast and the suspense high as Layla's discoveries add up, bringing real change into her own young life. You'll want to ride with her every mile of the way!

—**Robert Hershon**, editor of Hanging Loose Press, author of *Calls from the Outside World*

Céline Keating's debut novel, *Layla*, is a triumph of political literature. With mastery, Keating has fashioned a thrilling and moving tale of a young woman forced to discover the secret history of her family. Set in contemporary time, *Layla* reaches back into the tumultuous 1960s. It's the perfect novel for anyone in search of a serious, compelling read, as informative as it is impossible to put down.

—**Marnie Mueller**, author of *Green Fires*, *The Climate of the Country*, and *My Mother's Island*

I love *Layla*. I will give this novel, a precious gift, to my friends whose psyches were shaped by the idealism, hope, and chaos of the '60s. As a student of that period, I will also beg younger friends to read this emotional page-turner. Layla's coming to terms with her parents' dangerous activism is heart-wrenching due to Keating's delightfully drawn characters. This novel also serves as a compelling lesson in our values and how drastically they've changed. It serves as a better history than any essay or screed.

—**Susan Braudy**, author of *Family Circle: The Boudins and the Aristocracy of the Left*

play
for
me

A NOVEL

CÉLINE KEATING

SWP
SHE WRITES PRESS

Published 2015
Printed in the United States of America
ISBN: 978-1-63152-972-6
Library of Congress Control Number: 2014951328

For information, address:
She Writes Press
1563 Solano Ave #546
Berkeley, CA 94707

She Writes Press is a division of Spark Point Studio, LLC.

Epigraph: "Sonnet" from THE COMPLETE POEMS 1927-1979 by Elizabeth Bishop. Copyright © 1979, 1983 by Alice Helen Methfessel. Reprinted by permission of Farrar, Straus and Giroux, LLC.

Lyrics on page 152: "Drift Away," written by Mentor Williams.

To Mark
And Merren

"I Am in Need of Music"
Elizabeth Bishop

I am in need of music that would flow
Over my fretful, feeling fingertips,
Over my bitter-tainted, trembling lips,
With melody, deep, clear, and liquid-slow.

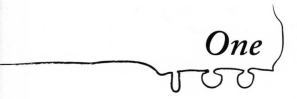

One

Lily watched her son walk away, the loose, jaunty shamble of him, the brave uptilt of his head, and felt just as she had when she abandoned him to kindergarten what seemed such a short time ago. He turned to wave, auburn hair bright in the sun, and then was gone, vanished, as if he had walked through a portal into another dimension.

"Oh, sweetheart," her husband said. Around them families bunched, kissing and parting in kaleidoscopic movement. Stephen touched her sleeve. She looked into his impish eyes and saw he felt none of her pain. In that moment she resented what she had always loved: his good cheer, his emotional maturity, his security in himself. Men!

But her son, walking into his future, was a man now, too.

"Ready to eat?" Stephen clasped her hand.

What was there to say? A son leaving home, starting college, a mother grieving—a cliché. But it was her cliché. And what she felt was not so much bereft and sad and teary, though it was all that. What she felt was drained and ugly, as if she'd been turned instantly into an old woman—sagging breasts, spindly legs, crooked back—well, it would all happen soon enough, wouldn't it?

Still. It was a storybook campus with beautiful, dove-gray stone buildings around a key lime–green quad. Colby would get a good liberal education here; he would be happy. But he would no longer sit with her at the kitchen table after school, unloading books and papers from his knapsack, as he told her about his day.

Stephen swung her hand back and forth as if to cajole her into better spirits. "That sophomore at orientation mentioned a restaurant."

Lily's stomach felt as if she had consumed the contents of her sock drawer.

"It will pass," Stephen said, in that way he had, sometimes, of reading her mind.

They jostled through people crisscrossing like random molecules, behind a couple in matching khaki slacks, blue fleece pullovers, jaunty cotton hats, the kind of couple she and Stephen—independent, strong—knew they would never be. But right now she wished they were more entwined, alike. Right now she hated feeling so alone.

"My life is empty," she said as they reached their car.

Stephen stopped short and guffawed.

"I'm serious." She didn't look at him as she unlocked the door and slid behind the wheel.

"You're always complaining you're too busy."

Her mind scrolled through images: her office, meetings of the block association, lunches. She shook her head.

"You'll feel better in a few days."

They pulled up to a timber-frame building with fading purple trim that must once have been a private residence. A hostess, who didn't make eye contact, seated them far from the bar, where body-pierced youths were making phenomenal amounts of noise. Would Colby come home at Thanksgiving with rings in his eyebrows and hair spiked like a rooster?

"In fact, you'll feel better in a matter of minutes."

He was not taking her seriously. In a matter of minutes, she was going to go from teary to cranky, and if this kept up, she'd be picking a fight in the car. She'd make a wrong turn, and they'd be lost in the Bronx, just like in *Bonfire of the Vanities,* yelling at each other. In fact, if she weren't careful, they'd be filing for divorce by morning.

"They have *croque-monsieurs*," he said and folded his arms. Case closed.

He knew her too well.

Lily woke feeling leaden, pressed down, like a chicken in an under-a-brick recipe. She had been dreaming of Colby. They were in Riverside Park, walking alongside the river, his hand in hers as small and warm as a bun. She heaved herself out of bed, her nightshirt clinging to her skin. The air was hot for late August. Stephen was gone, the bathroom still steamy from his shower. He'd made the coffee and scribbled a note on a Post-it propped against her cup.

She poured a cup and sat at the kitchen table. Moments alone in the apartment had always been precious, because at any moment Colby or Stephen would burst in. Interruption had been her way of life: broken thoughts, incompleted tasks. Now the murmuring and shuffling of a pigeon outside, on top of the air conditioner, the clicking of the refrigerator, seemed unnaturally loud. Her chest tightened, and she fumbled instinctively in her robe for her inhaler before her brain told her this wasn't asthma. These last few months she had focused so much on Colby that she hadn't realized her life was being irrevocably altered, too.

Better get moving before she collapsed into a puddle altogether.

Outside, the heat was a wet cloth covering her face, the subway platform suffocating. At least the office would be air-conditioned.

Lily had worked for MKT Productions ever since Colby was in day care. The MKT stood for Mike, Kevin, and Tom, the original owners, although only Tom was still involved. Soon everything would be totally digital, and MKT would make the transition to the new technologies, but for now they stored, edited, repaired, created, and shot footage on video. They were a small operation, which had its good and its bad sides. On the bad side, there were only eleven of them, which meant that there was a high probability at any given time that someone was getting on someone else's nerves. On the good side, everyone got to do a little of everything, from the scut work to the creative. After seventeen years, Lily was no longer challenged by making institutional videos, but she didn't consider leaving. She had long before given up the thought of looking for exciting work. In fact, she thought now, squished in the subway car, clutching her purse to her chest, she had long ago given up even *wanting* exciting work.

Was this what age did to you, she wondered—age, and having children? Stephen was a planner for New York City—a servant of the public, he laughingly called himself—feminist enough to do his share, but he was at the mercy of the mayor and the city council and a dozen others, while her job gave her much more flexibility. She had been the one to pick up Colby from school, help with homework. She thought a job that didn't demand too much was a job made in heaven.

She emerged from the subway and stopped short, shielding her eyes from the piercing sunlight. Was it only motherhood that had caused her to go from seeking challenges to avoiding them? Stephen was a parent, yet he thrived in the midst of chaos and uncertainty. She, somewhere along a line she could no longer remember, had become a creature of order, even stasis.

MKT's office was on Fifty-fourth Street between Broadway and Eighth in a building that housed a music school, an actors' studio, a costume shop, and, on the second floor, a gym. Gorgeous young people were always applying a moistened finger to their eyebrows or flexing their muscles at the security mirror inside the elevator. Lily had time to notice: She was convinced it was the slowest elevator in all of Manhattan—when it was in service at all.

Upstairs, she tossed her purse in a desk drawer. It pleased her that MKT was a small operation in a small building in the old Manhattan, the Manhattan of the garment district and seedy Times Square, before everything got glossy and sleek. The transparent partitions separating the workstations were so scarred and covered with pictures, they might as well have been cement, for all the visibility they allowed.

The office filled quickly, and against the familiar chatter of voices

4

and ringing phones she updated the status of the videos she had in various stages of production and slid the finished ones into their slots in the temperature-controlled storeroom: *HMOs for You and Me; A Day in the Life of a Longshoreman in Brooklyn, 1955.* The routine parts of the work always made her feel she was accomplishing something while she let her mind wander to important things—which class Colby would be in right this very minute, for instance. She glanced at her phone. Nothing. Should she text him? "Have a great first day!" she typed quickly. Her fingers hovered over the phone for a moment, and then she hit CANCEL. Back at her desk, she turned to one of the films she'd been putting off finishing, a twenty-minute short on the founder of a biscuit company, commissioned by his adoring wife. Lily popped it into her computer: shots of the factory, archival footage of the original 1934 building. Yawn. The wife would love it.

Close to lunchtime, an artificial chrysanthemum slowly rose over the partition between Lily's cubicle and the next and did a little jig.

"Two minutes," Lily called out.

Diana, her closest friend at the company, peeked around the partition. She had been on assignment and was dressed in her client clothes—which differed from her regular clothes in the addition of a loose-fitting jacket. Diana's answer to middle-aged weight gain was to get brighter and bolder—today, a burnt-orange top worn over flowing floral pants—while Lily took the conventional path of dressing exclusively in black.

They stopped in the bathroom before heading out, their faces registering identical grimaces as they faced the mirror. Diana slashed at her mouth with a lurid red lipstick. Lily ran her brush through her wavy gray hair, but it sprang right back out.

They headed down the street to their favorite pub-restaurant. Lily walked on Diana's right because Diana drifted left and they'd be banging elbows otherwise.

"I spent all weekend doing homework with Maggie." Diana dumped her oversize leather bag on the seat between them. "I couldn't wait to come in to work."

"Oh, that makes me nostalgic." Lily opened her menu.

"What, no romantic interlude after you dropped Colby off?"

Diana's round blue eyes lifted to hers. Lily hesitated. Should she unburden herself? Trouble her friend with her depression? Be a total bore?

"It was awful." She stirred her coffee madly. "I didn't expect to feel so—"

"Bereft?"

"Dead."

They stared at each other. Diana recovered first. "You poor thing. I can't wait until Maggie finishes high school. But of course you feel sad. Everyone does."

Lily shook her head. "This is worse. This is deeper."

Diana furrowed her brow. Lily knew she was trying to signal concern while she pondered how to be of comfort. Around them diners were settling in, rustling chairs, clinking silver against glasses, opening menus. Someone sneezed; a waiter dropped a spoon. A small pitcher of water jiggling with lemon slices arrived at their table.

"You need something to distract you. A trip! Let's plan something!"

Too late, Lily recalled why she tried not to complain to Diana. Diana loved to take problems in hand and shake them loose, like dust from a mop. Diana loved to travel, and Lily liked to stay put. When Diana brought brochures and travel books to tempt her, Lily saw beyond the beautiful vistas and mouthwatering food to the dirty bed linens and the missed trains and the sense of being totally lost and needing a policeman to help her find her mommy. Why hadn't she kept her mouth shut?

"Maybe you're right." She'd think of a way out later.

"Yes, definitely I'm right. We'll plan something."

Upon the arrival of their salads, Lily changed the topic. "What project are you working on?" She vigorously distributed the blue cheese, apples, and pecans into the chopped lettuce. She loved loved loved this salad. *How pathetic my life is,* she thought, forking a load into her mouth. The salty pecans exploded against the apples' tartness.

"Training seminar on sexual harassment."

Lily dug her fork deep into her bowl. The company would call a meeting, and they'd brainstorm about the video. There were only so many possibilities, given their limited budgets and the boundaries the clients set. She lifted her fork and stopped. Was this true of her life, too? Had she sealed herself into just a teensy-tiny existence in which to maneuver? Her elbow knocked her glass; water sloshed over her salad.

A soggy salad was not to be borne. Giving it up was unthinkable. Painstakingly, she began soaking up the water with her napkin, blotting lettuce leaves.

◄ ►

A soggy soul wasn't to be borne either, but sopping that up proved more difficult. Lily even found herself tearing up at Hallmark-card commercials.

Maybe it was only that her forty-ninth birthday was upon her. Stephen left a big box in the living room wrapped in shiny blue paper. Espresso machine? Juicer? Had she mouthed off something stupid about wanting to go on a liquid diet?

"Go on, open it." Stephen placed it in her lap. His sandy-colored eyebrows were lifted; the sprinkling of freckles across his cheeks seemed to dance.

The thick paper resisted her effort; she dug her nails in and ripped. A cardboard box with a picture of a camera was revealed. She sat back, mystified.

"A digital video cam!" Stephen removed the camera from the box. "It's not top-of-the-line, but for what you'd use it for, I thought this was just about perfect."

"Wow, this is incredible!" Why would he think she'd want a camera when she could borrow one anytime?

"You haven't been able to do anything artistic all these years. I think you've been a little bit bored. Unchallenged."

Lily knew that anyone with a real creative drive would have managed to find time.

"Now's your chance, with Colby gone."

"Thank you! I really don't know what to say. I'm just a bit stunned."

"I knew you'd be overwhelmed!" He pulled out the manual. "Let me show you a few things."

Lily had been a film student in college, but that was because it had been such a cool major. She hadn't truly been serious, had she? She couldn't remember the last time she had even thought about making her own films. Only someone serious deserved a camera this expensive. She should tell him they should return it.

"Lily?" His voice had a plea in it; his face had lost some of its animation. "I don't mean to pressure you to be arty. You can just have fun."

She moved the camera out of the way and wrapped her arms around him. "It's an amazing gift. It's so incredibly thoughtful of you." She wouldn't suggest they return it after all.

So here she was, two weeks later, lugging the camera along with her suitcase, going to visit Colby while Stephen stayed home and worked on a grant proposal. She assumed Stephen had instigated the invitation from Colby by letting on that she'd been depressed since he'd left home. The train ride was pleasant, the Hudson playing peekaboo out the window, small towns and suburbs whizzing by, and Colby at the end, reaching for her suitcase, giving her a hug, making her cry, already looking more mature than when he'd left only three weeks before. He even tolerated it when she smoothed a curl from his forehead.

"There's this cool bookstore-café where I thought we'd have lunch. I borrowed a friend's car." He loped ahead to a beat-up Volvo; the inside stank of sweat and corn chips. They drove to an area she hadn't seen before, past boarded-up storefronts and along a thread of river lined with spunky trees. In the bookstore, filled with chic, intense young people, lunch was a shared platter of hummus and vegetables and pita and olives and a slice of scrumptious spinach pie. Even the coffee was good.

Afterward, they walked around campus, and Colby pointed to

where he had classes. "Mom, you wouldn't believe how challenging and interesting the courses are. And get this—when the weather's good, we do classes outside!"

His face—like his father's, normally pale beneath his freckles—was flushed. He had always been shy, but he had found his niche, she thought. One day some perceptive girl would fall madly in love with him. With him, at least, she had not stinted; she'd done a job she could be proud of.

He shoved her gently onto a bench and handed her a card. "Happy birthday!"

She opened the card, and a ticket fell out. "What's this?"

"My surprise. Tonight, this very night, James Taylor is playing—the school is honoring him. There's another band opening."

Lily had played James Taylor songs for Colby as far back as the cradle. He liked sharing music with her, even through adolescence, when he introduced her to progressive folk singers like Rani Arbo and Dar Williams. Lily thought his taste was unusual for a boy his age, but he told her that this was what the "alt" types were into.

At her motel, just a few blocks from campus, she found herself humming "Carolina in My Mind" as she showered, remembering singing it and strumming her guitar as she pushed Colby's baby carrier with her foot. She'd had an OK voice once; she'd sung in her high school choir and been a backup singer in a local pop band. But when she became pregnant, her voice grew hoarse and wheezy. "Your body is going through changes," her obstetrician explained. "After you give birth, it might reverse itself, but right now you have asthma."

Asthma? From pregnancy? But the asthma never went away. The medication affected her vocal chords, and she was left with a limited range. It was a range that James Taylor's songs fell into, so she sang to Colby and rocked away. She joked that she had lost a voice and gained a son. It was a trade she never regretted.

When was the last time she'd gone to a rock concert? she wondered, as she walked through campus to meet Colby. Ten years earlier? Twenty? There had been a time when concerts were the high point of her life—when had that changed? She hardly listened to the radio anymore.

The auditorium was packed, loud, buzzing, working up a head of steam. Lily was suddenly aware of how much older she was than most of the audience. Not that anyone noticed or cared; she was clearly invisible. Still, she wished she had packed something dressier than her black pullover and pants, or at least brought some funky jewelry. The boys all looked so young, so . . . raw, somehow. She could almost smell the testosterone. And the girls—so pretty, so confident in their bodies. Or at least confident about showing so much. Why was it that when she was their age, slender and pretty herself, she hadn't felt that way? She slid lower in her seat.

"Hey, Mom, this is my roommate, Ian."

Tall and thin, Ian bobbed over her like a top-heavy sunflower. "Having fun?"

"Oh, yes," she said.

"It's so cool you could come." Ian seemed to genuinely mean it. In Lily's day, she wouldn't have been caught dead being seen with her parents.

The lights dimmed, and the MC came out. Lily settled back into her seat. "Here's up-and-coming folk rocker Blaise Raleigh, all the way from Colorado. Please put your hands together and give it up for Blaise!"

Onto the stage strode a small, wiry woman with spiky white-blond hair, dressed in tight leather pants and a loose, gauzy silver shirt. Her black guitar was slung low across her body, a large, ornate accessory, the strap studded with shiny, jewel-like baubles. Following her out was a slump-shouldered male guitarist with a long ponytail and a worn, raw face that looked dug out of the mountains of Appalachia. He wore a plaid flannel shirt rolled up to the elbows, revealing muscular forearms.

Without a word to the audience, Blaise said, "One, two, three," and they broke into an up-tempo rockabilly number. Blaise's voice was low and warm, with a ragged edge—like honey coarsened with salt, Lily thought, the rough, hand-harvested kind. The guitarist's voice was not as arresting but had an appealing soft quality that blended beautifully, providing just enough contrast.

Lily wiggled happily in her seat.

"Thank you, thank you all so much," Blaise said. She had a smoky speaking voice, with a trace of the Midwest. She ran her hand through her hair, spiking it more, then moved her capo one fret up the guitar neck. She came across as supremely assured, sexy. How did it feel to have the confidence to perform before such a huge audience? Lily wondered. "I'd like to introduce you to my guitarist, Jackson Johnson. Given what they named him, it seems his parents were hoping he'd end up being president, but, lucky for me, JJ had other ideas. See if you don't agree he's worthy of carrying the same initials as JJ Cale. We're going to do a love song for you now, one I just wrote, so we're a little nervous. Be nice."

The guitarist drew his pick in a diagonal line across the strings from treble to bass in a shimmer of notes, and Blaise began to sing. The song was lovely and plaintive. At the bridge, the guitarist sailed into an extended solo. Lily's spine stiffened. The guy was really good. She leaned forward. Amazingly good. She watched the play of fingers over the fret board, the seemingly effortless run of glittering notes up and down.

The performers ignored the lingering applause and charged into an R & B number. Again at the bridge the guitarist took off, but this time with a flourish of fast picking that went on through more variations than Lily would have thought possible to sustain. The crowd burst into such extended applause, they clapped over the beginning of the next stanza.

This guy wasn't just good, Lily thought, he was extraordinary. She didn't know if she'd ever seen or heard anyone better.

Their last song was a slow ballad. Lily fixed her gaze on the guitarist's hands: such supple movement, no motion wasted, every note as clear and sharp as a diamond. At the end of the song he pressed his pick into a string, bending it down and making it quiver like a drop of water before it falls, then released it.

It shot like an arrow straight to her heart.

Later, that was what she remembered. A sizzle of electricity shot through her body, and she was seared. One split second, and she would never be the same again.

Shaken, she stumbled from the concert hall, a mole surfacing into the light, and made her way to the ladies' room. She stood a moment with her eyes closed, leaning against the cool tile, until she came back to herself. In the mirror she looked flushed, so she splashed water on her face. Slowly she headed back to the auditorium to the merchandise table, where CDs were available for sale, and sorted through for Blaise Raleigh's most recent release. She looked up to see Jackson Johnson headed toward the door, pulling a pack of cigarettes from his shirt pocket. Her heart started to pound. She dropped the CD back onto the table and went after him.

He was just outside the door, lighting up. "Oh, hi!" she said, feigning surprise. "I really enjoyed your music." Close up, he was older than she had thought, possibly forty, but he had a tentative, gangly look about him, like an adolescent who didn't yet know what to do with his body. His eyes, slightly hooded, held a kind of sad, lost look. Or maybe it was the shape of the eyebrows, sloping down at the corners, that lent his face such appealing wistfulness, contrasting with its dug-out-of-the-earth aspect that made her aware of the bones under the skin, of something elemental.

"Thanks." He took a puff, offered her the pack. Camels.

"You should give those up."

"Yeah, I know," he said, sounding sheepish. He looked away, then lifted his chin, revealing a thick, muscular neck, and took a deep, lusty drag. "I've been meaning to."

"No time like the present," she said. What was the matter with her? It was that lost look that emboldened her.

He stared at her for a long moment, as if really seeing her. Her heart thrummed in a peculiar way. She noticed his eyes were hazel, green with flecks of gold.

He leaned in closer, holding her gaze, and pressed the pack of Camels into her hand.

"OK."

12

"OK what?"

"I quit." He yanked the cigarette from his mouth and stomped it with a black cowboy boot. "Thanks." He did a little bow, then began to walk away.

"Wait." She clutched the pack, not sure what to do with it. "Wait! Do you have any CDs—of your own playing?"

He turned back to her. "Yeah, one, but"—he shrugged—"I forgot to bring copies."

"Can I get it on Amazon?"

He threw his head back, laughing. "You're kidding, right? I just sell it at gigs."

The lights flickered on and off to signal that intermission was over.

"You're so good, you really should have your CD out there," Lily said, following him back inside.

"Blaise has a website; it's available there. Thanks again for your interest."

She watched him walk away in an unhurried, slouchy glide. The house lights flickered again. Reluctantly, she headed to her seat. She started to toss the Camels into a garbage can, then stuffed them into her purse. She spotted Colby chatting with two glossy-haired young women a few rows away. One stood and stretched, revealing a taut, tanned midsection. Suddenly Lily wanted—wanted so badly her bones ached—to be young like that again.

James Taylor's set seemed tame compared with the excitement of JJ's playing. Afterward, she and Colby headed outside into the warm fall air. There was a musty smell of fallen leaves, decay, a hint of woodsmoke from a nearby fire. She hugged Colby, felt the knobs of his spine through his thin cotton shirt. "What a fantastic birthday gift."

"Isn't this the greatest?" He spread his arms. Lily was thrilled to see him filled with the joy of being young and on his own for the first time, the whole world at his feet. So why were her eyes stinging?

As she followed him through the throng, voices wafting disembodied in the night, she felt unsettled, restless. They paused to watch a group of girls who were linking hands and flinging themselves around in an impromptu dance. Lily suddenly felt the urge to join in, to do something heedless and wild, to race through the dark as if on fire, feet barefoot on cool, slippery grass.

She wanted a second chance, a chance to do it all over. An extra life. A whole separate extra life. And she wanted it desperately. Greedily.

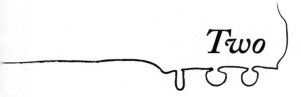

Two

On the train ride home the next afternoon, Lily felt overcome. There was an ache behind her breastbone where the notes of the guitar had pierced, as if they had done permanent damage, shifted her very DNA. Yet the feelings were also intoxicating, an intense itchy longing she was bursting to satisfy. This was all very strange. Was there a long-buried artistic urge inside her that she had somehow failed to notice? Was it that she wished she could have been a singer, could have been Blaise, with her low, sexy voice and thin, tanned arms? Would she want to be stomping around on a stage, wowing an audience? Or was it that she wished she'd studied music and were Jackson Johnson? She looked up with a frown from her magazine, which she was covering in doodles. The man opposite, sensing her intensity, gave a start. He resembled the Pillsbury Doughboy, his soft, round body demanding to be poked.

She turned to the window and the world rushing by—backward, as it happened. She had positioned herself to face away from where she was headed. Did this mean something? The concert had left her feeling even more off-kilter, her life as backward and blurry as the scenery. Had Colby's leaving home made her susceptible to the psychic force of the music, the way a weakened tree is vulnerable to lightning? How could a life feel basically satisfying one day and then, so suddenly, unsatisfactory? Was there some kind of equation at work, she wondered, as houses and telephone poles and trees flew backward, a mathematical formula that demanded a new variable be added every so often to keep things fresh?

Satisfying life = constant + constant + x (where x = freshness variable)?

Lily sighed. What was her problem? Stephen obviously sensed she had one and believed that his camera would help her solve it. He thought she needed a creative outlet.

Thank goodness she had remembered it—or, rather, Colby had. She'd left the camera behind in his room, and they'd had to go back for it and then do a perfunctory clip so she had something to show Stephen.

Stephen. Smart as a whip, reliable, responsible. Everything a woman would want in a man. Everything she wanted, appreciated, was totally grateful for.

Why was she going on this way, as if she were arguing with someone? She had a wonderful, enviable life. There was nothing whatsoever wrong with her life.

She squirmed, did a few neck rolls. "Your mother," Stephen had once said to Colby, "was a free spirit, so talented and artsy. I never thought I'd make her mine."

"I wasn't!" Those had been what passed as her wild days; she'd been a girl who stayed up late to party, walked barefoot on campus.

"She was," Stephen continued to address his words to Colby. "She looked like one of Titian's young girls, with the flowing curls and those sweet, soft cheeks."

"It was only that I had long hair and carried a guitar and had a tattoo." She had been imitating her favorite cousin, Renée, who had danced in the rain at Woodstock and carried protest signs at demonstrations. So what if all that was long over by the time she got to college?

"Where's the tattoo?" Colby had asked.

"Never mind." The stargazer lily was hidden just below her underwear line.

16

Even so, she liked that Stephen thought of her as creative. Of course she liked that. She just had so many enthusiasms when she was young; she tended to get excited by things. Stephen was drawn to that in her. But she knew down to her very core how ordinary she was. She lacked drive, and she lacked talent. But if there was one thing of which she was confident, it was that she could recognize real originality and talent when she saw it. She did not have it. That guitarist, though. He had it.

She felt a sharp stitch in her side and teared up. What in the world was the matter with her? She turned back to the backward scenery. They were in Yonkers now, hurtling toward the city, toward everything that had suddenly lost its appeal.

"So!" Diana popped around her cubicle, a cup of Starbucks in her hand and a squiggle of foam above her lip. "How was the big weekend? What was Colby's surprise?"

"A concert." Lily moved a stack of folders from a chair, and Diana plopped down.

"So, you were grooving with all the college kids. Was that weird?"

"Not as much as you'd think. Ever hear of Blaise Raleigh?"

"Country singer?"

"No, but she's a little like Lucinda Williams. Her guitarist was amazing. Jackson Johnson." Lily gushed on until Diana said, "Let's Google them," and stanched the flow.

Lily typed in Blaise's name, and her website came up. They scrolled through the photo gallery, touring dates, bio. "Cool," Diana said. "Well, better get to work. Oh, and I have some travel suggestions for you."

Fuck, Lily thought. "Great," she said.

She went back to Blaise's site and scrolled through the press coverage until she found a mention of the guitarist. "An impassioned performer . . . nearly upstaged Ms. Raleigh . . . skill like this doesn't come along often." Lily basked in the praise, as if she had something to do with it.

Diana returned with a few brochures and caught Lily staring into space. "I sent you some links. It's good we're going soon. I see you're not yourself."

No, she wasn't herself. Maybe the reactionaries were right and music *was* subversive. Maybe it could take a normal person and turn her into someone else, the way a tornado tosses buildings upside down and lands them far away.

She turned back to the computer screen. The photos showed Blaise at various festivals, mouth ecstatically open, head thrown back, hair catching the light. There were pictures of her as part of a five-person band, with a bass player, a keyboardist, a drummer, and Jackson Johnson on guitar. They called themselves the Rising Stars. Not *too* pretentious. From what Lily could tell, they'd been together as a group for about three years before breaking up. Artistic differences? Relationship quarrels?

She really should be getting back to work. A teetering stack of folders and flutters of Post-it notes reproached her. Instead she skimmed Blaise's song lyrics and lots of info on her make of guitars and other gear. Then she found what she realized she'd been looking for: a large shot of JJ. He was scowling ferociously down at his guitar, his fingers a blur. Excitedly she clicked below his image and came to his home page, but it contained nothing except a one-paragraph bio with three typos, a couple of lousy photos, and a mention of his CD, *JJ: Solo Guitar*, which, when she clicked on it, brought her back to Blaise's site and a PUT IN SHOPPING CART? icon. She clicked OK, but a message came up that the CD was not available. Two Rising Stars CDs were for sale, though, along with Blaise's new one. Lily made sure that JJ was listed on all three both before ordering them.

She sighed and forced herself to start in on editing two scripts. As she worked, a sense of pleasing anticipation crept over her, like the scent of coffee wafting into her consciousness in the morning. What was it? she wondered, and then she remembered. The CDs. Maybe they were already being loaded onto a truck and charging down a highway at seventy-five miles per hour, straight to her apartment.

"You're humming." Diana was standing at Lily's cubicle, bright paisley jacket draped over her arm. "That's a good sign. Did you pick something?"

"Not yet." She wanted to own up to the fact that she didn't want to take a trip with Diana but caved to cowardice. "I'll talk it over with Stephen tonight."

"With the fall foliage and all, we should make reservations well in advance."

"Got it."

"Tomorrow," Diana wiggled her fingers good-bye.

Was she really going to have to do this? Lily had a sudden thought and went back to Blaise's site. She was touring for the next month in the northeast at small coffeehouse venues and colleges. Lily's pulse quickened. She scrolled through Diana's travel links, checked back against the website. *Bingo.* Providence, Rhode Island.

Before she logged off, she clicked back to JJ's page and scrolled through again. A little button said CONTACT. She clicked, and it brought her to a window where she could leave a message.

Dear Mr. Jackson, she began. Too formal. *Dear JJ, I met you two days ago at a concert (I'm the lady you gave your cigarettes to). I'd like to buy your CD—can you let me know how to purchase it? Thank you, Lily.*

Her hand hovered over the mouse, ready to click. Should she sound more playful? She went back and inserted *pushy* before *lady*, and then hit SEND.

Outside it was warm for late September, with a rosy glow to the sky over New Jersey, across the river. Lily decided to walk. Living on Seventy-ninth Street was a godsend—close to Riverside and Central parks, the subway, and, best of all, the variety of food shops on Broadway. She stopped at Citarella's for fish and Zabar's for ham-and-cheese croissants. At the corner grocery she picked out a bouquet of purple and pink zinnias.

She handed them to Stephen and leaned into his kiss. He took the flowers into the kitchen for a vase, and they sat immediately and polished off the croissants. Lily licked the flakes from her fingers and used a moistened tip to commandeer every last crumb on her plate.

"Diana and I were talking about going off for a weekend—OK with you? I was thinking October seventeenth."

"Sure, as long as we don't have something. Do we have something?"

"I'll check." Lily got up to look at the calendar on their broom-closet door, but she really didn't need to. The second she made a plan, it was embedded in her brain. She didn't need a day planner, a BlackBerry, or any other electronic fruit or vegetable to tell her where and when she had to be somewhere. Probably this, too, said something terribly sad about her.

"What are you going to be doing? Leaf peeping?"

"I think we'll go to Newport to see the mansions." Why was she holding back? "We might go to a concert in Providence."

"Sounds like fun. I'll use the time to catch up on work. What concert?"

"You know the musicians I told you about who opened for James Taylor? They're playing that weekend, as it happens."

"Oh, that guitarist you keep going on about."

"His group, yes."

Stephen lifted an eyebrow. Lily felt ridiculous—not that it would stop her.

Later that week, the package of CDs arrived. She ripped it open and pawed through. Blaise was in the center of every cover photo, surrounded by male musicians. Inside with the liner notes, most shots of JJ were so small Lily could barely identify him, but in one he was standing by a tree, a guitar upright between his blue-jeaned legs, an expression on his face so tortured she wondered if it was supposed to be ironic.

She put Blaise's new CD in the player in the living room and sat down to listen. She stiffened as she recognized the first song from the concert. But something was different: Besides the vocals and guitar, there were fiddle, drums, and piano. The next track was a ballad with just voice and guitar, but where Lily had remembered JJ's long, incredible guitar breaks, these solos lasted just a few measures before the vocals began again. She listened to the end and then popped in the Rising Stars CDs, one after the other, but the music was missing a dimension. It wasn't like their live performance. There just wasn't enough of the guitar.

She was startled by Stephen's arrival. How had it gotten so late? He went immediately to turn down the music.

"What are you listening to?"

"Those musicians I mentioned."

"Good?"

"Not like the concert, but see what you think."

He went to change out of his suit and came back to join her in the kitchen, where she was hurriedly tossing a salad. He was wearing worn gray sweatpants and a T-shirt that said NO. 1 DAD.

"Well?"

"Well what?"

"Well, how do you like the music?"

He stood a moment, listening. "Lovely voice."

"I wish there was more of the guitar—that's what made them a cut above."

"I'll take your word for it."

There was no point in talking about this with him. She wanted to listen to the CDs again but decided to wait until he wasn't around. There was a funny sense of familiarity to her impatience and annoyance that puzzled her until she realized: It was just like high school, when she had to keep her noisy rock music away from her parents.

The next day, she and Diana spent their lunch hour planning their trip, choosing an inn and researching mansions. Lily's mind kept drifting. *Just three weeks. In just three weeks, I'll see them again. Hear him again.*

"We should dress for cold weather," Diana said.

Dress! What did she have that would look chic? But why on earth did it matter? She imagined JJ looking up as she approached to ask for his solo CD and seeing . . . Ugh. Why did she have to be so middle-aged, so thick around the middle, thick like a pudding? Not that it had bothered her before now. Men's stares had made her uncomfortable when she was young. She hadn't marked the moment when that had stopped, when she had become invisible, when she had felt she could finally breathe.

Twenty-three days. She could lose a few pounds in that time, couldn't she? She could buy new clothes. She'd find something that made her look hip—or at least interesting. When you were young, you tried to look beautiful. At some point you were grateful to feel attractive. Now she was just hoping to seem interesting. What was next—praying she didn't stink and offend too badly?

Well, she'd diet and walk home from work every day and lose weight and buy a new outfit. It was something. Then she remembered her date with Honor. High tea.

She and her college roommate got together every month or so, a ritual they kept up diligently. Honor was seriously overweight, not just settling downward. If Lily said she was dieting, Honor would take it as a rebuke. Somehow, she'd have to finesse it.

She had only a slice of melon for breakfast. As she greeted Honor outside the swanky Upper East Side restaurant, her stomach was yelping so badly she realized she should have eaten a full meal.

The three-tiered tray arrived fully loaded. "Oh my!" Honor's pretty round face went rosy. On the bottom level were three different kinds of sandwiches: egg salad, cucumber and cream cheese, and salmon; on the middle tier, various sweets; and on the top, scones. Clotted cream in a rose-patterned china server and little gold-rimmed dishes of butter and jam were placed around them. Lily salivated.

Immediately Honor deposited a scone on each of their plates and, spoon overflowing, said, "Clotted cream?"

Lily dabbed a corner of her scone with cream, took a tiny bite, and, to distract Honor, asked, "How's your mother?" while she surreptitiously slid the rest of the scone under her napkin. Honor's mother was suffering from Alzheimer's.

"Impossible!" Honor bit down hard, spraying crumbs. "They called three times last week!" She launched into a story of her mother's latest episodes at the nursing home.

"I'm so sorry," Lily said, lifting an egg salad sandwich from the tray. Eggs were dietetic, weren't they?

"So, how's Colby liking college?"

Lily indulged in a few minutes of maternal boasting. "I've been really cranky, though." That hardly covered it, but what else to call it? "Stephen thinks I need to develop a hobby. He gave me a video camera for my birthday. I don't know. I am plain dissatisfied lately. Me. My life. Everything."

Honor seemed to glare at her for a split second, and Lily felt instantly ashamed. Unlike Honor, she had that major coup, a wonderful husband. Honor's husband had left her without a word. She had come home to find his good-bye note on the refrigerator. It had been the cruelest breakup Lily had ever heard of. How dare she be dissatisfied?

But Honor's friendship instincts and social-worker analytical skills kicked in.

"Symptoms?"

"Depression. Irritation. An inexplicable desire to listen to music all day."

"What kind of music?"

"Does it matter?"

"Well, music aside, are you having hot flashes?"

"You think it's menopause?"

"Well, it's almost too obvious, isn't it?" Honor paused to lift a salmon sandwich onto her plate. "Colby leaves for college, and you can't have any more babies."

"But I don't want any more babies."

"Consciously, no. But I'm sure Freud would say otherwise."

"Fuck Freud." An image of the guitarist flashed before Lily, those hooded eyes.

"Besides," Honor said, moving on to the cucumber, "it's really

23

about loss. You might not want more babies, you might not really want Colby back home, but it represents a sense of time passing, the inexorable march toward death." She smacked her lips, lifted her cup to her mouth.

Lily fought the urge to stuff all the teacakes into her mouth at once.

"It's completely normal." Honor poked among the delicacies. "Oh, look," she purred, "strawberry shortcake and lemon bars, chocolate mousse cups, and a fruit tart."

The thought of smearing the mousse into her napkin made Lily shudder. She helped herself to the fruit tart. "Mmm," she said, making a show of eating the fruit while adding the pastry shells to the mess inside her napkin. She reached for the lemon bar. "I think I'll save this for Stephen. It's his favorite."

Honor bit into hers. "Delish—you'll be sorry. I've got a blind date next week."

"Really! That's great."

"Aren't you eating that?" Honor looked accusingly at Lily's strawberry shortcake.

"I'm actually feeling a little queasy," Lily lied.

A flicker of conflicting emotions played across Honor's face. "I really should lose some weight," she said, pausing. Then she frowned. "But if he wants a skinny woman, he's not going to want me anyhow." With that, she reached for the pastry.

Two pounds thinner, hair newly trimmed, an outfit purchased—black, of course, but the top had a flattering V-neck and a little colorful embroidery—Lily felt as energized as a windup toy.

Just that morning she'd checked her email and nearly went into cardiac arrest. There was a message from JJ in her inbox.

Hey Lily, of course I remember you! I'll mail you a CD. Give me your address. P.S. I like my women pushy.

Lily wrote back to JJ that as it turned out, she was going to be at the show in Providence, and—being pushy—was reminding him to bring that CD. Once in Newport, she and Diana checked in to their inn—small, charming, Victorian—and headed out for a walk down to the pier, where they had mojitos overlooking the water, drifted in and out of art galleries, and forked over for overpriced clam chowder and lobster. The next day they did the requisite tours of the mansions along Bellevue Avenue and the Cliff Walk along the ocean.

As the time of the concert drew closer, Lily hurried Diana to the point where Diana snapped at her, but even so they were too late to get seats right in front of the stage. The club was a run-down bar-restaurant in a deserted part of Providence. At the college concert, the guitarist had stood to the singer's left, so Lily chose seats on the right, hoping for a good view of his hands.

They ordered burgers and fries and beers, but Lily could barely swallow. She watched the room fill, surprised by the mix of young and middle-aged patrons. As she turned back to her beer, she did a double take and let out a little bleep.

"What?" Diana said.

"It's them—the musicians!" she hissed. Across the room, just like ordinary mortals, Blaise and JJ were eating. Shouldn't they be rehearsing? Pacing nervously? And if not, shouldn't they be dining by themselves and not in the midst of their audience? Lily didn't know what to make of it. She shot another glance, then whipped out her compact and checked her teeth. A few minutes before the concert was set to begin, Blaise and JJ casually sauntered to the stage and began fiddling with their gear. When they were satisfied, they gave a nod, and a man in a red velvet vest came up to the stage, kissed Blaise's cheek, and tapped a microphone.

"Welcome, everyone. Thank you all for coming out tonight. I can't tell you how pleased I am to have this young lady here with us. I've followed her career from the get-go, and let me tell you, she's going places. Without further ado, please welcome Blaise Raleigh and guitarist extraordinaire Jackson Johnson!"

The room burst into applause.

"How you all doing tonight?" Blaise drawled. "Everybody ready for a good time?"

"Yeah, baby!" a male voice boomed.

Tonight Blaise wore jeans and a simple tank top that showed off her slim shoulders, a total change from the glamour-girl look she'd sported at the larger venue. Her hair was artfully tousled, her eyes circled with dark liner. "We were strolling around Newport today. Wow!"

Newport? They were strolling around Newport? Lily could have seen them! She could have walked into a room in one of the mansions and found him at the window, looking out at the water. They could have had a conversation!

"Here's one from our first album, when we were with our band, the Rising Stars. It's called 'Three for the Road,' and we're sending it out to Joe and Marcy Reed."

JJ began a blues progression Lily now knew by heart, then did some fancy fingerwork that wasn't on the recorded version. They went on to a few early songs and several rousing numbers from the new CD, then slowed things down with a cover of Richard Thompson's "Dimming of the Day," the harmonies so lovely that Lily's teeth ached.

"We're about to take a break, but here's one to make sure you stay for the second set," Blaise said. The rock song had a strong, thumping pulse that called for lots of JJ's lightning-fast single-note runs. The applause was explosive. "See, didn't I tell you?" Lily whispered in Diana's ear.

"He's really good," Diana said. "I don't actually know a lot about guitar."

Seeing Blaise and JJ head for the back, Lily put her hand on Diana's arm. "I'll just be a moment." She jumped up, knocking into her chair, and rushed through the crowd, rubbing her thigh where she'd banged it. Blaise was already signing CD covers, but JJ wasn't at the table. Outside smoking a cigarette? Lily had stashed his pack of Camels in a shoebox at the bottom of her closet.

She headed for the door. Perspiration lined her forehead, and the hair at her neck was ridiculously damp.

26

He was coming in just as she opened the door. "You first," he said, holding it.

"No, that's OK." She wanted him to come in so she could trail him back to the CD table.

"Wait!" he said. "You're the one. You're Lily. I have you to thank for quitting smoking."

"You really gave it up?"

He brushed her cheek with his lips. "I did." Her hand went swiftly to her cheek, as if to trap the kiss. He leaned against the doorjamb as if he wanted to relax into conversation, so close she noticed the lines running from his nose to the corners of his mouth, the crinkles around his eyes, guileless and innocent.

"Did you remember to bring your CD this time?"

"Yes, it's inside. I'll sign it for you."

"Do you think you could play one of your compositions?"

"I don't know; it's really Blaise's call."

"What do you mean?"

"Well, it's her show. I'm her guitarist. She calls the shots."

"But you're so amazing. I mean, that's not really fair."

He looked amused and shrugged. "I'm not the singer or the song-writer. That's how it works."

"Well, I'll ask her, then!"

He laughed. "Come on." He pulled her behind him by the hand. "I'll get that CD."

Lily was barely able to keep from stomping on his heels. His palm felt warm and rough. Was her hand sweaty? He released it and went behind the table, where Blaise was holding court. He signed the CD with a flourish: *To Lily, with appreciation, JJ*. She passed him a twenty-dollar bill, but he refused it. "No, it's a thank-you. Just promise to enjoy it."

"I will. Of course I will!" Lily turned to Blaise. "I have a favor—I was wondering if you could do one of JJ's pieces from his solo CD."

Blaise looked surprised, gave Lily a measured look, and nodded.

"Thank you, thank you." She returned to her seat, gave Diana a big smile.

Diana narrowed her eyes at her. "Are you OK?"

The lights dimmed, and Blaise and JJ hopped onto the stage. "Ready for some more?" Blaise called out.

"Yeah!"

"I can't hear you!"

"Yeah!"

"Well, OK. We've had a bunch of requests, and we'll try to get to most of them. First, JJ's ready to wow you with one from his solo CD."

JJ stepped up to the mic. "This one's called 'Fields of Flames,' and I'm sending it out to the lovely lady Lily." He gestured to her with a sweep of his arm, and she felt her face flush. People craned their necks in her direction. Diana poked her hard in the side.

He drew his pick down hard and was off. Her brain seemed to set off sparks inside her like metal in a microwave. She felt the notes in her hair shafts, the soles of her feet. But she blanked out on whole measures of the piece—just as she had at Colby's grade-school shows, where her nerves prevented her from truly taking in the experience. When the song was over, she applauded so hard she thought the friction would cause the skin on her palms to burst into flame.

The rest of the second set went by way too fast. Afterward, she and Diana slowly followed the crowd filing out. Lily briefly considered going up to JJ to thank him for dedicating the song, but he and Blaise were surrounded by fans, and she was suddenly, inexplicably, exhausted. Outside it was overcast, with clouds dark against a darker sky, and as they walked in the chilly air and reached their rental car, Lily stumbled. This was it. It was over. She was never going to see them again. Him again. How was it possible? How could he and his music pass out of her life this way?

At home, Stephen greeted her at the door, wineglass in hand, something classical on the stereo. He hugged her hard and said, "I missed you." Lily stiffened. She had hardly given him a thought.

"How was your weekend?"

"Wonderful," she said, because it was true, despite her fraught state.

"Are you hungry? There's some leftover Chinese."

She followed him into the kitchen. "Get the proposal done?"

"Yeah, I worked straight through." He passed her the food cartons, poured wine.

"Tell me," she said, dishing out chicken with cashew nuts. As he described with gusto the ins and outs of a land deal he was working on, she thought about how important his work was—protecting neighborhoods, mandating vest-pocket parks—compared with, say, playing music.

"So, did you bring home any CDs?" he asked, surprising her.

Lily pushed rice around her plate with her chopsticks. "Yes, but let's wait till tomorrow to listen." She wanted to keep JJ's music to herself, to nurse it like a tender bruise.

Stephen didn't say anything for a moment, then reached for her hand.

"You seem cranky—are you OK?"

"I'm sorry. It was just a lot of driving."

"I hope that's all."

"What do you mean?" She tensed.

"Lately you've just been a little . . . I don't know."

She held her breath. Was he going to accuse her of having a crush? Had he noticed how completely carried away she had gotten?

"I was getting worried that you were pining for another child."

Lily nearly spit out her mouthful of food and took a sip of water to regain her composure. "I'm not pining." *Not for a child, anyhow.* "The next baby in our lives will be Colby's, and I'm not hoping for that anytime soon."

"I thought maybe you were missing motherhood. I guess you just miss him."

"Yes, I'm sure that's what it is," she said. "I'm sure it will pass."

But it only got worse.

She couldn't keep her hands off JJ's CD. His own music was unlike what he played with Blaise, but soon she was seduced by his compositions, by the slow melodies and intricate constructions and lush harmonies, all more sophisticated than what she would have expected from his scruffy-hillbilly look. She'd have guessed something bluegrass, blues, or country, even rock and roll, not this classical- and jazz-influenced, unclassifiable sound.

She took out her own guitar, a cheap acoustic she had bought in her teens, which had been entombed for years in its case, and replaced the strings. She tried out a few old songs, very simple ones that came back to her. But her fingers were like stumps, and her voice was a breathy whisper. She bored even herself.

At least once a day she visited Blaise Raleigh's website, ferreting out information. Were JJ and Blaise a couple? What were their lives like? How many days were they on the road? How often did they go home? She checked the touring schedule religiously. They had to come to New York City someday, they just had to. She had to hear them again. Lily could see how new dates got inserted into holes in their schedule, new venues grafted onto ones already there. Maybe when they were in Delaware, say, they'd get a call to play in New Jersey. She would just have to wait.

"Whatcha up to?" Tom, her boss, had come up behind her and was glancing at her screen.

"Oh, checking out a group I saw." Lily tried to sound casual. "They all seem to have videos these days." She hoped he'd think that what she was doing was work-related in some obscure way.

"That's an idea—maybe we'll go after that market once we upgrade our equipment. Meantime, we're waiting for you in the conference room."

Most of the staff was already assembled, a tray of cookies and coffee in the center of the table. Patsy, the receptionist, entered wearing a dark green silk shantung sheath with slits practically to her waist. Diana rolled her eyes at Lily.

"Let's start," Tom said. He swiveled in his chair, one of those expensive ergonomically correct ones that had so many adjustments you needed a manual to figure it out. Lily helped herself to coffee.

"Cookie?" Diana slid the tray closer.

"No, thanks."

Diana lifted an eyebrow—Lily, turning down food? Lily looked at Patsy and imagined herself in that slithery green dress at the moment JJ had said to her, "Wait! You're the one," or the moment from the stage when he had dedicated the song to her.

"Earth to Lily. . . ." Tom was holding out a sheaf of papers.

"Sorry."

"I think the time has come, the walrus said." He passed around the business plan. "It's gonna take a chunk of change to upgrade, but it's the only way to avoid downsizing. We're going to ditch Avid and switch to Final Cut Pro. Some of us will finish out current assignments while the rest transition to the new technology. We can't put it off any longer."

Everyone chewed pencil tips, tapped fingers. When she had started at MKT, they had made beta tapes using small cameras and a little mixing board for sound. They had graduated to the Avid editing suite. Now that, too, would be passé. She looked up and noticed Bruce's new glasses with the tiny frames. Bruce's eyes were hazel, a bit like JJ's, with those curious golden flecks. . . .

"Thoughts, Lily?"

She lifted the chart listing equipment, numbers, costs. "These don't add up."

"What do you mean—I had the accountant go over them twice."

"I meant the dollar signs don't line up."

Dead silence. Tom laughed. "You had me going there for a second."

"I'm feeling a little light-headed. I think I'll just take a moment."

She went to the ladies' room and lay down on the couch. She was beginning to frighten herself. Was this what happened in a psychotic breakdown? What broke in those instances, anyhow? Was the brain like a chain of molecules or cells, and if even a little piece wore off, everything just flew apart?

Oh, cut the dramatics, she told herself and sat up. *Get a grip!*

She washed her face and stared into the mirror. Worried brown eyes stared back at her. Was she just inventing all this angst out of thin air because her life lacked excitement? Was it that her life had gotten stale, or that she wasn't having enough sex? Could she have a neurological disorder? None of these rationales struck a chord. *Ha ha, a chord.* She laughed at herself in the mirror.

She recalled the moment of watching the guitarist's hands at that first concert, when something sizzled through her, as if transforming her—but into what? She swayed, grabbed the counter.

She had to take herself in hand. She strode back to the conference room. This had gone on long enough.

Cold turkey, she decided. She would not listen to any more of Blaise and JJ's CDs, and she would no longer check the website. At work she volunteered to try out the new software. She'd substitute one form of going nuts for another.

But her life, like the autumn trees, bled color. The new technology kept her busy, but it didn't fill the cracks of her deranged psyche. At last, Thanksgiving approached, and she could distract herself with preparations. Colby was coming home and bringing Ian.

She rushed Colby at the door, hugged him hard, then stepped back to look at him. He seemed taller; it was his posture, she realized. He was standing straighter. A long striped scarf was wound several times around his neck in some kind of fashion statement. He wasn't her little boy anymore.

"Mom, remember Ian?"

"Of course. Ian, great to see you again. Come on in."

"Can I get you guys a glass of wine?" Stephen asked. "I know you're not strictly legal, but we believe in the French tradition of starting kids out in the home."

Ian and Colby exchanged grins. "Sure!" Ian said.

"So, how's school?" Lily asked.

"I'm buried with work," Colby said. "My poli-sci teacher's a ballbuster."

"What courses are you taking?" Lily turned to Ian.

"A social science, bio, English, and The History of Rock and Roll."

"That's a class?"

"Yeah. And I'm taking From the Blues to the Moody Blues next semester."

"Lucky you!" She knew she should drop the subject, but instead she peppered Ian with questions until Colby and Stephen—auburn-haired, freckled bookends on the couch opposite—said in unison, "Enough!"

After dessert, Colby got Ian settled in his bedroom, then came to put away the card table, which they needed when they entertained, in the back of Lily's closet.

"Hey, I see your guitar is out."

"I've just been messing around. I'm not really enjoying it."

"Play something anyhow?"

"If you'll help." The temptation to sing with him, like when he was little, was too great to pass up. She strummed the chords for "You've Got a Friend."

"Nice," Colby said, as the last note died away. "Oh, guess what? That Blaise Raleigh we heard? She's playing near here soon."

Lily put her guitar down on the bed carefully. "When? Where?"

"January. I forget where exactly, but not far upstate."

To think she might have missed it. She had been trying to wean herself, but no way would she pass up a concert so close to home.

"I'll check the website."

"Website? You? You really are a fan," Colby laughed.

Fanatic, Lily thought, *that's what I am. An obsessed, middle-aged groupie fan.*

Three

The pungent scent of marigolds and decaying leaves always reminded Lily of the day she had realized she was in love with Stephen. She was working with her mother in the little garden plot in front of the house in the Bronx where she grew up. It was fall, and she'd just come home from her postcollege trip to Europe. She was chattering away about various men she knew and their many failings, when her mother paused, a smear of dirt across her cheek, and asked, "What are you looking for?"

Without thinking, Lily rattled off, "Someone strong and compassionate and smart and generous, with a good sense of humor. . . ."

"Sounds like Stephen," her mother said.

Lily inhaled sharply; the scent of the last lingering marigolds was heady. How had it taken her so long to see it?

She and Stephen had met in college and become close friends. Later he told her that he had known how he felt about her early on but knew she wasn't interested—yet. She was drawn to the lively, outgoing boys; he was far less charismatic—the solid, dependable type young women didn't fall for but whose mothers spotted right away. He told her he loved that she had such a zesty, open spirit cushioned by a tender heart. He loved that to buy the *Times* she would go blocks out of her way to patronize a particular Indian vendor because he was more polite than the others. Stephen, seeing her crash and burn through boys who were all wrong for her, was 100 percent sure no one would ever love her as he did and was equally certain that, although it might take her a while to know her feelings for him, she was the kind of woman who, once committed, would never waver.

They had married when she was twenty-six. Over their years together, they had grieved the deaths of their parents and had weathered the downs, and mostly ups, of parenthood. So, given everything, and given how reasonable Stephen was, how sane and secure he was in himself, there was no reason at all that she should be so hesitant about mentioning the upcoming Blaise Raleigh concert. Or that she wanted to go alone. She wanted to wallow undisturbed in the music. But like an alcoholic promising herself just one last drink, she would allow this final concert before reining herself back in.

Did she really need to mention it? she wondered, staring at Stephen. He was at the kitchen table, his reading glasses perched on his nose, papers strewn, laptop off to the side. He was barely aware of her as she took in his receding hairline, the paleness of his once-dark-red hair. He looked so . . . ordinary. She sighed. She never kept anything from him. "Have a sec? There's something I want to talk about."

Stephen's eyes went to the clock. "It's kind of late—maybe tonight? If it's not something you have to deal with this second?"

It had often irritated her when Stephen was distracted by work. Not today. The second he was out the door, she put JJ's CD in the player and sat on the couch, hands folded in her lap, eyes closed. She saturated herself with the music's streams and falls, snowdrifts of notes. She was obsessed with the sounds the guitar made—and maybe with the guitarist who made them. But that, she would not think about.

◀ ▶

"Honor," she said, when they were having their Christmas tea at Alice's Tea Cup on the Upper West Side, "do you think a person, a regular person who hasn't experienced any kind of trauma, can suddenly become delusional? Or, say, become so gripped by an obsession that, in a way, they're technically a little crazy?"

"I'm not sure I really understand what you're asking." Honor took a nibble of chocolate biscuit and lifted her cup daintily, pinky finger extended.

"Can you just suddenly go crazy?"

"Well, there are chemical imbalances, schizophrenia. Sure."

"If you know you are, can you pull back from it—choose not to go crazy?"

Honor frowned. "What's all this about?"

"Oh, we were just talking at work. I said I didn't think obsession was the same as madness."

"Well, someone famous said the next step after obsession *is* madness."

Lily coughed on her scone, a little fleck of cranberry caught in her throat. She took a sip of tea. "Like a downward progression?" She ferociously spread jam over the other half of the scone. "Where do obsessions come from, anyway?"

"All sorts of places. Unfulfilled longings." Honor lifted her eyebrows. "Is this about your music thing?"

"Of course not." Her obsession was making her unhappy, but what scared her more was the suspicion that life without it might feel worse. What if she liked living in her fantasy better than she did in her regular life?

"This menopause stuff takes a while to get through," Honor said sympathetically. Lily decided to change the subject.

"So, how did that blind date work out?"

"Oh, he canceled. Met someone."

They each reached for a sandwich and munched in silence. Lily thought about the holidays coming up, Colby home, all their traditions. She glanced at Honor, wiping her mouth with a napkin. Honor hadn't been with anyone since her husband left her.

Lily put down her cup. "Would you like to join us Christmas Day?"

"Oh, that's so sweet! But as it happens, I'm going out to Aspen. My friend Sarah and her family rented a posh ski house and are having a weekend-long party."

So much for my unnecessary and patronizing sympathy, Lily thought.

"Sarah has a dentist she wants me to meet." Honor gnashed her teeth together. "I've been doing whitening strips all month."

Lily parted from Honor on Columbus Avenue and continued on to West End. The air was sharply crisp, and Christmas decorations dazzled in the windows of the tiny, tony shops. The holiday hoopla was a waste of time and money, of course, yet it was all so pleasing. You saw the sparkle and the glitter and felt that holiday zip, that stirring of excitement from childhood, the magic of . . . well, presents. But maybe it went deeper, to the unexpected pleasures of promise itself. The Jesus story and the midnight sky pinpricked by stars, adding to the hush, the sense of mystery. Somehow, seeing the lights, hearing the music spilling into the street, you could convince yourself that it really wasn't all just about getting you to buy buy buy.

But Lily loved to buy presents. At a gift shop on Columbus Avenue, a small bell chimed as she walked into a crowded bazaar of colorful scarves and jewelry piled next to carved-wood boxes, jumbles of candles, tiny plush toys, glass figurines. Overhead dangled ornaments, a forest of glass baubles.

She found an enameled box for her niece Alicia; a necklace for her sister, Troy, with tiny coral beads; and a carved wooden knife for her nephew William. Near the register was a small collection of paperweights. One, cobalt blue with lines of sea green and gold, somehow said *Stephen.* Then a translucent cube with something wispy and white inside caught her eye; she lifted it and drew in her breath. The wisp was a little guitar with a line of notes swirling around it. She held it a moment; it fit her palm perfectly. She placed it in her basket.

Leaving the store, swinging her bag of tissue-wrapped treasure, she lifted her face to the chill and thought, *Everyone needs this. Everyone needs a little magic.*

Although it was Saturday, Stephen was on a work call when she came in. He nodded at her and said into the phone, "Listen, my wife's just gotten home, so why don't you email me the rest later?"

"So," he said, giving her a kiss, "how was tea? How's Honor?"

"Great and good, respectively. She's going to Aspen over Christmas."

"Can't imagine her skiing."

"Don't be cruel."

"I'm not making fun of her weight—she just doesn't strike me as athletic."

"It would be nice to sit in a lodge by a fire and drink hot chocolate."

Stephen crinkled his brow. "Do you feel it's too much having everyone over?"

"No. But change is sometimes good. I mean, we do the same thing every year. Same vacation in the Berkshires in the summer, same thing for the holidays. . . ."

"We do the same things because we like doing those things and look forward to them—at least that was my impression." God, he could be so stuffy, Lily thought. Did he have to sound so personally offended? "Well, don't we? I do. If you don't, then say so."

How was it they were suddenly having an argument? "I enjoy it, of course I do." What did she care about Aspen, anyhow? Tomorrow the house would be filled with people. There was cooking to do. She went to the kitchen and put on her headphones. As she chopped and stirred, Stephen receded from her mind, and she felt, as she did no matter how often she listened to JJ's CD, as if her chest had been cracked open for the music to pour into the very heart and soul of her.

◀ ▶

This was one of the things she loved: filling the house with flowers, cleaning until everything gleamed, then perching on a chair, glass of wine in hand, enjoying everyone enjoying her food.

Troy and her husband, Peter, were in the love seat: Peter lean and trim, with a headful of salt-and-pepper hair, Troy elegant and sleek, wearing the red cashmere turtleneck Lily had given her the previous

Christmas. It was a nice gesture. She and Troy had to work at being close; they were always trying, but never quite managing, to dispel a vexing wariness between them.

Stephen's brother, Raymond, a younger, slightly stooped version of him, and his wife, Susanna, petite and fair, were on the other couch. Their twelve-year-old, Alicia, swiveled in a chair next to Colby, whom she idolized, while William, their eight-year-old, was curled over a book.

"Try some of this cheese," Lily said to Peter.

He popped a cracker into his mouth. "Triple cream?"

"Sheep's milk."

"Listen to them," Troy said. Troy was a career woman with a capital *C*—or one without *C*s: not Cooking, not Cleaning, and not having Children was a point of pride with her. Lily thought she would be intimidated by Troy if she weren't her baby sister. She thought she saw through her tough exterior—her excessively feminine shoes were a dead giveaway. Though what, exactly, they gave away wasn't quite clear—her inner fragility? Frivolousness? Today they were red suede with demure black bows. Troy was an officer at a bank, while Peter was a freelance tech writer, as laid back and easygoing as Troy was tightly wound.

"Alicia, please stop twirling in that chair," Susanna said. Alicia ignored her and smiled up at Colby. "Come on, now," Susanna said more firmly. She was a fabric designer whose patterns—swirling lines, voluptuous flowers—were surprisingly bold.

"I was reading in the *Times* that the city is doing some interesting things with Governors Island," Raymond said to Stephen. "Are you involved in that?"

Raymond, a teacher, was interested in politics, and he and Stephen could talk for hours on end. Lily watched him caress his son's hair. She looked over at Colby, wishing he was young enough for her to run her hand over his head the same way.

The timer in the kitchen went off. Lily retrieved the crostini from the oven, slices of baguette moistened with pesto and layered with thin slices of mozzarella and sun-dried tomato, wonderfully gooey.

Stephen, busy pouring wine, looked up. "Can you stack more on the player?"

"Mom, play one of the CDs you bought from the musicians we heard."

"They're not very Christmasy."

"What musicians?" Peter asked.

Since she had made her decision to go to another concert, thoughts of Blaise and JJ were constant background noise in her mind, like a distant waterfall, and the desire to talk about them was as intense as an itch. "Blaise Raleigh—have you heard of her? Her guitarist, Jackson Johnson, is amazing."

"Lily's turned into a little bit of a groupie," Stephen said.

"*Our* Lily?" Peter raised his eyebrows.

"I'm not." Lily turned away.

"Yes, you are," Stephen said. The hardness in his tone took her aback.

"Not."

"This is getting interesting." Peter popped a cracker into his mouth.

"What's a groupie?" Alicia asked.

"A person who has a crush on a rock star," Susanna explained.

"Who do you have a crush on, Aunt Lily?"

"I don't have a crush on anyone." She bent to the tray so Stephen couldn't see her face.

"Lily, you really do seem . . . I don't know." Troy frowned, as if Lily were embarrassing her. Usually Lily was amused by Troy's attempts to be proper, but now her face burned. *What, I'm not allowed to be human? I'm not supposed to have any feelings?* She stabbed the OPEN button on the CD player. She knew she was overreacting. She slipped in Blaise's most recent CD and turned up the volume too loud, then headed to the kitchen. She should have made those shrimp vindaloo skewers she'd been considering, so spicy they would have shut everyone up.

She put the platter of spanakopita down hard on the coffee table. Stephen frowned. All her guests leaned in as if warming themselves around a fire.

"Did you hear about Renée?" Troy looked at Lily, lifting the appetizer to her mouth.

"No, what?" Renée, her favorite cousin. Lily was glad they were all focusing on someone other than her now, but she was disappointed that no one seemed interested in the music.

"Turns out Bob's been having an affair. She had no idea. She's devastated."

"No." Lily sat abruptly. "But they've been together forever. They're happy." In the background, Blaise was singing her favorite love song, the one with JJ's delicate arpeggios.

"He says he doesn't want to leave Renée," Peter said. "I don't know the circumstances, but they're seeing a marriage counselor."

Everyone was silent. "Right at the holidays," Susanna said.

If it could happen to Bob and Renée, Lily thought, it could happen to anyone. On the stereo, JJ was going mad on an electric. Disruption. Discord. Harmony turned cacophony. She grabbed her glass, downed her wine. She was suddenly sweating. Had she remembered to turn off the oven?

Holidays over, Lily got on the scale and winced. She had wanted to be svelte for the concert; she'd have to settle for less plump.

She rode the elevator with the receptionist, Patsy, sultry in a black pencil skirt and black suede boots. How did she keep that figure? If Lily was serious about losing weight—and she was serious, she told herself, oh so serious—then she was going to have to go on one of those programs.

Claire had lost a lot of weight. Lily went in search of wisdom.

"Weight Watchers," Claire said.

"But don't you have to go to those meetings where you stand up and say how you sinned by eating too much brie, and they weigh you in front of everyone?"

Claire laughed. "You're getting it mixed up with 12-step programs."

"You mean I wouldn't have to take Jesus as my savior?"

"You can take the Internet as your savior if you like. Register online. It's a cinch."

Lily registered, entered her height and weight, and was given a points allowance for each day, plus weekly extras. She looked up the corn muffin she'd enjoyed with her morning coffee. Eight points! More than a third of her daily allotment, and the day had barely begun.

Well, as long as she was online, she might as well visit Blaise's blog, *Rules of the Road.* As she scrolled through paragraphs of mundane details, she thought, *Who reads this crap?* Well, she did. But then again, she was crazy. She didn't count. Or were there dozens of other nuts like her? The thought upset her. She realized she was crazy enough to be jealous of anyone else who might move onto her crazy turf.

She exited the website just as Tom buzzed her to come into his office, and as she walked in, he motioned her to a seat. "I wanted to know how you're doing with Final Cut Pro."

"Fine, though I could do with a little more training."

"We just don't have the money."

"The company's doing OK, though, isn't it?" There had been some chatter in the office about downsizing, but, Lily realized, she'd been too preoccupied to pay much attention.

"Yeah, but—and please keep this between us—orders are down, and this conversion is costly. I'm counting on it panning out, but—"

"People will always need films made, and archiving. At least there's always money in converting video to digital, right?"

"Yeah, but more companies will eventually be able to do in-house a lot of what they outsource to us now."

"Our work is quality—we're professionals. We can't totally be replaced!"

"You're right, you're absolutely right. Ignore me—I'm making too much of it. I just didn't get enough sleep last night."

But his expression didn't relax, and uneasiness chased her all morning.

By lunchtime she was famished. Her two points' worth of blueberry yogurt was gone in thirty seconds. Was she so hungry she'd take the interminable elevator back down eleven floors, walk to the greengrocer at the corner, and wait again for the elevator, just for some lousy zero-points raw veggies?

At "Next came advances in engine design" in the middle of the script she was editing, she could take it no longer. Something unholy was roiling in her stomach, a thousand unleashed gases that usually lay calm and obedient. "Want anything from downstairs?" she called to Diana and Patsy.

"Candy bar," Patsy said.

"Chips," Diana called.

The elevator made its maddeningly slow progress downward, stopping at almost every floor, lithe young people gliding on. Why was it so hard to lose weight in middle age? She'd read that Mother Nature pulled the rug out from women in terms of attractiveness once they were no longer necessary for the propagation of the species. Men, of course, could procreate at any point. In case the world was coming up short with the next generation, in case all the young men were suddenly lost to wars or famine, those old geezers could step up to the plate.

Mother Nature? What mother would be so antifeminist, so diabolical? Lily was about to start gnawing at her fingers. She needed something to calm her down—something soothing, preferably chocolate. Why was she succumbing to cultural pressure to be thin and glamorous? She should be proud of her womanly curves. She should move to Hawaii. She'd read that they liked really big women there.

Carrots and celery got her through the afternoon, but she was too tired to walk home after work. On the subway she stood over a boy, slumped with eyes closed, a white cord dangling from his ear. She could hear crackling static, and her whole body was suddenly tingly. The concert was just weeks away. She couldn't bear waiting, but at the same time she wanted to soak forever in the glorious marinade of excitement and expectation.

Lily followed a mother and small girl off the subway and up the stairs. They headed to West End and, like her, turned down Seventy-ninth Street. As she walked behind them, she suddenly imagined following Blaise and JJ after the concert to wherever they were staying, trailing them in the morning to breakfast, seeing JJ bending over a plate of eggs, whites glistening.

Stalker fan.

Lily went about making dinner, sautéing low-fat chicken sausage, roasting zucchini. She realized she was fully capable of doing exactly what she'd imagined. *Stalker fan, stalker fan* repeated in her mind.

"You OK?" She hadn't heard Stephen come in. He took his tie off and hung it over the kitchen doorknob. "I've been talking to you."

"Sorry." She gave him a brief kiss. She'd been tuning out a lot lately, as if her mind and soul were residing in a parallel universe. Was this getting dangerous? Was this something like what had happened in her cousin's marriage? Lily had called Renée earlier in the day. She had told Lily that she and Bob had been drifting apart for a while, but that she hadn't really noticed.

"I was just thinking about Renée."

"How's she doing?" Stephen started setting the table.

"She blames herself."

"Because Bob's a jerk?" Stephen dished out the pasta.

"Well, it makes her question the marriage," Lily said. "I mean, how can she not?"

Stephen chewed, looked thoughtful. "You can't know what goes on in someone else's marriage," he said, "but Bob's always struck me as something of a little boy."

What would people be saying about her and Stephen if they were the ones going through this? They presented themselves as grounded and reasonable and good-natured and sensible. Who would guess that inside Lily was a ridiculous, obsessed stalker fan?

She watched Stephen swirl a corkscrew of pasta in sauce. She, alas, could not have another helping, not if she wanted dessert—two points! They had been together for so long that their way of being together seemed like the only way to be together. Things had worked out well—hadn't they? Besides all the obvious things they shared, there were the intangibles. Their senses of humor, their temperaments, the things they enjoyed doing—all of it meshed. But they'd known each other since college. How would she know if things weren't as good as they should be?

"Why are you staring at me like that?" Stephen asked.

"Was I? Sorry."

"You had this really odd look in your eyes."

"I guess I was just thinking of Renée and Bob."

"What part of it?"

"The part about how do you know whether your marriage is in good shape if nothing is obviously wrong?"

"I think you know."

"Renée says she thought everything was fine."

"What does Bob say?"

"That the problems are with him, his issues."

"Then the problems are with him."

"You really think so?"

"I really think so."

"So we're OK?"

"We're OK, Lily." He came behind her chair, draped his arms around her, kissed her on the side of her neck. "We're very much OK."

Finally, finally, finally! Lily had arranged to get out of work early so she'd have plenty of time to get upstate for the concert before rush hour. She didn't tell Stephen until the night before, mentioning casually that she'd just noticed the concert and thought it would be fun to go. She said wistfully, knowing full well he had a late meeting, "I don't suppose you could come with me?"

"Oh, damn, that would have been wonderful." He looked so sorry to disappoint her that she felt her face heat, and she had to look away.

When she got home from work she slipped *Cold Night Under a*

Hot Moon in the CD player, took a leisurely tub bath, and heated her curling iron. She'd bought a new top, made out of some strange, flattering material. Actually, she wasn't sure it really qualified as material. It seemed spun from plastic—recycled, she hoped—with flecks of something metallic running through it. Its magical stretch-like property seemed to tighten and tone and—dare she think it?—enhance her somewhat-less-than-full décolletage. It made her look, if not exactly sexy, like someone who might once have been. That was as good as it was going to get.

She smoothed concealer under her eyes, lined them with dark-gray pencil, and twirled her hair around the iron, remembering the very few times she had spent this much time primping—her prom, her wedding. She picked up the framed photo that stood on top of the bookcase. She stared at her young self, her smile big and ecstatic, as if she and Stephen had the keys to all the secrets of the universe. Her skin was the color of toast, and her light brown hair lifted in the breeze. She was squinting into the sun. She and Stephen leaned slightly into each other, hands clasped. Her body was strong, curvy, perfect in the simple dress that hugged her torso and then swept out around her like seafoam. Yet she couldn't remember the day in much detail. It was a blur of comings and goings, Troy and her mother and girlfriends in and out of her bedroom, palms and armpits that wouldn't stop sweating, mascara that kept running. Lily bit her lip and returned the frame to the bookcase.

It was late afternoon when she set out, the traffic light going up the West Side Highway and over the George Washington Bridge, the sky just beginning to glow. She popped a Rising Stars CD in the player and sang along, belting it out as if she were Blaise.

She exited the Palisades at Stoney Point and drove through a mile or so of sprawl that gave way to a curious little town with a postindustrial feel. She drove up and down the streets, noting Christmas decorations that hadn't been taken down, handwritten signs in shop windows, a riverfront park. There were smoke stacks from a plant whose function she couldn't determine, three churches but no synagogues.

Off the main street, which was lined with antique stores, a pharmacy, and a few restaurants, a crooked, steep road led to the folk club. She parked and walked uphill, turning her coat collar against the chill. The club was a two-story building with a restaurant. Was the concert space upstairs or on the ground floor? She peered in a window and then jumped back as if scalded. They were there. Inside. Just the two of them. They had turned when they saw there was someone at the window. She prayed she'd been too backlit by the sun for them to identify her.

She scampered away. What was she afraid of—that they were going to chase her down the block? They must be doing sound check. Oh, to think they were doing sound check and she was right outside! For a brief second she considered asking if she could watch, but that was way too brazen. Sacrilegious, even.

Lily scooted back to the main street and into a McDonald's. She'd barely eaten all day, so she squandered her points on a double cheeseburger and fries and enjoyed every caloric mouthful. Then she went into the bathroom and dug in her makeup kit for her travel toothbrush, brushed her teeth, and washed the grease off her hands. Her face in the mirror was pale, as if all the blood had fled her body, so she applied more blush. She was chilled from nervous excitement. It was time. This was it. This was finally it. But now she wanted to hold off, savor the anticipation. What she would feel like later, after it was all over, she refused to contemplate.

When she walked back, the club lights were on and the door ajar. She paid the cover, then headed downstairs to a large, open space where waitresses were bustling about, R & B was thumping from the jukebox, tables were already filling. Lily took a seat close to the stage, yet a little on the side, wanting, and not wanting, JJ to spot her. She ordered a glass of merlot and gulped it down. She would go up to JJ at the break and tell him how much she loved his CD.

A couple settled in opposite her at the table and smiled, asking if she had heard Blaise before. "We adore her music!" The woman leaned in confidentially. They chatted about favorite albums and compared shows they'd been to until the club manager came out, announced the lineup of future acts, and said, "Please put your hands together for Blaise Raleigh and Jackson Johnson!" JJ hopped onto the stage. Lily felt her pulse beat in her throat. He was wearing a tattered flannel shirt and worn jeans; he nodded at the audience and then reached into his pocket for a pick and ran it over the strings. Briefly blocking her view, a woman with a brightly patterned scarf draped dramatically around her shoulders slipped into the empty seat on Lily's left. "Yeah, JJ!" she called out and gave a wolf whistle.

Lily stiffened. How dare she? Who did she think she was? JJ barely glanced up; he was tapping his monitor with the toe of his boot. Maybe she was just a fan. She probably thought she was his biggest fan. Well, she wasn't. Lily was the best fan. No one could be a better fan.

Lily felt her shoulders slump. Of course there would be other fans clamoring for him. She should be pleased. Didn't she want the whole world to acknowledge his fabulousness? Why then this uncomfortable, burning emotion?

Loudly amplified sound brought her back to the music. JJ and Blaise were checking their high E strings against each other; everything seemed to coalesce around that note. JJ played a few bars, and finally Blaise began to sing. It was "Shady Lady," one of Lily's favorites; she went warm with pleasure. Tonight Blaise's tone was a little thin, but JJ's voice snaked around it, cosseting it. His guitar playing was crisp and fast, and Lily sat barely breathing, watching his hands thunder chords up and down the neck of the guitar. When the song ended, Blaise said, "JJ sure is hot tonight!"

"He's amazing, isn't he?" Lily burst out to the couple.

"He's one of the best there is," the know-it-all woman with the scarf chimed in. Lily wanted to smack her. She was going to monopolize JJ between the sets, Lily just knew it. Then an even worse thought occurred. What if JJ wasn't hooked up with Blaise; what if this woman was his girlfriend? But why did it matter? What did Lily think—that she was going to kidnap him and take him home with her?

Blaise and JJ played one after another of her favorites, as if she had written the set list. She forgot the woman with the scarf and inhaled every note, every gesture. What was it like for JJ and Blaise, inside that musical hemisphere? How did it feel not to just visit that space, as she and the audience did, but to reside there?

"Thanks, y'all, we'll be taking a short break," Blaise said. "Come chat with us."

The woman next to Lily jumped up, sending fringe into her face. Lily wanted to yank the scarf from her shoulders. Following her, Lily threaded her way through tables, burning to know who she was to JJ. But the woman headed straight to Blaise and threw her arms around her.

Lily stopped dead, flooded with a delicious surge of relief. She spotted JJ standing across the room, an expression of polite interest on his face, talking with a man who was gesturing wildly. Now was her chance. As she approached, JJ's eyes flicked to her and away, and then back again as recognition dawned.

"Hey, Lily," he said eagerly. Was it that he was pleased to see her or just wanting to escape the man he was talking to? "Thanks for coming out tonight."

"I love your CD, I wanted to tell you. It's really really wonderful. I love it."

"Well, thank you so much." He smiled, his head tilted slightly to the side.

"I wanted to know"—the thought popped into her head—"do you ever do solo shows? You know, just of your own music?"

"No—Blaise and I are pretty busy." A woman touched him on the sleeve to get his attention. "Sorry," he gave Lily a rueful smile, squeezed her shoulder. "Thanks again for your support and interest."

That was it? Weeks of waiting and longing, weeks of being deranged, all for "thanks for your interest"? Lily slunk away.

She headed down the long passageway to the ladies' room. It was time to get over all this silliness. She'd enjoy the second half of the show and go home and regroup, reclaim her life. Near the end of the corridor a man stepped out of a side room, leaving the door ajar; as he passed her, she glanced in and spotted an open guitar case. Without

50

hesitation she slipped inside. The room was small, cramped, with two guitar cases, other gear, and outerwear strewn about. Opposite was a closed door.

Taped inside the lid of one guitar case was a partly ripped-off photo of a dark-haired woman. On a chair was *A Life on the Road,* by Julian Bream. Lily tiptoed to the closed door and slowly turned the handle. The door swung in soundlessly. Her guess was correct: It led directly onto the stage. An idea did a little jig in her brain.

Lily went back to retrieve her tote, leaving her coat draped over her seat. She waited near the ladies' room until the musicians were back on stage and then raced back to the green room, blood rushing to her ears. She took her camera from her tote and turned it on, fingers trembling. She had taken it with her just in case she could work up the gumption to ask to tape a song.

Her chest felt as if it were caught in a vise, but nothing was going to stop her. From the angle of the doorway, she couldn't see or be seen by the audience, but she had a perfect view of JJ from the side. She zoomed in on his hands, trying to hold her camera steady.

She meant to film just one song, but she found herself staying for the next, and then the next.

"Tonight I've decided to let JJ flaunt his chops," Blaise said. "This is one we'll be including on our next CD, which we hope will come out this summer." She stepped out of Lily's range of vision. Lily trained her lens on JJ's fingers, zooming in to capture the blur of speed, the thirty-second notes, the loud vibrato.

The applause was thunderous. Just as Lily lowered the camera, Blaise moved past the doorframe and glanced her way. Her eyes widened. Lily froze. "Get the fuck out," Blaise hissed. "I want to see you after the show."

Blaise marched to the front of the stage and grabbed her guitar out of its holder. Lily's whole body began to shake. She wanted to dive headfirst out the window. She shoved her camera back into her tote. Should she just run away? But there was no way out except through the audience. Blaise might even make a scene, humiliate her from the stage. Back at her seat, she slumped down as far as possible. After the show, she gathered her things and slowly headed to the back room, holding her coat against her chest, as if for protection.

Blaise was pacing in the room and wheeled on her as soon as she approached. "How fucking dare you?" Her hair, stiff with mousse, was in lethal-looking spikes.

"I'm so so sorry," Lily burst out. "I should have asked. Please forgive me."

"What the fuck did you think you were doing?" Her small, thin body was rigid. "You think you can do an unauthorized video of my concert? I could sue your ass from here to the next century."

"I'm terribly sorry. I'm just a fan, and I just wanted to tape one song. I didn't mean any harm. I'm really sorry." It occurred to Lily that Blaise could demand the camera's memory card.

"What's going on?" JJ came in from the stage, holding his guitar by the neck. Lily, face burning, turned away.

"This woman was taping the show."

"I should have gotten permission, but I just wasn't thinking. I only wanted it for myself. To watch. Alone."

"You're damn fucking right you should have asked." Blaise leaned into Lily's face, and Lily saw that her pale blue eyes were slightly dilated.

"Don't rake her over the coals." JJ's voice was laconic. He sat on the arm of the couch with loose grace. "She's the one made me quit smoking. I owe her."

"You might owe her, but I don't!" Blaise folded her arms across her chest. She wasn't about to let this go.

Lily, still clutching her belongings, was at a loss for what to do.

"Look, she's a friend; let her be," JJ insisted.

The word *friend* spread warmth through Lily's body. JJ's soft tone seemed to calm Blaise. Her arms relaxed against her sides. Still she didn't take her eyes off Lily. "Who are you, anyway? How do I know you're telling the truth?"

"Me? I'm nobody. My name is Lily Moore, I'm a huge fan. . . ." God, could she sound any more inane?

"Tell her what you do, so she doesn't worry you're scamming her," JJ said conversationally. "You know, for a living."

"Well, actually . . ."

"What? What do you do?" Blaise's eyes narrowed.

"Well, um, I work for MKT Productions. It's a small outfit, really, nothing glamorous, we don't do music videos . . ."

"Wait a minute. You work making videos?" Blaise's voice rose slightly.

"Please, please believe me, I wasn't trying to do a commercial project—"

"I've been thinking of making a professional concert film," Blaise's tone had shifted entirely.

"You have?" JJ said. He frowned slightly.

"Are you any good?" Blaise asked Lily, ignoring him.

"Well, I'm competent, sure," Lily said. "I've been doing it for, like, seventeen years." Possibility began to dawn on Lily. She loosened her grip on her coat. "Actually, if you like, I could do one for you. The company I work for has all the latest technology, we have teams of people who write and edit . . ."

"Great idea!" JJ said. "She should come along. That's inspired."

"Forget it. I can't afford to commission one." Blaise turned her back to Lily. "Go. Hold on to your precious little tape. I won't prosecute." To Lily's surprise, she removed her blouse, revealing a lacy black bra, and pulled a T-shirt over her head.

"Hold on. Wait. I'd love to do it. I'll do it for free. It can't be a high-end job—you'd need two or three cameras and a sound person for that. But I can do something pretty good, and if you like what I do, it's yours. Free."

"Free?" Blaise turned, hands on her hips, and stared at Lily, appraising. "We're leaving for upstate tomorrow morning. If you can make it, fine."

"Tomorrow?" Lily squeaked.

Blaise turned away and clicked shut the latches on her guitar case.

"I'll make it. When do you want to get under way?"

"Noon. We're staying at the Best Western in town here. Be on time, or we leave without you. Bring your own car. I'll cover your meals and hotels. You can tag along for a week or so."

Lily glanced at JJ. He raised his eyebrows and gave her a slow wink.

"Till tomorrow, then," Lily said, bolting from the room before Blaise could change her mind.

Outside, she let out a shriek and ran all the way down the street to her car.

Four

Lily's drive home was a blur of rain-slicked road, taillights streaking color across the windshield, the sound of the blood beating in her heart, reverb beating in her head. She could pull this off, she could. She had no big projects pending at work—new orders had slacked off anyhow—and she and Stephen didn't have any plans that couldn't be postponed. By the time she hit the George Washington Bridge into Manhattan, she felt as if she'd run the entire way: her knees thudded, her skin was clammy, her breathing raspy.

She found a parking spot right away, a miracle. She stumbled getting out of the car and steadied herself against the door, then bent all the way over. As the blood flowed to her brain, she clasped her knees and waited for her head to clear. She righted herself. It was so unexpectedly quiet—no cars on Riverside Drive at 2:00 AM, no dogs barking, no wind, even, cajoling the trees' sparse leaves into movement. Inside her building, the doorman sagged, half-asleep. "Hi, Mrs. Lane," he said, straightening. She felt irked to be called by Stephen's surname, then alarmed because that had never bothered her before. Moore was her maiden name, retained to declare her feminist independence. But it had just as much to do with disliking the alliteration of Lily Lane, with not wanting to sound like a pretentious Hamptons address.

Upstairs, she opened the apartment door slowly so it wouldn't squeak and wake Stephen. She pulled off her shoes, slipped to the bedroom, and stood over him. She had always loved to watch him sleep. He was curled on his side, features relaxed, mouth slightly open. Lightly she brushed his hair off his forehead. Her heart swelled with tenderness interlaced with apprehension, as if she teetered on a surfboard facing a towering wave.

In the kitchen she warmed milk in the microwave, dosed it with a shot of Kahlua, and sipped while she made a road map for the morning. *(1) Explain to Stephen.* How much time should she assign to *that*? How, exactly, was she going to explain she was leaving that very morning to go on the road with Blaise and JJ? She wrote *30 mins.* If he objected to her going, even thirty minutes wouldn't cut it. Was she prepared to go anyway? To leave if he was upset with her?

(2) Pack. As she listed *warm sweater, toiletries, cash,* she had to fight to keep out the intruding thoughts, like *You're about to go over a precipice—get back now!* She focused instead on outfits and shoes and whether it would be quicker at 8:00 AM to get a cab or the subway to the office, where she needed to borrow a more professional camera. Finally, fatigue began to blur her mind's edges, then filtered in like dappled shadows, and she stumbled to bed, setting her alarm for six thirty, a little before the time Stephen usually got up, feeling guilty to deprive him of sleep.

"What? What?" Stephen cried out when her alarm went off.

"Shush, go back to sleep." He zonked right back out. She was showered and dressed by the time his alarm went off. She was ready to go, bag packed. At the last minute, she had put the paperweight with the filmy guitar inside her bag for good luck.

"I need to talk." She handed him a cup of coffee and sat on the edge of the bed.

"What's going on? Did something happen? Colby?"

"Everything's fine." Oh, how very very evil she was! "I got this fantastic opportunity, Stephen. But I have to leave today. Now."

"What are you talking about?" He lifted himself up on one elbow, peered at her from behind a flop of hair. Curlicues of chest hair peeked from the V of his T-shirt. Lily felt her eyes well up. Her stomach clenched.

"Blaise Raleigh? We got talking after the show. She asked me to do a performance video. Can you believe it? I'm scared shitless. But it's great. You know what you said when you gave me the camera—that I should try and do creative work."

"Wow, that's amazing," he said slowly. He didn't look upset; her stomach unclenched slightly. "That's super, Lily. I didn't know you were doing much with the camera, or even thinking about any of it."

"Well, it's been floating around in my mind . . ." *What a fucking liar I am,* Lily thought dispassionately. It didn't really matter if it was a lie, though, did it? She sure wanted to do it now, and it was, after all, his bright idea. It never would have happened otherwise. "But I have to go today."

"Whoa, hold on a sec. Where exactly are you going? And for how long?"

"I'll follow them around for a week or so. Upstate. I'll call you later, as soon as I know the details." She kissed him, held him in a tight hug. "I love you."

"Me too."

Lily called a rental company to arrange for a car, since Stephen would need theirs, and then left a message on her boss's voice mail to say she needed a big favor.

"What's up?" Tom said, as she came flying in. "Is everything OK?"

"Everything's fine. I just have to take some time off."

"Lily, you're making me nervous. Explain."

"I got a chance to do a concert video. It's a great opportunity. You can take me off the payroll for a week and save money." At that, his expression looked wary. For a second she hesitated; was she running a risk by taking off when they were having money troubles? She brushed the worry aside. "Can I borrow the Sony PD170? I'm going to be shooting in low light; I need the stabilization, too. My Canon won't quite cut it. And could I borrow a tripod? I'll use my own shoulder rest. And I'll absolutely put our logo on the video. We'll figure that out later. Whatever you say. But I have to go."

"OK, OK." Tom was laughing. "I've never seen you like this. Go, enjoy, do a good job."

"Thanks. I adore you," she called over her shoulder.

By the time she'd picked up the rental car and was heading up the West Side Highway, she was drenched in sweat. It was 10:10. She was already behind schedule. If she didn't make it on time, they would leave without her. All of this would have been for nothing. She had the Best Western's number, but she was sure that even if she called ahead to say she was late by only seconds, Blaise would not wait.

She drove over the speed limit the whole way and, at exactly five minutes to twelve, screeched to a halt in front of the motel and ran in to the lobby desk.

"Has Ms. Raleigh checked out?"

"No, she hasn't."

"Can you call her room, please? I'm supposed to meet her."

The clerk nodded, scrolled through his computer screen, then dialed.

"Ms. Raleigh, a—what's your name?—a Ms. Moore is here to see you." He listened, nodded. "Go on up—room 214."

Lily took a deep breath, straightened her shoulders. She walked briskly up the corridor, trying to convey confidence.

"So, you made it. Didn't think you would." Blaise looked bleary, as if she had just woken up. Devoid of makeup, her face was excessively pale, and her curious light blue eyes seemed far less piercing. She gestured for Lily to come in. Clothes and toiletries were scattered around the room, a suitcase open on the bed. Clearly the noon departure was a little loose.

"Sit. I can't concentrate," Blaise ordered. "Tell me about yourself while I pack." She moved about the room, picking up garments, rolling them into lozenges, and placing them in the suitcase. She was almost scarecrow thin, with knobby shoulders and no hips, but she had the kind of sexy grace that comes from being very comfortable in your own skin.

"Well, what would you like to know?" Lily hedged. What about her life could Blaise possibly find interesting?

"Anything relevant," Blaise said. Her speaking voice was a gravelly drawl.

"Well, I'm a big fan of your work," Lily said, for the zillionth time. When that got no reaction, she went on. "I live with my husband in Manhattan, I have a son who just started college, and I work, as I told you, at a video production company. I was a film major." She added as an afterthought, "I play a tiny bit of guitar."

"Sing?" Blaise asked suspiciously.

"No voice," Lily said.

"But you know a lot about music, about the music world?"

"I'm eager to know more." What else could she say that would sound plausible? "This is the area I'd like to branch out into, which is why your offer is so exciting to me."

Blaise looked skeptical, paused in the process of wedging a toiletry bag into her suitcase. Lily waited. Had she sounded convincing? Would Blaise send her home? She rotated her wedding band. The skin underneath felt itchy and dry.

Blaise sighed. "Fine." Had Blaise taken her measure, known Lily would kill to do a good job? Or was she just lazy, and figured Lily was already here, a bird in the hand?

"Go find JJ. He should be in the lobby. Tell him to get the car."

"Sure," Lily said. "We'll talk later, then? About what you want with the video?"

"Yeah." Blaise yawned widely. "I need to wake up first."

Lily closed the door behind her and rested her head against it for a moment to calm herself. Could this really be happening? One day she was a normal person, the next she was traveling with a rock star, like the kid who wrote for *Rolling Stone* about traveling with bands like Led Zeppelin. OK, so Blaise wasn't quite a star. But still.

JJ was slumped in a chair in the lobby, watching TV, wearing a thick gray sweatshirt. At the sight of him, something sizzled up her back, as if his fingers were playing scales along her spine.

"Can you believe this bullshit?" he said by way of greeting. "American culture is really sick." He shook his head in disbelief.

"What is it?"

"They're letting people claim SUVs as business vans for enormous tax write-offs. So it's cheaper for people to buy big-ass gas-guzzlers than low-emission cars."

"That's awful." Lily needed to process this unexpected environmental awareness. "I just came from Blaise's room. She asked me to ask you to get the car."

"OK." He snapped to attention with the suddenness of a pen clicking shut. "Let's go, then."

"Where are we going, exactly? I mean, I can follow you, but I should have the directions and address, in any case."

"Sure. Come with me." She walked with him to a blue Mazda rental that was parked not far from her silver Opal. He pulled a file folder from the trunk. "Today is a travel day. We'll make it upstate to Plattsburgh—it's about a five-hour drive—and have tomorrow to hang before the gig. You get off at exit 36 of the Northway. We're staying in a Ramada Inn. You should book yourself a room. Here's the number."

"OK, I'll do that now," Lily said. "Don't leave without me."

"Where are you going?"

"I left my cell in my car."

"Here, use mine." As Lily made the call, he leaned against the car, biting a cuticle, watching her. In repose he had that lost, troubled look, the look that got to her, that said, *Help me, please.* What was it? Probably just the form his eyes took, and the set of his mouth and chin, nothing more. It tugged at her just the same.

"Thanks," Lily said, handing him back his phone. Their fingers almost touched. Lily backed away slightly. "She said she'd be right here."

"Oh, she loves to be a bitch. She loves her little power trips."

"She does?" Lily was taken aback that he'd criticize Blaise to her. She felt a disquieting sense of pleasure.

"I'm sorry, I shouldn't have said that, but she drives me crazy, you know?"

"I won't say anything." *Tell me more,* she thought. *More and more and more!* "She's difficult to be with?" She thought of Blaise removing her blouse in front of him the previous night. Were they a couple or not?

"Oh, yeah, big time. And it all just fucks with my head. I can get kind of wrapped up in my own mind, and, OK, I can be kind of paranoid, but even so . . ."

He was talking to her as if they were confidants and he felt he could unburden himself to her. Crazy. Was he like this with everyone?

"Is it hard, being together all the time and then having to perform?"

"Well, there are days and there are days." His tone shifted abruptly. "Hey," he called out, straightening, and Lily turned to see Blaise. In an oversize parka and with her hair covered in a purple watch cap, she looked nothing like the glamour girl of the stage.

"Off we go," she said to JJ. "See you there, Lily."

JJ got behind the wheel; Lily hurried to her car. She expected him to shoot off, but he waited until she had her seat belt on and had pulled up behind him.

In what way did he mean that Blaise was a bitch? Lily wondered, following JJ onto the highway. Just for being late? Did that really make her a power freak? Though Lily did get that vibe from her. Maybe it went with the territory, with being a star, or trying to be one. How big a success was Blaise, anyhow? Clearly she wasn't huge, but was she on a tier with, say, Dar Williams or Nanci Griffith? She knew from following Blaise's website that she and JJ had plenty of work; she assumed the steady touring meant their music supported them.

Ahead of her, JJ and Blaise seemed to be talking. They seemed to be getting along just fine. Good. She didn't want them breaking up just when life was getting interesting. Maybe JJ was just one of those people who liked to vent and then forgot all about it.

Lily relaxed and settled into driving. Years ago, she and Stephen had gone away many weekends, and driving gave them a chance to have long conversations not interrupted by chores or phone calls. They would stop someplace they'd never been to break up the journey, sometimes to eat, sometimes to take a short walk. One time they found a pine forest to explore. The needles were spongy underfoot, wonderful to walk on, and they came to a small enclosure like a fairy-tale glade, with sunlight filtering in. They rolled their jackets behind their heads and rested against a log. She put her head on his shoulder, and he turned to kiss her. Suddenly they were removing their clothing and making love in the middle of the afternoon, the coolness of the air against her skin in delicious contrast with her internal heat. But once Colby arrived, there was less space for serendipitous moments.

The Thruway ended near Albany, and she followed the blue Mazda onto the Northway. She was suddenly starving, but the apple and tiny bag of air-popped popcorn she'd purchased on the way to picking up the rental car that morning would have to do—she wasn't about to stop and lose Blaise and JJ. What did they do about eating? What were their routines? How did it feel to be them day to day, filling up the car, stopping for a burger, and electrifying an audience in between? What a strange life.

But then again, the music! It must be like a drug, something so exquisite and exciting you became addicted, you had to have it, and it was worth everything. Worth driving long distances and eating bad highway food and living in motel rooms with boring TV and spending time with someone you maybe didn't even like very much.

Exhausted and famished, Lily pulled into the Ramada Inn parking lot behind JJ and Blaise.

"Ride OK?" JJ called out.

"Great. You made it really easy to follow. I was wondering—do you two want to have dinner and go over everything?"

"Let's talk in the morning. I'm bushed," Blaise said. "I'm gonna order room service and veg out." She grabbed a small bag and her guitar and went on ahead.

"You'd think she was the one who did all the driving," JJ muttered to Lily, pulling out the large suitcases. "I'll have dinner with you, but let me get this stuff inside first."

Blaise was at the counter, getting her room key. Clearly she and JJ had separate rooms. As if in answer to her unspoken question, JJ said, "She likes her space." Lily didn't know if that meant they weren't a couple or that they were but Blaise liked having her own room anyhow.

"A half hour?" he asked.

Lily was beside herself. Dinner with JJ! Alone with JJ! He liked her! He seemed to like her. Could this be true? It wasn't just her imagination? Well, he had dedicated the song to her, and now he was offering to eat with her. She dragged her rolling suitcase down the corridor and into her room and began quickly sorting through her clothes. In fact, he had seem pleased, almost as if . . . But no, she was too sensible to think he could be interested—of course not. And she didn't want that, of course not, she thought, choosing a loose apricot silk shirt she had planned to save for the next night. She loved her husband; she wasn't that kind of person. But she could enjoy the idea of being liked by him, couldn't she? That was OK, wasn't it?

She showered quickly and dressed, trying to be at least a few minutes late, so as not to seem too eager, but got to the lobby exactly on time. JJ was already there. He looked up, and his glance swept appreciatively—it seemed appreciative—over her body. She had lost six pounds and could actually touch her toes without feeling a roll of fat around her middle.

JJ stood. "There's a Mexican place the desk clerk said was good—OK?"

Mexican? Luckily, she'd had only the apple and popcorn. "Wonderful. I haven't had Mexican in an age."

"Me neither. I get it every chance when we play out West. Maybe it's risky to try it here in the boonies?"

"Let's live dangerously," Lily said. "Your car or mine?" What had gotten into her?

JJ raised his eyebrows, smiled. "Mine," he said.

The restaurant was in a small brick building in an old section of town whose streets teemed with college-age kids. JJ stood just inside the door, lifted his head, and sniffed. "Smells great."

The yellow walls were decorated with shawls and large tin ornaments, and the wooden booths were painted orange, purple, and green. "Love this place," Lily said. They sat opposite one another in a small booth. She couldn't focus on the menu and ordered the first thing she saw, shrimp fajitas. JJ ordered chicken mole and a pitcher of sangria. "We need to get drunk."

Uh-oh.

"Just kidding." He leaned forward. "I'm trying to cut back on that, too. First the cigarettes, thanks to you, now the alcohol. One thing at a time. It's hard, when you're on the road, to really take care of your body, you know?"

She nodded, keeping her eyes on his, trying not to think about his body. The sangria arrived, and he poured first into her glass and then into his own. She watched his hands, long-fingered, movements graceful, almost feminine.

"Don't worry," he said, misunderstanding her fixated gaze as he poured, "I don't have a problem with alcohol, per se. But as a musician you're always in the clubs—it's like part of the job, you get to hear from the fans, you hang out with other musicians—and so you're drinking. But you get to a certain age, you can't keep that up. I can't tell you how many musicians I know who've kicked the bucket lately, one thing or another."

Lily didn't want to know all the depressing parts of his world, at least not until she had gotten to soak up some of the cool parts first. She took a long swallow. The alcohol surged through her body.

"But playing . . . the music—that must be amazing for you, right?"

"I love performing, sure. And an audience . . ." He closed his eyes briefly, then held her eyes, as if eager to convince her. "I know it's a cliché, but it's a high like you can't imagine."

Please, please help me imagine, Lily thought. She was starting to relax. All the questions she'd been pondering for months, she could finally ask. "Tell me, how do you go about composing?"

"I don't really do it in any particular way."

"You don't consciously work on it?"

"No, I just mess around on the guitar sometimes and see where it takes me. Sometimes on the road, but more when I'm home, between tours. It's kind of like doodling, only with strings."

Given the complexity and beauty of his pieces, it was hard to believe they began as something as prosaic as doodles. "Even when you're writing a song with Blaise?"

"Wait"—he put his glass down abruptly—"you're not making the video about me, are you?"

"Well, no—but isn't it a partnership?"

"That's how I used to think of it, when we had our band. But the group split—Blaise was with the bass player, and then she and I got it on for a bit, and the band disbanded. Usual story, right?"

Lily nodded and carefully put her fork down, as if it might slip from her fingers otherwise. "For a bit." Did this mean that JJ and Blaise were no longer a couple?

"She wanted to go in more of an alt-country direction anyhow," JJ was saying. "She liked how we sounded together and asked me to be her guitarist. She's the one with the voice, so . . ." He shrugged. He poured them more sangria, then smiled. "What were we talking about?"

"You were explaining why you don't want the video to be about you. Why you think you're not a team, how she's the singer and you're the . . ." *Lackey* ran through her mind. "Lead guitarist."

"Yeah, right. See, songwriters are the stars. Their guitarist is *their* guitarist. The video has to be about her."

"But your sound is your sound together. That doesn't seem quite right."

"It is what it is. Shit, I get to play most nights of my life. I get to make a living doing what I love. When I get fed up, I remind myself of that."

Lily leaned forward. "I do want to film you, too. It doesn't have to be part of this video. I mean, your playing is incredible. People should know about you. Couldn't—" She stopped herself. *Couldn't you have more backbone and insist on a more equal role?* she wanted to say. *What am I talking about?* she thought. *What do I know about anything?*

"I appreciate your interest," he said. He was always saying that:

"Thank you for your interest." *Thank you for your slavish devotion* was what he should be saying.

Their dinner arrived. She glanced at her sizzling onions and peppers and wished she hadn't had so much sangria. She took a small bite of shrimp and waited to see if her stomach would cooperate.

JJ sawed energetically at his chicken. "I hate all that cult-of-personality stuff. When I was first playing, my musician friends would argue—Keith Richards is the best guitarist! No, Eric Clapton is best! That's bullshit. It's not just a matter of chops."

She wasn't sure exactly what he was getting at, but she nodded anyhow. "Do you ever think about having a solo career?"

"No. I always wanted to play with other people. But lately . . . sometimes I do wonder if maybe I should have."

"Is it too late? I mean, what would it involve?"

"A ton of work—I'd have to do everything myself, like book the gigs. Managers aren't interested in instrumental players. Leo Kottke can support himself, not me."

"But couldn't you do a solo show once in a while?" she said plaintively. How she longed to hear his music live, to see the relationship of hands to strings, strings to chords, chords to notes. How did he make that quivering vibrato, that bright piercing tone, that throbbing bass?

"Nah, doesn't work that way. See, if I had my own gigs, I'd have to fit them around Blaise's schedule. Then, if a show of hers got added and it was on the date of my gig, she'd be super pissed. I mean, either I'm her guitarist or I'm not."

"It's a shame for people not to hear you!" Lily's fork smacked her water glass.

"It is what it is."

Lily lifted her fork again, took another tentative bite. Her stomach seemed OK. "Maybe you have more power than you think. Maybe you could make a few demands on her. Tell her you want to play one or two of your own instrumentals at every show. I mean, it's not like she can go out and get anyone nearly as good as you."

"Not what she says," he laughed. He pushed away his plate. "She likes to tell me she can replace me in a minute, that guitarists are just lining up to take my place."

"That's horrible!"

"Lily, you can't say anything about any of this to her. I really shouldn't have been dumping on you like this."

"It's fine, really." *Dump, dump away!*

"You're a really good listener."

"Wow, thank you," she said, flattered for an instant, and then deflated. Did he see her as a therapist, not a woman? She pulled herself up short. *Whoa, girl!* What was she thinking? She shouldn't want him to think of her as anything other than the unavailable married woman she was.

Still, there was an undeniable ease between them, she thought, as they moved on to other topics, an undeniable connection. There was something, she was sure of it. It had been there from the first, when she had seen him outside the school auditorium and admonished him to stop smoking. For her, it began the moment on stage when he paused, placed his pick just so, and released the note that shot into her like Cupid's arrow. Or was it a poison dart that had lodged in her heart like a tick, burrowing, feeding on blood? She laughed inwardly at her metaphor; clearly the wine was going to her head.

"Have some more sangria," he said.

Back at the hotel, she couldn't fall asleep. It was as if being with JJ had given her an electric charge; she was over capacity and needed to let the battery run down. She ran the conversation with him over again in her mind, wondering about his and Blaise's relationship. Even if they weren't a couple, they seemed a lot more connected than just bandmates. Maybe JJ was one of those men who complained about the women who had so much control over their lives, the women they were ensnared by. It didn't mean that they didn't want to be with those women, that they didn't want to be ensnared, that there wasn't some sort of sick, warped attraction. She thought of the casual way Blaise had removed her shirt in the green room. JJ and Blaise could be together, right this moment, making love. He could be one of those men. She didn't know him. He might very well be the kind of man she didn't respect at all. Clearly, though, that would have nothing to do with whether or not she liked him. Or whether or not she had, maybe, just a tiny little crush.

There. She'd said it, if only to herself, if only to her pillow. Just a silly little crush on top of the worship she felt for his talent. She must be confusing the adoration for his talent with a crush on him. Because she had just admitted she didn't really know him, hadn't she? In fact, what she did know about him did not at all fit the kind of man she would squander her emotions on. He was not grounded like her husband, her husband whom, she recognized, she hadn't been in the mood to speak with earlier, for whom she had left a chirpy little message to say where she was and that everything was OK before she had headed out to dinner. Unlike Stephen, JJ was indiscriminant—he should never have talked to her about Blaise the way he had. How did he know he could trust her? It was patently stupid and showed a terrible lack of judgment. He was a blabbermouth—how could she have a crush on a blabbermouth?

Funny: She had heard that people were usually disenchanted when they met their idols in the flesh. But having met JJ, she was even more enthralled.

Stop it, she told herself, turning over, wiping her sweaty hair off her neck. *Concentrate on your meeting tomorrow with Blaise.* Reluctantly she pulled her mind from JJ's slender fingers, his troubled eyes. She focused on her Blaise checklist, like counting sheep, until she fell asleep.

◄ ►

The next morning Blaise answered Lily's knock wearing white from head to toe, a slinky satin lounge outfit that said, *Let me dazzle you.*

Like Lily's room, hers had the standard hotel decor of matching curtains and bedspread in a muted floral, a tweed rug that wouldn't show stains. She also had a little window alcove that looked out on the highway, the cars moving up toward Canada.

"Let's have coffee." She gestured to the alcove and sank into the cushions, leaned back in a supple stretch. With just a touch of makeup, she was striking. Her narrow face and small, sharp features saved her from a too-facile beauty, Lily thought.

"Have some strawberries," Blaise said, seeing Lily eyeing the bowl.

"Great, thanks." Lily slid a few onto her saucer. Why did she feel as if taking anything from Blaise, anything at all, would be a mistake?

"So, what would you like in the DVD?" Lily asked. "Just concert footage?"

"You have some ideas?"

Lily had surprised herself, during the drive to Plattsburgh, to discover that she did have ideas. "I think we should include some of your background, your life." *And not just because I'd like to hang around and ask a lot of personal questions to satisfy my prurient imagination, either.* "We could show you arriving at a given town, exploring a bit, sound check. I'd like to film you working on songs—how you go about the arrangements, that kind of thing. How do you and JJ work together?"

"Usually I write something and have a vague idea of the kind of sound I think would go with it. At some point I turn it over to him, and he works it up."

"Well, that could be really interesting to film."

"We don't have studio time scheduled at the moment."

"You said at the concert you're hoping to have a new release by this summer. Do you still have to record some of the new material?" Lily had heard them perform only a few new songs. Visions of watching them in the studio danced in her head.

"We have a month off in March to work on stuff before we head for Europe."

They were leaving? Europe must have gotten added to their touring schedule since she had last looked at the website.

"How long will it take to produce the DVD?" Blaise popped a strawberry into her mouth.

"Well, there's the postproduction work. The editing. That can take a while." At work they turned things around fairly quickly, but who knew how long she would need? "Figure at least a month or so."

Blaise stood up to signal that their time was over. They would do their first formal interview the next day. "When you're done, if I like it, we'll sell it through my website. I'll give you royalties. That's only fair."

"That's not at all necessary! Doing this film is truly an honor." *Forget royalties,* Lily thought. *Just, please God, let me not fuck this up.*

Lily sailed through the afternoon as if on a giddy marijuana high. She checked and rechecked her equipment, making notes and blocking out some of her ideas, and then shot footage near the hotel until five o'clock, when she drove to the down-at-the-heels theater where Blaise and JJ would be playing. They were on the stage already, tapping microphones with forefingers, asking for more guitar in the monitor—that odd box on the floor that JJ poked with the toe of his cowboy boot. She made a mental note to find out what it was actually for. As they went through parts of a couple of songs, starting and stopping, Lily tried out distances and lighting options. She zoomed in on Blaise's fishnets and boots, then up to the little O of her mouth as she sang high and low to check the sound, then on JJ's fingers going crab-like up the frets. She tried the tripod in a few locations before deciding on one that would give her the best angle. For other positions, she would mount the camera on her shoulder. Lily choose one setting for the tight close-ups of Blaise, one for the middle distance, and one for JJ's guitar, and saved the settings.

"How's it sound, Lily?" JJ called out. She couldn't read his expression; was he regretting how much he had told her the previous night?

Lily hesitated. "The instruments maybe overshadow the voices just a little bit."

"More vocals, Ted," Blaise said. Lily glowed.

Sound check over, JJ jumped off the stage and with a wave disappeared down a hall. "Catch you later," Blaise said to Lily over her shoulder, following him. Lily had hoped for an invitation to dine with them, but clearly that was not to be. She packed up her gear and walked slowly from the musty little theater, drove around until she found a diner, and ordered a chicken Caesar salad, six points. She got back to the theater way too early and fussed more with her equipment, trying to stay calm.

The door opened, and JJ walked in. Spotting her, he came over. "All set?"

"I think so—how about you?"

"Yeah, I got a chance to chill a little."

"What do you do beforehand—practice scales or something?"

"No, I just do some stretches."

"Really. Stretches."

"Or take a bath."

Don't go there, Lily thought.

"Anything to get loose."

"After all this time, you still get anxious before a show?"

"No, I meant loosen the muscles, to play more fluidly." He jiggled his shoulders.

The door opened again, and Blaise and the theater manager came in, Blaise in her black leather pants and an off-the-shoulder paisley top, a sort of urban-cowgirl look, followed by the ticket takers. Something went rat-a-tat-tat inside Lily's chest.

"Now, don't forget: Don't shoot too much of me. She's the client," JJ said.

"OK, boss." He was just too adorable.

Finally the doors were flung open, and the theater started to fill. How different everything was from just two days ago, Lily thought, watching people drift to their seats. Just two days ago she sat alone in the audience, envious of the woman with the elaborate shawl. Now, as people glanced her way, she imagined herself as they might see her—a cool lady with a camera, who got to go to lots of great concerts. How wrong impressions could be. She wiped her lens for the twentieth time, made sure the mic was on. Had she checked the battery? Steady now. The thought of blowing it in a big way sent sweat trickling down her sides.

The MC hopped onstage. Lily pressed the ON button. He had a wiry beard that reminded her of the scrubby she used on her dishes, and he wore a flat wool cap. Why did folkies favor tweed caps, as if they had just gotten off the boat from Ireland?

"Hi, folks, I'm Adam Loran, president of the North Country Folk Coalition. We've put together a terrific series of acoustic music, as well as some slightly more rock-oriented shows, like our guests tonight. Let's welcome Colorado singer-songwriter Blaise Raleigh and guitarist Jackson Johnson!"

The applause was less enthusiastic than it had been at the venues Lily had attended. Perhaps in this rural area people weren't so familiar with Blaise's music.

"Hi there, Plattsburgh, we're so happy to be here!" Blaise said. "I spent some time today checking out your town, and I have to say, you have some of the prettiest scenery I've ever seen."

Her usual line, Lily knew now. Blaise hadn't ventured from the hotel. "Nicest people, too." The applause was louder. Lily swiveled to pan the crowd.

"Now, I hope you like our show tonight. I have with me the greatest guitarist you're probably ever likely to hear—you tell me if I'm wrong—Mr. Jackson Johnson. And I hope you all will clap real hard, because Lily here is taping the show. Hit it, JJ!"

Blanggggg! JJ's guitar went, shaking the dust from the decaying theater carpeting. *Waaaa.* JJ did a run up the guitar so fast Lily couldn't keep up with the camera, and the crowd was already hooting. Blaise hadn't opened with a JJ solo before. It was almost as if she had heard Lily's complaint of the previous night. JJ wouldn't have told her what Lily had said, would he? She had been so busy promising him she wouldn't tell Blaise what he told her that it had never occurred to her to ask him to extend her the same courtesy.

Besides, she hadn't said anything that couldn't be repeated. Had she? Lily moved the camera to JJ's face, back to his hands, pulled back. Blaise probably had sensed the tepidness of the crowd and decided to wake them up, that was all. She had correctly guessed that a rocking bluegrass flat-picking instrumental would do the trick.

"What did I tell you? Thank you, thank you all. Now we'd like to shift gears and do an R & B number off our latest album. It's called 'Take Pity on Me.'"

JJ and Blaise went through the familiar opening chords, the familiar harmonies, the familiar pauses. Each time Lily heard the songs there were slight variations, little things JJ did differently. She'd have to remember to ask him about that.

At the break, Lily went to the bathroom, washed her hands, took a few deep breaths. She played back the last minute of the tape to make sure it was OK. The lighting was a bit off, and she adjusted it. She could tinker with it afterward as well.

She went outside to the lobby to find something to drink.

A man sidled up to her. "Are you a producer?"

"I'm a video-camera person," Lily said. *Video artist* would be way overstating it.

"Have you done anything I would have seen?"

"I do mostly industrials." He had probably missed the one on employee health-coverage packages, *PPO or HMO? The Choice Is Yours.*

"It must be exciting work."

"Yes, I'm very lucky," Lily said, not wanting to burst his bubble.

"Well, nice to meet you. I'm sure you're quite talented."

I wish, Lily thought, then wondered, did she? Did she wish she were talented? She wasn't sure how much fun it was to be talented. She thought guiltily of Stephen, of pretending she was getting serious about film. She knew it wasn't true. But she sure was really liking it tonight. Was that just the glamour? Or maybe she hadn't had a subject she found sufficiently compelling before. Then again, maybe she just hadn't had the guts, and telling herself she wasn't talented got her off the hook.

Lily sighed. It was too much to think about right now. Now she had to focus on the task at hand so she could earn her place on the road for this one unbelievable, incredible week. She went in search of JJ and Blaise to film them autographing CDs.

She taped the second set plus two encores and still had about twenty minutes left on the second tape, so she filmed a few minutes of Blaise and JJ schmoozing with the audience. She trailed them backstage and filmed them packing up their instruments. She filmed them trekking out to the car.

"Enough already," Blaise snapped. "Put the damn thing away. Let's go drink." Excited to be included, Lily followed Blaise and JJ to the bar. She left the tripod in the trunk but took the very expensive camera in with her.

The bar, with neon signs from the '60s and creaky wood floors, was filled with scruffy neighborhood kids and men who looked as if they'd been drinking there since World War II. Blaise plopped into a booth and slid over, patting the seat next to her for JJ. "God, that was good, wasn't it, Lily?"

"Everybody loved it, you could tell."

"We sold sixty-three CDs. Amazing. Those folks weren't the kind with a lot of discretionary income, in case you didn't notice."

"I noticed," Lily said.

"We made some real fans tonight. That's what counts. You build your fan base slowly, but once you have them, they're yours for life—unless you fuck up and put out a bad product. So, what are you drinking? Should we splurge on champagne?"

"Sure! It's on me."

"God, she's great, isn't she, JJ?" She leaned into him.

"She sure is." He put two fingers to his lips, kissed them, and blew them to Lily.

"He likes you," Blaise said. "I can tell. That's good. I like when JJ likes someone. He has good taste."

"Blaise," JJ said, a plea in his voice.

Lily felt uneasy. "I'll just go get that champagne."

"You're frightening her away," Blaise said.

"Blaise," JJ said again.

When Lily returned, Blaise's arm was slung over JJ's shoulder. He looked unhappy but resigned. Resigned to what? Blaise looked drunk, but they hadn't had anything to drink yet.

"A time for champagne," Blaise quoted one of her song titles, lifting her glass.

"You have great titles," Lily said.

"What others do you like?"

"Well, 'Sweet and Sour Sensation' and 'Shredded Melody,' for starters."

Blaise and JJ burst out laughing.

"What? What is it?"

"We got those off a Chinese menu," JJ finally explained.

"You're kidding, right?"

"No, really. It should have been 'Shredded Medley.'"

"Creative." Lily tried to sound hip but felt like an idiot. To regain her dignity, she dredged up a question she'd been meaning to ask. "How do you see your music fitting in, in the larger sense? For instance, where do the radio stations place you?"

"Oh, please," Blaise said, "don't get me started." She flicked with her fingernail at her glass, making it ping.

"Radio sucks," JJ said. "Forget radio. The radio stations are controlled from the top; the hosts are told what to play. Only the big labels have the dough to buy time."

"But I've streamed radio shows from links on your website."

"Oh, we've been on small independent stations, college stations. But as far as getting real airplay? No way." He began doing a little drumming motion on the table.

"Can we just forget this?" Blaise grabbed the bottle. "Can we just put this out of our minds for one fucking night?"

"Sure, sorry," Lily said, stung.

"Whoa, Blaise." JJ's fingers stilled on the tabletop.

"Brown Eyed Girl" came on the jukebox. "I love this song," Blaise said abruptly. She glanced at the group of college-age boys in the booth next to them, slid her blouse a little farther down her arms, revealing more of her shoulders.

"Hey, you there," she called to a shy-looking kid with blond hair. "Come here."

The boy looked at his friends and then got up and walked over to Blaise. She pulled his head down next to hers and whispered in his ear. The boy stiffened, shook his head, moved away. She stared after him a moment, then turned to JJ and reached out her hands. "Well, *you'll* dance with me."

"I'm really not in the mood."

"JJ."

JJ stood, his face a mask. He stood aside for Blaise to get out of the booth, then followed her to the jukebox. They moved into each other's arms, JJ's back rigid. Blaise's hands cupped the back of his neck. Lily wanted to look away. She fought the urge to get up and leave, but she knew Blaise wanted an audience.

They swayed to the music. Lily remembered her college bar, of times she was the one pressed up against a strange boy's body, holding herself as steady as an instrument for gauging depth or temperature, afraid to move, remembering the confusion because the boys never talked; you never knew what they were thinking or feeling.

JJ and Blaise returned to the booth, arms around each other's waists. JJ didn't meet Lily's eyes. Blaise filled her glass to the brim, downed it. She had emptied the bottle, but Lily was not about to buy another.

She was suddenly furious.

"I think I'll head out," she stood. "I'll see you both tomorrow."

JJ looked up. "Good night, Lily. Thanks for the champagne."

"Yeah," Blaise said, not glancing at her.

Outside the cold air was like a slap, a sudden shock to bring her to her senses. The camera strap bit into her shoulder. She walked quickly to her car, cold cutting through the thin cloth of her slacks. She felt like a voyeur, soiled and scummy. What was going on with those two? And did she really want to know?

She drove the few miles to the hotel, made her way, still shaking from the cold, into her room, and ran a hot bath. She threw off her clothes. Steam from the tub wafted into the room, and the scent of orange bodywash filled the air. She lowered her body into the water, the heat instantly warming her. She rested her head back, slid lower into the water.

It was only then that she remembered she had promised to call Stephen.

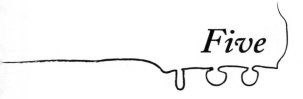

Five

Lily awoke to a line from a favorite poem: *Beautiful my desire, and the place of my desire.* Roethke. The night before came flooding in, and to dispel that aura she picked up the phone to call Stephen.

She caught him just as he was leaving for work, so he asked her to try him later. Just hearing his voice was like a cooling tonic on her skin, skin that had been overheated by JJ and Blaise. Stephen was real-world, she thought, though she wasn't clear what she meant by that. JJ and Blaise wouldn't last a minute in his world of meetings and negotiations and position papers.

Yet she imagined their world to be more colorful, perhaps more meaningful, than her own. As if hers—the dailiness of work, cozy Sunday mornings with bagels and the *Times,* walks in Riverside Park—were a pastel pastiche in comparison.

Ouch. If she truly felt her life was so lacking, maybe she should do something about it.

She showered, dressed, ran gloss over her lips. Well, even if her fantasy was way off, she could chalk this experience up as an interesting chapter in her pleasant but unremarkable life.

A knock on the door relieved her of more painful reflection.

JJ greeted her with a tentative smile. "I'm real sorry about last night; I know it was pretty awkward. But I warned you what she's like. Want to catch some breakfast with me? She's not ready to greet the world just yet."

Yesterday the prospect of time alone with him had sent tingles to every nerve center in her body. Now all she felt was apprehension. "How late did you stay at the bar?" she asked as they walked down the carpeted hallway.

"Not too. I had to pry her loose from the bottle."

The hotel dining room was stirring with activity, busboys and waiters hurrying to and fro, children spilling Cheerios, crowds around the buffet's Sterno-lit chafing dishes.

"Let's go off in the corner so we can be private," JJ said. He gestured for her to precede him; as she threaded her way among the tables, she straightened, conscious of how she must look from behind.

They decided to skip the buffet and order off the menu. JJ was quiet, staring down at his place mat, tapping a beat on his coffee cup with his forefinger.

"There's something I need to explain." He looked up. "But you have to keep it confidential. I have to have your word."

"Of course."

"Blaise isn't in great shape." He leaned forward. "She sees a shrink when she's home, has phone sessions when we're on the road. She drinks too much, she does drugs—even with the meds the shrink prescribes, which is really, really messed up."

"I had no idea." Lily remembered Blaise's eyes the night she caught her taping their show. She had thought they were dilated from anger.

"She's a major handful. Sometimes she's better than other times, but lately . . ."

"She's worse?"

"I'm not sure. I'm not sure if she's worse or if I've just gotten more aware of it, you know?" He bit at a cuticle. "We've been playing together for twelve years. In the beginning, it was all just part of the show, part of being young and in a band. We sure had some crazy times, it was fun, but you get older and you realize a lot of that is really fucked up, right?" He looked at her with the pleading intensity she found so compelling.

The waitress arrived with their omelets. She had a gray bun covered by a hairnet and the calves of a twenty-year-old.

"I'd appreciate some ketchup when you have a moment." JJ gave the waitress a smile that would have melted a price sticker off a bottle. *No wonder I can't help liking him,* Lily thought. She watched him douse his eggs with salt and pepper.

"It must be difficult."

"I have to tell you, I think about quitting. I know I denied it the other night, but I do think about it lately."

"But you said you couldn't really go solo."

"I guess I'd look for a new band, but that sucks because I'd have to settle for just the few little guitar parts I'd have with most bands. Or I could team up with another singer, but the established artists have their own guys already. I don't want some singer who's just starting out. And it's got to be a woman. My voice goes better with a woman's. Plus, male singers have even bigger egos than Blaise has. They'd cut my solos to, like, ten seconds. That's the dilemma."

"Well, what do you think you really want? I mean, ideally? Do you think you're so unhappy you'd be better off leaving, or would you rather try and work things out with Blaise?"

"Yeah, exactly. If l could tell you that, we wouldn't be having this conversation."

"Here you go, sugar." The waitress was back with the ketchup.

"You're a doll." He smiled up at her, whacked the bottom of the bottle. "Reminds me of my mother," he said to Lily. "She worked all her fucking life, as hard as this woman probably does. When I think of that, I can't believe I'm bitching and moaning like I am. Ignore me, please."

"No, it's tough, what you're facing."

"But what I wanted to say to you is that Blaise doesn't know enough to protect herself from looking like an asshole. I'm asking you—as a favor—not to film her when she's out of it. She holds it together for performances, but other times . . . well, I hope you'll be a little judicious."

Judicious? Lily was impressed by his vocabulary. "You love her a lot, don't you?" It came out before she thought to censor it.

"Love?" JJ said. "Where did you get that idea? I hate her guts."

"Hate?"

"OK," he grinned, "so that's too strong. I respect her music, but I don't respect her. She's an amazing talent, and we work really well together. I do care about her, I don't want her to drink or drug herself to death, but I don't love her. She's a narcissistic, self-involved egomaniac."

"But you said . . . and you had a thing together. And last night—"

"She goes through men like wrapping paper—covers you in something glossy, then rips you to shreds, throws you away. I told you, we had a thing when we were in the band. Afterward we stayed together professionally because we were good together musically and could handle it. But what you saw last night is her playing at seducing me— it's just a game."

"Why would she do that?" Lily hit her elbow on the table, jostling her juice glass. She took a hasty sip.

"Because she can. Because she likes to exert her control over me."

"But why?"

"I told you, she's the act, I'm the hired gun. I mean, let's face it, she's a hot little number. But she's bad news. Usually she picks up guys when we're traveling. But when she's not getting any, or when she's insecure, she gets weird and likes to screw with my head. That's what you saw last night."

This was too convoluted; Lily filed it away to think about later. "I'll edit out anything that isn't appropriate. You have my word." Given what he was telling her of Blaise's shenanigans, how did he manage a love life of his own?

"Thanks," he said fervently. Fingers laced, he lifted his arms over his head and stretched. "I feel so much better." He smiled at her over his coffee. She smiled back. A warm feeling pooled between them, like sunshine on a table.

"You feel you have to take care of her, don't you?"

He looked momentarily startled. "I guess. I mean, I think of it as protecting my own career—I do it for myself as much as for her. I'm not always in such great shape myself. I've even been thinking of going on something for anxiety. I work at staying sane. I mean, even without Blaise, this life's a crazy mix of highs and tedium—sometimes in the same day."

Ecstatic highs between troughs of boredom—that part was familiar. "Sounds like motherhood: intense joy and then changing diapers and playing hide-and-seek."

"That's right"—JJ wiped his mouth and leaned forward—"we haven't talked about *you*. Your son is in college, right? Blaise told me. I have to say, you don't really look old enough to have a son that age. Your husband made you a child bride, didn't he?"

"Ha," Lily looked down, "you're quite the charmer, aren't you?" Out of the corner of her eye she saw Blaise skirting the buffet and heading their way. Lily didn't know whether she felt disappointed or relieved to end the conversation. "Blaise is here." Even in faded jeans and a sweatshirt, Blaise owned the room, striding toward them with confidence.

JJ looked up at Blaise and smiled. "Hey." His voice sounded perfectly comfortable, as if he hadn't been trashing her just minutes before.

"Man, do I have a hangover." Blaise slumped into a chair. There were dark shadows under her eyes. "I didn't think you got hangovers from champagne."

"Might have been the vodka you had after it," JJ said.

"Don't start."

"I have some aspirin," Lily offered. "I think tomato juice is supposed to help, too."

"Lily, so thoughtful, so wonderful to have around." Blaise sounded sincere rather than snotty—or maybe both? She grabbed a piece of toast off of JJ's plate and buttered it top to bottom in four precise strokes, like a lawn she was mowing.

"Do you want to get started on the interview after breakfast?" Lily asked. *After a couple of cups of black coffee and before you get into any more mind-altering substances,* she thought.

Blaise wafted a hand in the air. "Whatever."

"I'm going into town," JJ said. "I'll meet up with you later, then."

81

Blaise glanced up at him briefly and then stirred her coffee vigorously. *She has feelings for him,* Lily thought, startled. *JJ was completely wrong about her. Blaise might not even admit it to herself, but she does.*

Takes one to know one, a voice inside her said. She swatted that away.

◄ ►

Blaise had spruced up by the time Lily came to her room after breakfast. In jeans and a stretchy multicolored top that reminded Lily of the hook rug her grandmother had had in her foyer, Blaise looked remarkably good for someone who had awoken with a hangover. Lily was envious. She herself was at an age where her face showed every minute of lost sleep. "Let's just chat for a bit first, OK?" she said.

"Sure." Blaise plopped into the cushioned seat in the alcove, her back to the window and the highway. She tossed her head back as if she were posing for a shampoo commercial.

"I'll film our conversation, just for practice. It'll give me a chance to test the light and the angles. This way, you'll get comfortable with the camera and forget it's even here." This, of course, was bullshit. She did not need to fuss with the equipment, and Blaise would never forget a camera. Still, she hoped it would loosen Blaise up. "So, tell me: Did you always want to be a singer?"

Blaise straightened slightly, poufed her hair with her fingers. "Since I was a girl. I sang in my choir, and school shows."

"Did you enjoy that?" Lily stayed a distance away but zoomed in.

"Sure, it was fun. It taught me to listen to the different musical voices. I try to get some of that in my own songs." She continued to attack her hair with nervous gestures, but her voice was a little more animated. Lily moved closer.

"Where? In, say, a ballad like 'Whisper in My Ear'?" It was a striking song, with beautiful harmonies that wrapped in and around each other.

"Yes, exactly!" Blaise put her hands together, steeple-like. Her nails were painted a deep purple shade. "The bass as well as the main melody. JJ harmonizes with that."

"Can you point to other influences that your choir singing has on your music?"

"Well, obviously in how I use my voice"—her hand gestured to her throat—"as well as the training and the discipline."

"When did you start writing songs?"

"Not till college. I had this music teacher, he was really cool—big brown eyes, played keyboard—he encouraged me. I started writing poetry, and then song lyrics." Blaise had given up the glamour-girl posture now and was leaning forward.

"Your lyrics are really compelling. It's a difficult art form, I would guess?"

"Yes. You have to say so much with so few words. And of course the meaning and the feeling have to work with the music to communicate."

"What about your parents? Were they musical?"

"No, although they encouraged me. Mom and Dad were always very supportive."

Blaise looked down and pulled at her top. Sensing her discomfort, Lily decided to drop that line of questioning. She switched to asking about how Blaise got her start, how she liked touring, her plans for the future. She was enjoying this. It was like creating an appetizer plate; later she'd play it over and decide on the most promising bits. The interview portion would end up being twenty minutes, tops, of an hour-long DVD, which she'd have to edit down from at least ten hours of interviews. The sound checks and performances would be three or four times that.

"Had enough for today?" Lily asked after an hour.

"I'm dying for some air. Let's take a walk."

Lily went back to her room, bundled up, and met Blaise in the lobby. Outside, the winter sun was silvery on the dusting of snow that had fallen during the night.

"That went OK, don't you think?" Blaise asked. Under her knit cap and oversize down jacket, she looked more waif than diva. It was the first time Lily had heard her sound less than sure of herself.

"Absolutely. You're a natural on camera."

Blaise set off at a brisk pace. "I find it all so stressful. I don't know why I can't just enjoy things. My shrink says I have to lighten up, but of course that's easy for him to say."

"I know what you mean," Lily said. Telling someone to lighten up was like telling a hysterical person to calm down—it just sent her further over the edge.

They walked single file to pass a woman and small boy coming the other way. "I bet it's great being behind the camera," Blaise said, looking over her shoulder at Lily. "You get to do the looking, and there's no pressure to perform."

Lily almost laughed out loud. "Well, it's performing in a way."

"You know what I mean."

"But don't you love performing?" Lily came alongside her again. "I can't imagine you could be that good at something without enjoying it." *Damn,* Lily realized. This was what she should have gotten on camera.

"I love it and it's hard, both." Blaise finally sounded genuine, as if she had decided to trust Lily and drop the rock-star persona. "I love when I'm singing, when I'm in the moment, but the rest of the time I'm worrying about my career, and what types of songs I should be writing, and where I am on the charts." She stopped abruptly, and Lily almost tripped. "You can't use any of this. It's too personal."

"OK," Lily said, hoping she could get Blaise to change her mind later. "Don't you have a manager or someone to worry about all that for you? Someone to guide you?"

"I have a manager, but I'm a very hands-on person. I do some of my own travel arrangements, I deal with the publicists—you've no idea how many details there are!" She pulled hard at the ends of her scarf. "Everyone will cheat you or fuck things up if you're not watching."

"Hmm," Lily said. Was this what JJ meant by overcontrolling and paranoid?

They came abreast of a furniture warehouse on two stories. Couches and gigantic dining room sets were displayed in the windows.

84

"Hey, let's go in here," Blaise said. "I need a couch."

"Wouldn't you want to buy one closer to home?"

"I live in the sticks, so if I see something, I can have it shipped."

"You'd have to have a pretty big house to fit this furniture," Lily said as they wandered through the showroom. "The scale is huge."

"You live in Manhattan, right? I guess you're used to tiny spaces."

"You're right," Lily laughed. "I lose sight of the norms."

"What's your husband do?" Blaise paused at a large square-shaped oak dining table.

"He's a planner. Works for the city."

"How long are you married?" Blaise ran her finger over the table's glossy surface.

"Twenty-three years."

"Wow." Blaise stopped dead, stared at her for a moment with those curious blue eyes. Then she looked down, ran her finger along the fabric of a sectional covered in an apricot-colored suede. "This is nice. Probably costs a fortune."

What was a fortune to her? Lily wondered. After all, despite her success, she had to pay for the hotels and the meals and the car rentals and her health insurance and everything else. That had to come to a hefty piece of change. Lily located the ticket. "Forty-five hundred."

"Well, it'd be double in Boulder," Blaise said, but she moved off. "So you and your husband were just kids when you got married. That's a long time. Pretty impressive."

Lily never knew what to say to that. What did people find impressive? That they had stayed in love? That they'd been lucky to fall in love with the right person? Or did people assume a lot of work and sacrifice must go into sustaining a marriage, and give them credit for that?

"I can't imagine what that must be like. I've never been in a relationship longer than a couple of years. That's really long for me."

"Is that good or bad?" Lily asked. They reached a soft gray leather couch just begging to be sat upon. Lily complied. Blaise, after a second, joined her.

"I don't know. Mostly I get bored. Relationships take so much out of you. But sometimes I think it'd be nice to have someone to come home to after a tour. A guy who worships the ground I walk on. But I'm never home long—a few weeks over the holidays, a break in summer, a day or two here and there. So when would I see him?"

"Is it better to be involved with whomever you're playing with, then?" *Like JJ*, she refrained from saying, hoping Blaise didn't suspect she was fishing. "I mean, if you met a musician you liked, couldn't he join your band?"

"Well, there you go. Is a solo artist going to join my band and play second fiddle to my talent and vision? Am I going to do that for him? No. Or if it's just a backup musician, there's the whole ego thing. Maybe if it's the guy who's the lead and the girl who's backup, it can work, but with the female being on top? Forget it." She took her cap off and stuffed it in a pocket.

"So you're saying it's a choice—long-term relationship versus career?"

"That's kind of what it's looking like."

Of course, your difficult personality doesn't help matters either, Lily thought. On the other hand, right this moment Blaise's personality didn't seem all that difficult. Had JJ overstated things? Maybe he was the one with the problems. Or maybe they were both screwed up. Maybe it wasn't possible to be normal in this profession at all.

"Are you happy, Lily?" Blaise said abruptly. "Or do you get bored shitless by having a quote-unquote 'normal' life?"

Lily tensed; she didn't want to answer that —not to herself, not to Blaise. "I've been pretty happy." She gave a little laugh. "But somebody like you would probably go crazy in a life like mine."

"Hmm. Maybe we could both do with a little of each other's lives. That would be fun—like that movie *Trading Places*. I get to have the adoring husband and son and interesting job in trendy Manhattan, and you get to be the rock star."

Lily pictured herself in Blaise's black leather pants and guffawed.

Back at the hotel, Lily saw her note reminding herself to call Stephen.

"I'm in the middle of a meeting. Can I call you back in fifteen?"

A half hour passed, and he still hadn't called. She was used to his thinking an hour had passed when it had been two. It rarely bothered her; she knew he was just busy and engrossed. But it pointed to an imbalance she rarely thought about: Her own life hadn't engaged her as deeply.

Finally the phone rang. "I didn't forget you. We're in the middle of a problem. Can we talk in an hour or so?"

"I'll be leaving for sound check and all that. It'll probably go late."

"Well, you sound good, you sound like you're having fun. Let's talk in the morning, then. By eight, though—I have a breakfast meeting."

Lily lay down, set the alarm just in case, and closed her eyes. She was happy not to talk. She wanted to quarantine herself, hug the experience of being on the road with no outside contact. Her mind was on overload, filled with everything Blaise and JJ: with the spikes, like blond meringue, of Blaise's hair, the feel of the cushy leather couch, the drumming of JJ's fingers on his coffee cup. This was more stimulus than she was used to. Much more. How did the two of them manage to go from city to city, club to club, day after day after day? They must find a rhythm somehow; they must develop a groove. She wondered if living this way made them feel isolated or if they kept alive in their minds the subculture of all musicians—performers in the next city, musicians who played the club they were in the night before, musicians at festivals, musicians at small jam sessions. Did they feel part of a vast web, connected even to the musicians who worked in the local music store?

That was what JJ had said he was going to do—check out the local music and record stores. You'd think he'd want to get a break from it. She hoped the day on his own had done him good. He had sounded so unhappy this morning, almost desperate. She rolled over, punched the pillow. Should she have encouraged him to leave Blaise, strike out on his own? Why hadn't he already? He was too good to be burying his talent this way. She assumed you didn't break out at, say, the age of forty-five. So if he were thinking of doing it, he would have to do it soon.

She pulled herself up short. What did she know? Who did she imagine she was to give advice? What if she encouraged him and it didn't work out? It would be all her fault!

Yet they both seemed to need some kind of help. Top-notch performers with serious careers though they were, they seemed lost.

Focus on yourself, Lily's inner voice cautioned her. *Get your own life together, why don't you? You're in danger of trying to live through the two of them.*

But they're so much more interesting than I am, she thought.

The little voice didn't have an answer to that.

Word had gotten out from the previous night's performance; tonight was a sold-out crowd.

Lily sensed Blaise and JJ felt the jolt of excitement, too. Some shows, she saw, as she focused her camera on Blaise's movements around the stage, were more wonderful than others. This was one. The energy was electric, yet she couldn't figure out what was different. The notes were the same, the lyrics the same, their voices the same. Yet there was something more, something that brought everything up a notch.

Tonight the music seemed to weave a net over the audience, tightening little by little, until the room was pulled together into a solid entity that breathed and clapped and stomped as one. Lily filmed the hooting fans along with Blaise's flying hair and JJ's flying fingers. She filmed like a madwoman, not stopping for a second, swapping out her battery for a backup. By the time it was over, she was slick with sweat.

The crowd didn't want to let the musicians go. They came out for an encore, left, came back out again. JJ threw down a gauntlet of notes that built and built until everyone was stomping their feet so hard Lily thought the floor would cave in. Finally the lights came on and the audience dispersed slowly, talking in low voices, as if wrung out, too.

Lily's mind was jammed with images and incoherent thoughts of how to present what she'd filmed. She hurried to the green room, gushing. "That was incredible."

"It was good, wasn't it?" JJ's face split open with his smile.

"What did you do? How did you do that?"

"Just happens," he shrugged. "You can't plan it, you can't force it. Something just happens, and you ride it, it takes you with it. Just like a bronco, or a wave." He clicked open his guitar case. "What am I talking about? I don't fucking have any idea what riding a bronco is like, or riding a wave, either, for that matter."

He nestled his guitar into its satin bed. Involuntarily, she moved toward it. "What kind is it?" It was a pale blond color, with dark sides and back.

"A Martin D-18. Some people think it's better for recording than as a road ax, but not me. I leave my good guitars at home."

"You don't use your best one for performing?"

"Can't chance it with plane travel. But this is fine. It has Sitka spruce, which gives it a nice tone, and the back and sides are mahogany."

"Can I touch it?"

JJ laughed. "Sure."

She ran a finger along the neck from the bridge to the sound hole. The wood felt satiny. There were tiny scratch marks where he'd hit the body with his picks.

Blaise threw open the dressing-room door. Her eyes, as if reflecting the sequins on her top, glittered like ice chips. She was followed by a cluster of people.

"Hey, Bruce." JJ stood up to shake hands with a barrel-chested older man in a cowboy hat. "I didn't see you in the audience. We would have dragged your sorry ass up on stage if we'd known you were here."

"Well, that's why I was hiding. Great show."

JJ made the introductions. Bruce was a country singer, the short, plain woman was his wife, and the three other men were his manager, the director of the theater, and the president of the music association that had sponsored the concert.

"Lily is our video artist, everyone," Blaise said.

The manager, a slight young man who was already balding, turned to Lily. "What else have you done?"

"Lily has extensive experience, but we'll be her first performance video," Blaise said, saving Lily the embarrassment of saying, *Nothing*.

They piled into cars, drove to a nearby bar, and took a big table in the back. Blaise ordered shots of tequila and pitchers of beer. Lily found herself seated next to the country singer's wife on one side and the president of the music society on the other.

"Speaking of the blues, that was a terrific riff you did in the first number," Bruce said to JJ. "You were on fire tonight."

"Don't think of stealing him away," Blaise said.

"No chance. I'm not as talented as you—he'd overshadow me."

"You're so smooth you could sell condoms to the pope," Blaise said.

"Speaking of smooth, any of you heard of the Yellow Curries?" the manager asked.

"Derivative," Blaise sniffed.

"No way!"

Bruce's wife tapped Lily's arm. "Do you enjoy making videos?" Lily wished she could listen to the shoptalk but didn't want to be impolite. "Yes, especially this one. And how about you—do you enjoy traveling with your husband?"

"I'm not a big fan of traveling. While we were raising our family, I worked at my kids' school. But now that they're grown, I keep Bruce company on the road. We go home to Nashville next week, and I can't tell you how much I'm looking forward to that."

"Is it tough if you're not a musician?"

"It is, but, to be frank, I learned long ago it's wise to go anyhow. These musicians are cut off from everything, and even the ugly ones have adoring fans. It's just something that happens with women and musicians. So if you want to hang on to your guy, you figure out pretty quick that you better stay close. Of course, if you don't, it's also a small world—word gets around. The wives find out, and they make life hell for their men. Or they leave them."

Lily glanced at Bruce, who was leaning on one elbow, listening intently to Blaise.

"It's nice you can be together, then."

"I'm lucky with Bruce—he's a family man at heart."

Blaise was looking a little looped, Lily noticed. How in the world would she ever cut back on her drinking? What could she do, coming off a performance high—sit alone in her hotel room and watch late-night television?

The manager and JJ seemed to be having a private conversation. Could the manager be interested in JJ? Or was JJ seeking advice? He had his head down, looking thoughtful. His expression was respectful, a child taking in the wise counsel of an elder—though the manager was probably a good ten years his junior. What was up?

"So do you think you'll use the footage from the concert tonight?" the music association president suddenly boomed in her ear.

"Absolutely—the show was fantastic," Lily said.

"You'll make sure to include that we sponsored it?"

"Of course. In fact, I should get your email address." Lily pulled out her pen.

"We're a pretty big organization." He cradled his beer mug in his hands. They were meaty, with thick fingers, as if he were a road worker or lumberjack. "We have members from all over the North Country, a huge fan base for bluegrass, new acoustic—you name it. Even young kids. They like the White Stripes and Coldplay and all the rest, but a lot of them have been brought up listening to traditional. Shit, they do country square dances and go to county fairs. So it's fertile ground, so to speak."

"Terrific," Lily said. She noticed Blaise seemed to be cozying up to the theater director. He had shaggy long hair and wore a black velvet jacket, as if aping the styles from the Beatles' era. JJ was still deep in conversation with the manager.

"Well, I've got an early day tomorrow." The music association president stood and shook Lily's hand. "Nice meeting you. I look forward to your video."

"Sue and I should be going, too," Bruce said. Everyone began to stand.

"I think I'll stay," Blaise said. She turned to the theater director. "You'll give me a ride, won't you?" He tucked a piece of her hair behind her ear in response.

Lily trailed the others from the bar, everyone calling out good nights. JJ and the manager walked off in the opposite direction from where she had parked.

She was bone tired, but she didn't want to go to bed just yet. She decided on a hot bath and ran the water, dimmed the lights, and poured a disgraceful amount of bath gel into the tub. The scent of apple blossom filled the air. She would probably associate it always with this strange, exciting interlude she was having, she thought, sliding into the warm water, smoothing the slick stuff over her skin. She closed her eyes, felt her muscles relax, and rewound the evening, from the first moment of JJ's fingers on the strings. *Beautiful my desire, and the place of my desire.* When her own fingers were wrinkling, she got out and wrapped herself in the thick white terrycloth robe the hotel provided. Wet tendrils of hair clung to her neck, escaping from where she'd tied them on top of her head. She felt as fragrant as a geisha.

There was an abrupt, hard knock on her door. She rushed to it, heart pounding, thinking, *Colby!* She hadn't given Colby a thought in days, and now something had happened.

But it was JJ, lounging against the doorframe. What had made her mind go straight to calamity?

"I hope I'm not bothering you." His glance took in the wet skin and the robe. Most people would have said, *You're indisposed, I'll come back.* He didn't.

"You're not bothering me. I was just . . ." Well, it was obvious, wasn't it? Now was when she should say, *I'll just go get some clothes on.* "Come on in."

He threw himself into the only chair, so she settled on the bed, her robe pulled demurely around her. Although it struck her that this was a little . . . unconventional, in some strange way, it felt perfectly normal and comfortable.

"God, I just don't know what to do. I'm so glad I have you to talk to."

Well, she hadn't exactly signed on as his shrink, but she wouldn't point that out. "Something with that manager, right?"

"He's encouraging me to break from Blaise, to let him manage me. God, she'll kill me if I do that. It'll devastate her."

Lily just looked at him. It would devastate Blaise? Didn't this contradict everything he'd been telling her? Maybe it was him it would devastate. She decided not to suggest that to him. "What does your gut tell you?"

"My gut is churning like an egg beater's gotten into my stomach."

Lily laughed. "Did you feel a jolt of excitement before all the anxieties hit? Can you take yourself back to that first second's response?"

JJ closed his eyes and tilted his head back, exposing his strong, long neck. Did playing give him muscles there, too? Her eyes traveled to his arms, which were flung behind his head. The sleeves of his flannel shirt were rolled up to reveal his massive forearms. His hair, in its usual ponytail, gleamed in the light from the night table.

"I don't think so. I think it was more a sick feeling, like when someone tells you to do something you don't want to do but that might be good for you."

Lily knew that feeling exactly. It was the muse of duty she'd followed millions of times in her life. "I know the feeling. Was that all?"

"I get where you're going—that you can tell what you want from that very first reaction. That's makes sense. But I've already lost that. God, I'm feeling so crazy and shaky. You don't have any tranqs, do you? Probably not—you're probably one of those people who gets by without taking drugs. How do you do it? You're so calm and wise and centered. I've really got to work on that. I've really got to get calm and centered."

He jumped up, began pacing the room, then plopped down on the edge of the bed. She knew she should move away, just a little. She wished she hadn't dimmed the lights. It scared her to have him so close. But she didn't want to move. As if he were a bird she was trying to get a good look at, she didn't want to startle him away.

"What would you do, Lily? What do you think I should do?" He grabbed her hand. There was nothing sexual in it. She knew that. At least, she thought she knew. But the erotic charge momentarily cut off her breath.

"I think you should wait and let the ideas settle a little." Where was this font of advice coming from? "I think you're too"—*unstable,* she almost said—"upset at the moment, and that's never a time to make a decision. There's no rush. That manager isn't going anywhere. You want to make a decision quickly because you want to get the anxiety over with. But you need to live with all the feelings this churns up, not run away from them. It's uncomfortable, I know, but it's what I think you should do."

"Oh God," he said, "you're so right." He pressed his face against her chest, shocking her into immobility. "Thank you so much."

She felt his breath against her bare skin above the V of the robe. She stared down at his tangled ponytail. She fought the urge to stroke it. Then it hit her, why this all felt so oddly familiar: It could have been Colby she was comforting, Colby she was giving advice to, Colby who, conflicted and confused and unhappy, needed to press himself against her.

He was looking for a mother.

Lily bit her lip, hard. As if he sensed her emotions, he pulled back and looked at her. He touched her cheek with his fingers. Smiled. What did the smile mean? Her heart was hammering.

"Sweet Lily," he said.

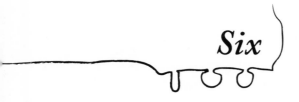

Six

Lily had spent her teenage years, when she wasn't out partying and getting as close as possible to getting into trouble, lying on her bed, listening to the radio, and reading the day away. *Finding yourself,* they called it. As if "yourself" were over there, in the bushes maybe, or in the flowerbed, and you had to follow the clues of your personality, sniff your scent, to track yourself down and discover who you were. She enjoyed the music of her own day, but she loved most the songs of her cousin Renée's Woodstock generation—Janis Joplin, Neil Young, Fleetwood Mac, Bob Dylan.

So when JJ began singing, "Lay Lily lay, lay with your man awhile," her eyes smarted. He was teasing her.

"Out you go, you flatterer. It's late."

He stood immediately, like an obedient child. As he opened the door he turned, and in his "sweet Lily" voice said, "I really do adore you, you know." And he was gone.

She lay awake for hours. Her sleep, when it came, churned with dreams both erotic and confused. In the morning her eyeballs felt bruised, her mouth dusty. She dialed Stephen, her heart beating so hard she almost shoved the phone down before he could pick up.

"Glad you caught me," he said, the normalcy of his voice steadying her. "So, details. How has it been filming the concerts?"

"Good. Fun. OK, I think." She smoothed the bedspread, pushed the image of JJ lying next to her from her mind. That was a detail she didn't think Stephen would appreciate hearing. "How are *you? W*hat's new?"

"Good. Nothing much new. There's a little bit of mail. A package from Amazon."

More CDs, probably. She'd gone a little crazy.

"Work?"

"The usual."

Had Stephen ever unburdened himself to her the way JJ had last night? Lily tried to imagine Stephen throwing himself on her, nuzzling for comfort, and snickered. But it was nice to feel so important. She could just imagine what Stephen would think of JJ. Not so much that there was a sexual threat—she very much doubted that would cross his mind, and for many good reasons. No, he would think that JJ was absolutely, unequivocally, a nut job. He probably was.

"Well, I'd better run. When are you coming home?"

"We're headed to New Hampshire—a concert in Keene, a small venue this time. We go to Boston after that. I would guess that'll wrap it up. So, Sunday."

"Well, call me. I miss you."

"I miss you, too." Suddenly she didn't want to put down the phone, and a chill stole over her. "Stephen?" she said, but he had hung up.

It was getting late, the sun already leaching what color there was in the bland striped wallpaper. She dressed, packed, and decided to take her suitcase with her to the dining room so she could go straight to her car after breakfast. She had better keep her distance from JJ.

She heard a soft tapping, and her heartbeat spiked.

He leaned on the doorjamb, wearing her favorite of his flannel shirts, with teal intersecting navy blue. "Hey," he said. The gold flecks in his eyes shone. Clearly *he* hadn't been up all night. He gave her a big, goofy smile.

"Hey yourself," she said. She had to smile back.

"Thank you for last night. You're a godsend."

"Well, I like you," she said. Already she was forgetting the distance she had promised herself. "I mean, I want to help."

"But why?" Funny he hadn't wondered about this before, as if he took her interest totally for granted.

"Your music's given me so much. I know that sounds hokey, but maybe it's as simple as that."

"So it's not that you fancy me a little?"

She felt her face flame. "JJ, you must be ten years younger than I am," she sputtered. Hearing the shock in her voice and seeing JJ's expression, she realized he probably thought she was horrified by what he said. *Au contraire!*

"I'm forty-three. How old are you? Like, forty-five?"

Oh, she wished! She hesitated, but she had never lied about her age. "Forty-nine," she mumbled.

"Older women and younger men are all the rage," he said. "Don't you want to be trendy?"

"You know I'm married," she said, unable to take the conversation as lightly as she knew she should.

"Then why has your husband let you run away with me, huh?" He took her hand with his left, her suitcase handle with his right. The skin of his palm was pleasingly rough against hers.

"Oh, is that what I'm doing?" she said, finally able to laugh.

"Let's pretend it is," JJ said. "Come on, it'll be fun."

He pulled her down the corridor, swinging her hand, until they reached the elevator. Blaise stood waiting, arms crossed. Lily quickly removed her hand.

"Lily has agreed to elope with me," JJ said. "She's going to solve all my problems."

"A tall order," Blaise said dryly. "Even our inestimable Lily might not be able to pull that off. He's certifiable, I hope you realize?" Blaise stabbed the elevator button.

"Just highly neurotic," JJ argued.

The elevator doors opened. Blaise marched in; they followed like sheepish children. No one said a word until they were seated in the coffee shop. Blaise hoisted the large laminated menu in front of her face.

Lily decided to take the professional tack. "I'd like to set up another interview, Blaise—will you have time later?"

"Today's no good," she said from behind the menu. "By the time we get there, I'll need to rest."

"Tomorrow, then?"

"Tomorrow morning I want to see Keene. JJ will drive me around. Maybe in the afternoon, after we get to Boston."

"Fine." Put in her place, not invited for the drive. *Just as well,* Lily thought.

After breakfast, supplied with directions and a map, she set off. She was glad to have the day to herself. She was suddenly feeling suffocated by tension and emotion.

She crossed into Vermont, then turned south. The Adirondack peaks across Lake Champlain to the west were dappled with melancholy early-morning cloud shadows, broken by occasional glints of light off patches of ice near the mountain summits. At Rutland she headed east to New Hampshire. The roads, lightly traveled, snaked through snow-filled forests. She and Stephen had camped often in Vermont in their first years together. She could almost smell the pungent smoke from campfires, feel the early chill as she emerged from the tent in the morning. She had grown up in the Bronx; Stephen was from Michigan. He had taught her everything about being out of doors—how to gather kindling, how to read a trail, how to recognize even the simplest constellation. They had put their wine bottles in streams to cool, made meals on a Coleman stove. After Colby came, that had all tapered off. She hadn't realized how much she'd missed it.

It was hard now to remember the self she was before becoming a mother. But being on the road was like revisiting that long-lost person. She hadn't felt the urge to be in touch with Colby since she'd left; maybe that was why. In college she had fantasized about being an artist or a career girl, not a mother. But there was something appealing about an image of herself barefoot in a field of poppies—no, poppies wouldn't do, but something else red, or at least colorful—with a long flowing skirt and long flowing hair and an adoring infant gazing up at her, an infant she carried in an embroidered cotton sling in a carefree fashion as she walked through a meadow, singing softly, brimming with mothering essence like nectar from exotic fruit. When she got pregnant, those fantasies were abolished in the hatchet stroke of reality. But she discovered she loved being a mother. She loved the scent, like fresh grass in the spring, of Colby's skull, the tightness of his fingers grasping hers, his curious wrinkly knees. She loved her competency with the bottle and the bathing and even the diapers. She even loved staying home, cutting out recipes, and making dinner.

Over time she grew into the practical skin of a mother, like the tough exterior of an avocado. She laughed, seeing herself in her mind's eye, a rounded avocado body with her head on top. Was that old pit inside capable of sending forth a brand-new shoot? Was she becoming a new self she wasn't so sure she wanted to be?

Maybe this journey was a mistake and she should head home, she thought, reaching the border of New Hampshire. But it was already three o'clock, the sun low in the sky, the shadows long and somber, the air frosty as hell, pressing in against the car windows. There were only a few more days of the tour. She just had to keep her focus, her distance, not go out after the concerts. And not answer her door if JJ knocked.

The thought of him knocking. The thought of him coming back into her room. Her hands on the steering wheel did a crazy, nervous dance.

As the last of the sun's rays were scalding the sky with orange and raspberry, she pulled into the driveway of the inn they had booked for two nights. A large Victorian, it stood on trim grounds with a garden lightly dusted with snow and punctuated with a few defiant plant stalks. The calm beauty was comforting. It was so civilized and charming, Blaise and JJ would fall under the genteel spell and behave themselves. Things would be OK. There'd be no men picked up in bars, no sneaking into and out of bedrooms.

She walked into a small foyer and pressed the bell for service. A woman came from behind a swinging door with a big smile of greeting. Blaise and JJ had not yet arrived. The woman took her up carpeted stairs to the third floor, where her tiny room with dormers and pink floral wallpaper made her feel she had stepped back in time. The wooden plank floor was covered with hook rugs, and the bed was a canopy, with fringes that ended in little pompoms. Her bathroom was across the hall. Lily was coming out of the shower when she heard a car door slam from the parking area below. She went to her bedroom window, which looked over the back of the inn, and saw Blaise marching toward the building. JJ was still in the driver's seat, his head on the steering wheel.

Uh-oh, Lily thought, then cautioned herself: *Stay out of it.*

Still, she circled her room like an edgy cat, back and forth to the window, until she saw that JJ was no longer in the car. She realized she didn't know where the club was or what time they were doing sound check. Each time she heard sounds in the hallway, she poked her head out.

Finally, Blaise was coming down the hall. She was already dressed for the show in tight jeans and her sparkly top. Her expression was grim, her mouth set.

"OK for me to come to sound check?" Lily asked.

"Fine." Blaise's voice was clipped. "We'll leave in a half hour."

"Everything OK?" JJ hadn't spilled the beans and told Blaise of the manager trying to lure him away, had he?

"Oh, hunky-dory. Just peachy."

"What's wrong?"

"JJ being JJ. He can be such a jerk."

Lily was silent; she was afraid to ask anything more.

"Come with me. Let's talk," Blaise ordered.

Lily followed Blaise down the wide, curving staircase to a lushly carpeted sitting room. The walls were painted a dark green with pale yellow molding above the wainscoting; somehow it worked. They helped themselves to the tea that was set out on a sideboard.

Blaise plopped into a chair and sat cross-legged, jostling her tea bag with her spoon so vigorously Lily was afraid she'd break the flowered china cup. Blaise set the cup down on a side table without tasting her tea. "He's such a narcissist, constantly needing his ego stroked. He's so fucking insecure. He gets bent out of shape by everything. Like, he didn't think he got enough credit on our last CD. He's the fucking coproducer, for God's sake. He wants more artistic control of the next one. But only one of us can have artistic control, and that someone is me. I think he's just pissed because I got it on with that guy last night. He's not getting any, and he's jealous."

Lily felt a spasm in her belly. Was that what had been going on last night? And that morning, him swinging her hand—had he just been trying to make Blaise jealous?

No, surely no. Surely she couldn't have misread the situation that grievously. If it had been comfort he'd been looking for, OK. But if he were using her . . .

She took a deep breath. "It sounds like you two could maybe use some help working out these differences. Are there people in the music business who—"

Blaise snorted. "Yeah, right, and this person, this advisor, should travel with us to give us this advice?"

"Well, no, but—"

"Actually"—Blaise squeezed her tea bag with her fingers—"maybe you could talk to him. He seems to like you. Maybe you could make him see reason." She didn't look at Lily, placed the spent tea bag on her saucer.

Lily hesitated. "About what, exactly?"

"Well, convince him that I do appreciate his talents and that I want him properly compensated and that I'm happy to give him tons of credit. Find out what he's really looking for, and then tell me, and then we'll see if we can work out some kind of compromise. You know, like they do in arbitration or whatever it is."

"Mediation." Stephen was involved in mediation all the time. She knew exactly how it worked.

"I have so much to deal with; I'm so stressed." Blaise's voice climbed to a higher register. Her cup rattled in its saucer. "I can't take this! You have to help me!"

Lily was startled. "Of course, of course I will. I'll do what I can."

"You're so great, Lily." Blaise's voice went instantly back to normal. She smiled at Lily, lifted her cup to her lips, and finally took a sip.

Lily's face felt tight. "It's getting late. I'll go get my stuff."

The venue that night was a coffeehouse, tucked away on a side street in downtown Keene, that probably couldn't accommodate more than fifty people. Lily had asked JJ why they played such disparate places, and he had explained that once they had an important gig in one location, Blaise's manager would hunt around for other places in the area, even if they were small. With the costs built in to travel, it was the only way touring was economically feasible.

During sound check, Lily could feel the chill between Blaise and JJ from across the room. She kept her own distance, kicking herself for being manipulated into getting involved. "More of my guitar in the monitor, please," Blaise barked. JJ's guitar was not loud enough, but Lily said nothing. They were so lackluster, she stopped taping. Blaise and JJ stalked out in separate directions for dinner.

She picked a spot in the small space to set up the tripod and went off to grab something to eat. By the time she came back, the club was filling up. The crowd was more colorful than the working-class audience in Plattsburgh. This was a college town, with bookstores and boutiques and antiques dealers. Here were grown-up hippies with stylish jewelry, as well as kids Colby's age who looked straight out of Urban Outfitters, wearing cargo pants and chunky hand-knit hats from places like Ecuador.

The hum in the room intensified, that buzzing, intimate sound that was created in places with low ceilings and small tables jammed with people. There was a crackle of anticipation, bursts of laughter, the clink of bottle against glass, and finally the coffeehouse owner went onstage and tapped the mic.

"Hey, Keene, are you ready? Please welcome the lovely Blaise Raleigh and her faithful sidekick, Mr. Jackson Johnson!"

Blaise strode gracefully to the stage, glittery shirt sparkling, lifted her guitar from its stand, and slipped the strap over her head. "Thank you, everybody. We're sure happy to be here in the loveliest town in this very beautiful state. We'd like to open with a few tunes from our last CD. Testing, one, two. More of JJ's guitar, Sam. Everyone, a hand for Sam, the sound guy."

They began with one of their usual openers. Somehow JJ was less forceful, and Lily thought she heard Blaise say, "Come on, JJ," and he seemed to wake up. Was he doing something deliberately, or had he lost concentration? It must be hard to be 100 percent all the time. Even when you felt you were, maybe it didn't always come across. You had a toothache, you were distracted. You were at odds with your singing partner.

Lily switched to her medium-distance setting and pulled in a little. Of course, even at 80 percent, JJ was a thrill to watch: a fast tremolo here, a run there, a charge up the fret board with an intricate set of chords.

There was very little interaction between Blaise and JJ during the show, and JJ's laughs in response to her little jokes seemed forced. The audience was respectful, but the applause trailed off quickly after each number. During the break, Blaise and JJ stood at opposite ends of the merchandise table. The second set was a bit more up-tempo, the crowd more engaged, but there was little of the ecstatic stomping and hollering Lily had come to expect.

As they exited the stage, Lily could feel their sense of anticlimax. The crowd drifted out quietly, and she watched the sound guy fold up his big square box of knobs and wires and dials and lock it. The waitresses bustled about, cleaning up. The house lights came on, revealing the empty glasses with lipstick impressions, the crumpled napkins and stained tablecloths.

Lily was folding her tripod when Blaise and JJ emerged with their guitars.

"Give JJ a ride back," Blaise said. Wordlessly, Blaise stretched out her hand to him, palm up. Was she so pissed she wouldn't ride with him, or was she just trying to engineer Lily's promised talk?

He fished in his jacket pocket and dropped the car keys in her palm, then stood staring after her as she walked away, before turning to Lily.

"Let's find someplace quiet. I need a drink."

"Sure." So much for her promise to herself to keep her distance. Outside it was clear and bright, with a slice of moon so sharp it looked scissored from the sky. They walked to the main street, where people were clustered outside a bar, smoking. Inside they found a table wedged into the corner near the bathroom. While JJ went to get their drinks, Lily was thinking furiously. If she raised Blaise's concerns, wouldn't he feel she was taking her side? But if she didn't, what excuse could she give Blaise?

"What a bitch of a day," JJ folded himself into his seat, handing her an Elm City beer; he had told her he liked to buy from local breweries when he traveled. "I'm fried. That was one of the hardest gigs I've played in a long time."

"What's going on?" Lily asked, feeling duplicitous. The table was so small, their elbows nearly touched.

"We had a knock-down, drag-out. We both said a lot we shouldn't have. I really lost it. I usually can keep a lid on my feelings—you see how careful I am around her. But, man, she pushed my buttons." He tilted his head back and took a long swallow.

"You didn't tell her about the manager's offer, did you?"

"No, but I came close. I came close to quitting. She knew she'd gone too far."

Lily was silent. This wasn't squaring with Blaise's take. "What did she say?"

"It all started because she wants to add another guitarist on the next CD, to expand our sound. I think that's exactly the wrong way to go. Not to mention it really diminishes my role. Plus, she was thinking of having some male guest singers. Not for backup, like me, but to duet. She thinks it'd be a hotter sell—you know, like, if she could get Ryan Adams or someone like him. I told her she was just being insecure. She doesn't need to ride on someone else's coattails. She should trust her talent—mine, too. And our two guitars are enough guitars. Give me a break." He took another swig.

"Hmm," Lily said. How did any of this fit with what Blaise had said? And how to broach the issues she had raised?

"Do you think she's afraid you want more credit or personal glory, and she thinks that's the reason behind your objections?"

"I don't know. Why would she think that?" He tapped the beer bottle with his nails.

"Well, sometimes people project. You know, she's the one who's all concerned about stardom, so . . ."

"Maybe you're right. I never thought of that. Yeah, sure, that could be part of it. She's fucking paranoid and such an egomaniac that she thinks everyone else is, too. I don't give a shit about credit—I've been on plenty of albums. I'm more interested in doing another solo recording anyhow."

"You should tell her that."

"It won't help. I truly believe she's going to disappoint her hardcore fans by trying to be what she's not. It's fucking crazy. She's great as she is."

Lily was surprised by his reverence for Blaise's talent, given his negative feelings for her. She hadn't even thought about what his professional opinion of Blaise might be. But of course he wouldn't be lending his talents and energy to someone whose work he wasn't excited by. And clearly Blaise was totally off base about him.

"She does appreciate you, you know," Lily said.

"She thinks there are a dozen guitarists just as good."

"No, she doesn't. Really. When I've interviewed her, she's told me how much she values you."

"She says that?"

"Yes, and I believe her. I think she just likes to be in control."

JJ made a face. "You're probably right. I shouldn't get so bent out of shape. Why should I give a shit, really?"

Lily took a big gulp of beer. She felt more relaxed now that she thought she had a handle on things. "Maybe just concentrate on your next solo CD?"

"You're right. I let myself get too wrapped up in her crap."

"Have you been able to compose on the road?" Lily was eager to turn the conversation.

"I noodle around every now and then. Sometimes first thing in the morning, right after I get out of bed, sort of an extension of that dream state. But mostly I work when I'm home, in between touring."

"Where is your home, exactly?"

"Do you know Colorado?"

"I've never been there."

"Well, I live near Boulder." He leaned closer. "The mountains are so incredibly beautiful, you have no idea. I have a little house—really little—that looks out on a valley. It's on a dead-end dirt road surrounded with fields and trees. It's so quiet. I mean, there's nothing around. You should see it."

"I wish I could," she said, too fervently.

They were silent, looking at each other.

"Well, you'll just have to come out and visit."

Lily felt heat rise to her face. "I'd love to film you playing your own music. Not for the video. Just for myself. Would you play for me one of these days? I'll try not to be dysfunctional to your process."

JJ threw his head back and laughed. "My process—that's a good one! I have no process. I never know what the fuck I'm doing."

"Your pieces are exquisite. That makes no sense."

"I get lucky sometimes."

"I think you really are a genius," she said.

"That's bullshit. But I will play for you."

"Promise?" Even the bottoms of her feet were tingling. To watch him play, up close and personal. She imagined sitting opposite him, so close she could reach out and touch the slick gloss of his guitar.

"What's a nice woman like you doing with crazy people like us, anyhow?"

Lily laughed. She imagined telling him the truth, about how strong a connection she felt to him, her passion for his music. It would frighten him. Or if it didn't, she'd be in even deeper trouble than she thought.

"Oh, I'm not as sane as I appear."

"Really? Like how?"

"You'll have to take my word for it."

"OK, I will. So tell me about your life. You like city living?"

"Yes, the energy, the range of people. It has its downsides, but the trade-offs are worth it."

"And your husband? Does he feel the same way?"

"Definitely. He works for the city as a planner—you know, an urban planner. To some it's a very dry and bureaucratic field to be in, but he loves it."

"I had to get a variance to build my deck," JJ said. "Are we talking about that kind of thing?"

"Yes, but with big projects."

JJ went to get another round. Lily amused herself by imagining having JJ over to dinner with some of their friends, the conversations about the mayor and city council, the politics of everyday New York. She imagined passing him crackers and the creamy Morbier, with the line of ash. Would JJ hate their world? Find it pretentious? Stultifying?

"You gotta see this." JJ placed her bottle on the table and grabbed her hand. He led her to the other side of the wall she had been sitting against, where there was a huge old-fashioned jukebox. "Isn't it incredible? A gaudy, gorgeous piece of history. We've got three songs. I've already picked two. Your turn."

"What did you pick?"

"Doesn't matter. If you pick one I picked, we'll listen to it twice."

"Fair enough." Lily studied the choices; there was a Lucinda Williams favorite, "I Envy the Wind." She punched in the numbers and then, too late, remembered the lyrics.

The first song up was "Unchained Melody." JJ put his bottle on a shelf, grabbed her hand, and swung her into a slow Lindy. Lily, stiff and uncomfortable, kept stumbling. She hated being so uptight. JJ persisted, and by the end of "Bird on a Wire" she was beginning to give over to the music.

"I envy the rain that touches your skin," Lucinda sang. JJ put one hand on the back of Lily's head, cradling it gently, and pulled her close. "I envy the wind that blows through your hair," he crooned. Lily removed her hand from his and wound both arms around his neck.

She could hear the beating of his heart where her ear rested against his throat. She willed herself to keep it together.

The song ended, and they broke apart. "Well," she said, trying to laugh.

He grabbed her hands, didn't release them. He stared at her. She stared back.

"OK," he said, dropping her hands.

She took a deep breath. "That was fun. So, I guess we should be getting back."

They walked in silence to the car. Her thin-soled shoes slipped a little on the icy sidewalk; he reached out to steady her. What was he feeling? Loneliness? Lust? Whatever it was, it probably wasn't truly about her. She had to keep reminding herself of that.

In the car, he surprised her by asking, "Do you want to talk?"

She turned the heater on and sat back. "Do you?" She could barely swallow.

"Is your marriage solid?" he asked. "Are you completely committed?"

She looked down. "Yes."

"OK, then."

"But you know that . . . that otherwise . . . Still, you can't possibly—"

"Lily, you know what I'd like. Don't pretend."

"But I'm over the hill, let's face it."

"Well, I'm no teenager. I'm attracted to you. I know you're attracted to me. Let's at least be honest."

She felt her skin burn, grateful that he couldn't see her face in the dark.

"You know, I was married myself for a while." He leaned back, put his arms behind his head. "It was a long time ago. She was great; she was willing to make a home for me, to be there when I came back between tours. But I cheated on her. It was like I had two separate lives: my life on the road and my life at home. You really can't separate it like that and have it work. So it got back to her, and it really hurt her, and she divorced me. I really messed up. I miss being married, having someone."

108

Play for Me

"But you must, well, meet a lot of women on the road."

"It's not the same. And you get tired of it." He looked away.

Lily imagined that wife at home in Boulder. Watching TV alone, standing by a window, looking out at an empty field. Going alone to a dinner party on a Saturday night. Doing the laundry, pushing a cart through a grocery aisle, plunged into her own thoughts because there was no one with whom to discuss what to make for dinner.

She thought of the musician's wife the night before, picking at her napkin, clearly bored by or lost in the conversation at the table and happy to have Lily, another woman who wasn't a musician, to talk to. That alternative seemed no better.

"I've never lived in one place or had a regular job." JJ turned back to her, and his face was suddenly illuminated by lights going on in a nearby house. "Lots of musicians who are always on the road are totally fucked up. I don't want to end up like that."

"Could you play fewer gigs and maybe sell more CDs to make a living?"

"Springsteen, yes. Me, no way."

"Besides, you like performing."

"I couldn't live without performing." His voice was low, soft.

"It's a much tougher life than I realized." She turned down the heat, which was fogging the car windows. She didn't want to break the moment by driving back.

"People are drawn to the romance of it all—and it can be pretty exciting. But there's a lot of loneliness and just plain tedium. I mean, it's an alternative lifestyle, really, and you can really only share it with others living the same way. Like it must be with Hare Krishnas," he laughed. "But then, when you do go back home, because you're not there long, you can't connect to anything. Sad to say, the truth is, you're kind of bored by all those regular people's regular lives. Their kids and the dentist appointments, the doings at the church. It all seems awfully dull. You feel that way because you don't share in any of it. You're an outsider. I always want to go home, but after I've been home for a few weeks, I'm always really ready to go back on the road."

He was looking down, frowning. She stared at him, indulging herself in being able to drink him in. "I understand." When he didn't say anything further, she said, "I guess we should get going."

She drove carefully through the nearly deserted streets of the little town and then the dark rural roads, focusing on not getting lost. She pulled into the inn parking lot, but before she could turn off the engine, JJ put his hand on hers.

"It's been so nice having you along this week. It's been so much better; it makes me aware just how unhappy I've been. Having you around has eased things. I wish you could stay—maybe a little longer?" The jolt of pleasure Lily felt alarmed her. His fingers traced hers lightly, down to her fingernails and back up.

"I've . . ." *Enjoyed it? Enjoyed* wasn't the right word. "It's been good for me, too." But that wasn't it either.

"I'll leave you alone," he said. "I'll behave."

She couldn't bring herself to speak because she was too afraid to hear what she might say. Still, she didn't take out the key.

He paused a second. "Are you really happy in your life?"

"I thought I was," she said. "I mean, I was, I am."

"But?" he said. "There's a 'but' in your voice—I hear it."

"I guess I'm just a little confused at the moment."

"You don't have to talk about it if you don't want to. But maybe it'll do you good to keep touring with us. Can you tell your boss you need more time on the film? And your husband, he's a reasonable and really nice guy, he wouldn't mind, would he?"

"How would you know that? He is, but what makes you say that?"

"Because I can see what kind of person you are, and I'm kind of, I don't know, not psychic, but maybe I have a little of that ESP thing going for me. I'm just sure your husband is the kind of man who trusts you and wants what's best for you, and isn't a crazy jealous needy dependent type like I am."

She felt an involuntary shudder through her back and shoulders. She forced herself to laugh. She was taking him way too seriously. "You're altogether too charming for your own good," she turned the key decisively, shutting off the motor. "Go, get out of here. I'll see you in the morning."

"OK, I get the message." He laughed, too, getting out of the car. What a seducer!

"Here, let me carry that." He reached for the tripod, and she followed him up the walkway. The inn was dark, so late the front door had been locked.

"Shit, can't find my key. Do you have yours?"

Of course she did. That was the kind of person she was, the kind who had put the key securely in an inside pocket of her purse the second she had gotten it. They went up the creaky stairs on tiptoe so as not to disturb the other guests. Their rooms were on different floors.

"Well, good night," she said, her voice sounding a little hesitant to her ears.

"Good night, Lily." He leaned the tripod up against the wall and started up the next flight, then bounded back down and grabbed her in a tight hug that lasted a second longer than it should have.

Lily didn't take sleep aids, but she kept Benadryl in her purse in case of allergies. Now she took two. She didn't want to spend another night tossing and turning. As she lay in bed, waiting for the drug to kick in, she didn't even try to put her mind where it should be. She reimagined every moment of dancing with JJ, the warmth of his hand cradling her head, the feel of his chest against her face, and she flipped over and back and over again in the bed. A small, whelpy moan escaped from her, embarrassing her.

She awoke with the alarm, groggy and disoriented. She got into the shower and stood waiting for her head to clear, but it didn't. It could be ages before the antihistamine wore off. It was as if her head were filled with packing peanuts.

The inn's small breakfast room, overlooking the back garden, was decorated with floral wallpaper and shelves running along the molding, displaying teacups and saucers in hundreds of patterns. There was no sign of Blaise or JJ. Lily seated herself by the window at a table for two.

"Coffee?" The innkeeper, a stocky woman in a white blouse with a Peter Pan collar, gave her a high-beam smile.

"Please!" When the coffee came, she drank it so quickly she burned the top of her mouth.

No other guests had come down yet. She listened to the sound of the wall clock, watching out the window at a small sparrow that went back and forth from a tree branch to the ground. "Are you happy?" he had asked, and she had said, "I thought so." How could she have said that? Of course she was happy! She rotated her wedding band on her finger. The skin was even redder, more irritated. She'd meant to apply a cream. She had noticed for the last several months that it seemed a little tight; now it felt downright uncomfortable, even with the weight she had lost. It couldn't be symbolic, could it? Psychosomatic? She couldn't have been just going through the motions with Stephen all these years; it wasn't possible that if she weren't happy she wouldn't have noticed.

But what if you're not happy now?

Well, then, it's just temporary. It will pass.

She suddenly felt chilled and pulled her sweater more closely around her. What if all of this with JJ was more serious than she had assumed? What if it was more than just a little passing silliness?

Her omelet came, a perfect, lightly browned ten points of savory paradise. Thank God you could always count on food.

On the drive to Boston, she turned her mind firmly from JJ and focused on what to ask Blaise at their interview that afternoon and on ideas for the DVD. Should she use sequences of full performances or collages of images and snippets of songs, like what floated behind her eyes every night before she fell asleep? Unless she considered staying on, tonight would be her last concert taping. Tomorrow JJ and Blaise would be heading up to Montreal for a few weeks before flying to Europe. She would be heading home. Home, where she would watch her video footage over and over, trying to make that suffice. Her stomach twisted. How was she to bear it?

It was a cold, damp, raw day. She checked in to the nondescript motel on the outskirts of Cambridge and took the T to the Museum of Fine Arts. She viewed several video installations, hoping for inspiration, but they were arty black-and-white ones with repetitive scenes and variations so subtle they didn't hold her interest. She gave up and roamed through all the exhibits, up and down stairs, into and out of different wings. When Colby was growing up, she had often taken him to museums; he particularly liked Kandinsky and Matisse, and also the surrealists. She loved to get him talking about what he saw in the paintings, finding a little window into his imagination. On impulse she began to dial his number, then stopped. How could she talk with Colby when she was in this heightened state over JJ? She and Colby were so attuned to one another. Maybe he would access her thoughts and feelings, feelings that seemed like a betrayal of him as well as of Stephen.

Back at the motel, Blaise was waiting, a basket of cheese and fruit on the table.

"How was your day?" Lily asked. *How was JJ?* was what she really wanted to know.

"We window-shopped; I got a few things. Fun." She poured coffee for Lily. "So. Whatever you said to JJ worked. He backed off the sole-producer thing. He's coming around to my point of view on some other stuff."

Lily started to explain she hadn't actually done what Blaise had asked, but she decided she didn't want to risk giving away too much of what she and JJ had discussed.

"That's good, then."

"I want to do something for you in return; what would you like?"

"I'm happy if I was able to help."

"No, I insist. JJ and I will think of something."

"Just like the video when I'm done. That's all I really want."

"I'm sure I will. I wish I had more new material, though. I want to launch a whole new direction."

"Wait, don't say another word. Give me a sec." Lily hurriedly set up, steadied the camera on her shoulder. "OK, Blaise, you were just saying that you would like to launch a new direction in your music—what would that be?"

Blaise's voice became forced, as it always did at the beginning of their taping. "I'm beginning to get attracted to some other forms. I would never venture too far from my core sound, but I think we can shake it up some."

"How would you characterize your core sound?" Lily asked.

"Folk-based, with an emphasis on ballads, rock-and-roll influences, blues." Blaise sounded prim and formal; her posture was stiff. "But there are some interesting things in world music that have been attracting me lately. After this tour, I'll be spending a lot of time in the studio, some creative time." She smiled broadly, wooing a thousand fans.

Was "world music" code for adding other players to their lineup—and what JJ worried would take Blaise too far from what made her special?

"Will your fans be pleased by the new direction?"

"Your fans are the reason for your success. You never want to disappoint them, never," Blaise said. "But you have to grow as an artist, and to do that, you have to push the boundaries. You have to stay fresh, always searching. I would hope my fans would understand and appreciate that." Her tone had become officious. "The bottom line is, if what you end up with is good, and is a natural outcome of your growth as a musician, then it'll work for the fans, too. I sincerely believe that." She sat back. Lily knew the interview was going to come across as forced, that the viewers wouldn't buy Blaise's confidence.

"Are there any topics we haven't covered? Something I've missed?"

"Well what about these babies?" Blaise lifted a leg to reveal soft turquoise boots.

"Wow, stunning! So, what is the one question you've been afraid I'll ask?"

"I'm not afraid of anything," Blaise said curtly. Then she added, more softly, "Except not succeeding."

"Are you succeeding?"

"I'll let this film speak for me." Blaise lifted her chin high and looked into the far distance, as if she were ready for stormy seas, hands steady at the helm, hair flying in the wind.

Lily turned off the camera.

Blaise grabbed a chunk of cheese. "Let's demolish this food." She plopped her booted feet onto the edge of a side table. "God, I'm feeling crazy. I get crazy when I'm close to going home. We've been nonstop for seven weeks."

"What's your life like at home?"

"I see friends. My mom lives not too far away." She took another cube of cheese, popped it in her mouth, and stretched out on the couch.

Lily had trouble imagining Blaise with a mother. If anyone had been born full-size out of the head of Zeus, it was Blaise. "Where are you in Colorado?"

"North of Boulder. Not too far from JJ, so we can get together when we need to."

"Do you ski, hike?"

"Nah. You wouldn't think so, but I'm kind of a homebody. I like being by myself, as a—what do you call it?—antidote to all the socializing on the road. Sometimes I go into my own head too much. But I've got my shrink there; he keeps me sane."

Lily saw Blaise glance at the clock. She stood. "I guess we should work out the next steps. I mean, after I get home tomorrow and edit this thing, how we'll proceed."

"What?" Blaise sat up abruptly. "Aren't you coming with us until the end of the tour? Didn't we say that?"

"I thought you only meant for this week," Lily pressed her hand to her stomach, to calm her leaping insides. "I told my boss I'd be back."

"Well, could you call him? Please? It's been really good with you around."

She shouldn't stay; she knew she shouldn't. "Let me think about it."

"But then tonight would be the last concert!" Blaise's voice was squeaky; the little girl was back, the captain of the ship vanished. "We haven't played our best. We haven't played even one of the big venues!"

"Your performances have been fantastic. Put the video out of your mind tonight. Don't think about anything but performing."

"How come you're so fucking smart about everything?"

"We all have our talents," Lily said. "Mine's being a smart-ass."

Back in her room, Lily threw herself on the bed. Her mind and emotions were swirling. These two were a mess—it was clear. So what drew her to them? Why did she hate to wean herself off them?

It was like the hard time she had giving up cigarettes. She loved the feel of the pack in her chest pocket, the little strand of cellophane as she opened the box, the strike of the match against her jeans' zipper, her coolest move.

She put a pillow over her face. Blaise and JJ probably weren't good for her either, but she was just as addicted. It was heady to be the altar boy to the high priest and priestess, close to the holy sacrament, the source of the mystery. To God him—or her—self.

She didn't even believe in God. What was she talking about?

Lily flung the pillow away. The music was powerful, and power was seductive. Maybe that made the two of them powerful and seductive. In other words, she was caught up in some odd equation. Searching for God, she was traipsing around with a couple of loser musicians.

She laughed. She had to keep that ironic distance, or she would be in danger of losing herself completely. But she wanted to stay deep under the spell, like a crocus hidden beneath the snow. She wasn't ready to awaken.

Lily sat up, giving up on the idea of a nap. Her nerves were too jangled; she was—she might as well admit it—too excited to sleep. Should she call Tom and ask for another week off? Test Stephen's good graces even further? As she stripped for her shower, she caught a glimpse of herself in the full-length mirror. What would someone—JJ, for instance—think? How bad did she look, objectively? She straightened her shoulders, pulled in her stomach. In the mirror, blessedly lit low, was a woman of average height and weight, a bit more flabby and curvy than society's ideal, and a soft face with pleasant, though not particularly noteworthy, features. On the plus side, there were few wrinkles, the brown eyes were soft and eager, and the lips looked somewhat inviting. Maybe how she looked would depend on just how drunk that someone was, she decided.

Seven

The Boston club was a funky old warehouse with wide-planked floors covered in sawdust and a huge mirror over the bar. JJ had walked in and hooted loudly, then clapped his hands. "Hear that?" he said. She didn't, but she was impressed that he could tell with a clap and a hoot something about how good the acoustics were.

She circled the room with her camera. Blaise had family in Boston, and tonight there were two tables of guests seated near the stage, including a group of musicians called Ticker-Tape Parade. Lily filmed them, as well as the sound engineer fussing with his knobs, the crowd streaming in, even the photos on the walls of previous performers. She swiveled, and JJ was suddenly at her elbow. She hadn't seen him since the night before in New Hampshire. "I came to say hello," he said. "I've gotta take a piss."

"Thank you for sharing."

He glanced at her long-sleeved velvet top, the one she had saved for her last night, and said, "That's very pretty," his eyes on her chest.

"So. Blaise. She said you worked things out."

"I caved." He put his hands briefly over his face. "If I'm not about to make any big changes, then fuck it, I've got to just accept the situation."

"I see."

"I mean, look at this place. This is a historic landmark—it has an incredible history. Look at the pictures on the walls. Hendrix played here. Dylan. Without Blaise, I wouldn't be here."

119

"I don't know about that."

"Ah, Lily, that's why I love you." He kissed the top of her head and went off to the men's room, leaving her singed.

Tonight Blaise and JJ charged onto the stage with all the energy they had lacked the previous night. Blaise wore tights and a long crimson tunic with overlapping horizontal pleats—she must have gotten it on the shopping foray with JJ—along with the turquoise boots. She looked absolutely wired.

"JJ and I want to thank our video artist for all her hard work trying to make us look good. To Lily—this one is for you."

Lily's eyes smarted. JJ began the delicate picking that was the opening of her favorite song—well, one of her favorites, she could never choose—and she couldn't hold the camera steady. She pressed the OFF button and just stood and listened, every note reverberating, shimmering through her like sheets of water over a windshield, every chord raising the hairs on her arms, closing up her throat.

She couldn't concentrate after that, and it was almost a relief when, at the beginning of the second set, Blaise called the members of Ticker-Tape to the stage. Lily kept filming even though she probably wouldn't use this footage. The group was good, though: a banjo player, a piper, a Dobro player, and a striking female bass player with a headful of dark corkscrew curls, who positioned herself next to JJ on stage.

After the concert, Lily headed backstage, where the musicians and family members were congratulating Blaise and JJ.

"Time to part-ee!" Blaise said. "I'm dying of thirst." She looked manic. Was it just relief about a great show after the poor one the night before, or was she on something? Lily edged toward the door, remembering her promise to herself, after dancing in the bar with JJ, that she would keep her distance.

"Don't even think of ducking out," Blaise said.

What was one more night? Lily followed the cavalcade of cars to a bar near Harvard, where Ticker-Tape was pulling together tables. Lily squeezed in next to a man who turned out to be Blaise's cousin. "She's fabulous, isn't she?" he said loudly in Lily's ear. "I spotted her talent years ago, when she was a little girl."

"Really?" Lily said politely. JJ was talking with the bass player, whose curls danced with every movement of her head.

"She was always strutting her stuff. 'She's gonna go far'—that's what everyone said," the cousin continued in her ear.

"She sure will," Lily said. She heard Blaise say "completely wasted," and the piper say "fired the publicist," and JJ say "backup for his last album."

Ticker-Tape's Dobro player, on her right, leaned over. "It's cool you're making a DVD for Blaise. Have you done a lot of those?"

"A lot of video, but not concert video. Do you have one?"

"Not yet, but I'm thinking of making a teaching one. A lot of musicians sell them through their websites. You teach a few licks that your fans want to learn. Plus, it helps pay the rent. Do you have a card? I'll call you if I get my act together."

What the hell? She dug an MKT Productions card from deep in her wallet, brushed off the dust, and handed it over. He passed her one in return.

"What kind of music does your group play? Something similar to what you did tonight backing Blaise?"

"Yes. We're considered alt or newgrass—we use traditional instruments—but with a kind of Neil Young vibe, given Wallie's vocals. Suze and I sing backup. We've been talking with Blaise about maybe doing a tour together."

"I didn't know about that."

"Yeah, it's cool."

So this must be what Blaise had been cooking up. Was JJ upset? Lily glanced over. His head was bent attentively toward the bassist. He didn't look the least bit troubled.

She felt her shoulders sag as if under an avalanche of wet snow. She took a long swallow of her beer, wiped her mouth, and then, liking the sensation as the alcohol hit her almost-empty stomach—she'd had only twelve points so far today, she'd been so jumpy—she took another long swallow.

Time drifted. She drank some more. People stopped having side conversations as the musicians talked. Their plans, makes of guitar, types of amplification. Good studios and bad, good producers and bad, good CDs and bad. Lily ordered another beer. Words danced. The sound became muted, and she watched the shapes of the mouths as they opened and shut, as eyes widened or narrowed, hands gestured. She drank some more.

Suddenly they were all leaving. She scrambled to get up and nearly keeled over. "Oops!" she said.

"Are you OK?" Blaise frowned.

"I think I had a little too much to drink."

"You'd better come with me. JJ can drive your car back."

They headed to the parking lot. Lily lurched from one parked car to the next, keeping a hand out to steady herself.

"Open the window and hang your head outside. I don't want you puking in here."

"I'm not going to puke; it's just, things are a little . . ."

"Been there. Just keep your head out the window."

Lily breathed in the cold air deeply.

"God, what a night!" Blaise said. She said other things, but the words swam past Lily like fireflies she couldn't quite catch. Blaise probably just wanted to hear the sound of her own voice anyway.

"Are you going to be all right?" Blaise parked the car.

Lily got out, concentrated on putting one foot in front of the other. "See, I can walk a straight line."

"Barely." Blaise took her arm.

"I'll be fine. The cold air is helping."

Blaise walked her in. "OK, then. See you in the morning."

Lily collapsed on the bed and let the room revolve around her for a while and tried very, very hard not to think about JJ. He was supposed to leave her car keys at the reception desk, but they hadn't been there when she and Blaise had come in. Had he gone somewhere with the bass player? Imagine if she and JJ were together—she'd be jealous all the time he was on the road. It would be torture. She was lucky. Lucky she was married, lucky she was older. For if she weren't married, and if she were young and could actually win him, these terrible feelings were what she'd have to live with all the time and accept as the price she had to pay.

It was not a price she would be able to pay. Good. That settled that, then.

Settled what? What was she thinking?

There was a discreet tap at the door. She froze. Maybe it was the reception clerk with her keys. Maybe it was him. She should pretend to be asleep. She was in no condition . . .

"Lily? Lily, it's JJ. I came to see if you're OK."

"Coming," she croaked, struggling to sit up, fluffing her hair.

"I'm sorry, did I get you out of bed?" His eyes took in her state of dishevelment. Why had she gone and gotten drunk? She looked a mess, and she couldn't think clearly. She tugged her top down over her hips.

"I was a little worried about you."

"I'm all right. I think. I never drink like that."

He was holding a bottle of seltzer. "This ought to help."

They stood facing each other in the doorway. Finally she stepped aside. He walked into her bathroom and found a glass, poured her some seltzer. "Go ahead, lie down; I can see you need to." He shoved her down gently on the bed, and then, as casual as a cat, settled next to her and stroked her forehead. "Poor Lily. So you don't get drunk too often, huh?"

"I'm never doing it again."

"Drugs are so much better," he said. "But I got a little too friendly with coke for a bit, so now I'm strictly grass. I'm weaning myself off that, too."

"You're weaning yourself off everything," she mumbled.

"Not off you," he said, sliding his head down onto her chest. "I don't want to wean myself off you."

Lily's breath cut off. She stared at his head, the dark brown hair. There was nothing she could do but put her hand on that head; it had a will of its own, her hand, and that's where it went. She stroked his hair lightly, then stilled.

"Please don't leave tomorrow." He touched her shirt, the pretty velvet paisley, felt the fabric between his fingers. A moment later his hand slipped inside her blouse. She didn't know how that had happened. *No*, she thought, *no, I can't do this*.

"JJ," she said, her voice sounding strangled.

He rolled on top of her, pressed his full length over hers. "We won't make love, OK, but just let me hold you."

She breathed into the side of his neck. His skin smelled like the sea, salty and fresh; she felt his pulse against her lips. After a moment, she put her arms around him and pulled him tight to her. She didn't know how she was ever going to let him go.

At 7:00 AM Lily sat up, wide awake, heart racing. She stripped and stood under the hot spray of the shower until she felt boiled. She had to leave, and leave now, before she did something irrevocable. She had passed out with JJ on her bed, then awoken to hear him clicking shut her door.

Lily threw everything into her suitcase. She wrote notes to both Blaise and JJ, left them at the reception desk, and rushed to her car.

She had never seen such a hard, brittle sun. It glowered, sent needles of light like glass into her eyes. She was shaking so hard she could barely get her suitcase in the trunk. She couldn't make the key fit in the ignition. The only time she remembered feeling this shaky was after her mother died.

She had to leave. She knew she had to leave. She had to leave now.

The car started up. She eased it from the parking lot. She entered a roundabout, going around and around until she finally managed to exit in the right direction. As she drove she tried to concentrate on Stephen, her job, her apartment, reminding herself where her world was centered. On Colby. But her life wouldn't come into focus. She put on the radio, but every guitar note scraped her soul like a jagged nail, so she switched channels until she found NPR. A bank robbery, a tax scandal, a report about the marshes in Iraq that had been drained and the people who had lost their homes, their very culture . . . suddenly she was sobbing. She turned off the radio.

With every mile she put between herself and Boston, it got harder to keep going, and her panic intensified. She kept failing to keep the pressure on the gas pedal and decelerating to the point where people were passing her on the right. Finally, a few hours out, the truth hit with the force of a pothole. She didn't want to go home.

She had taken the Mass Pike into New York and onto the Thruway, and so she pulled into the next rest stop, a little south of Albany. She sat in the sprawling fast-food complex, nursing a Starbucks coffee. Around her were harried families grouped around mounds of fries, wads of crumpled paper, enormous cups of sugary liquid. *This is America,* she thought. The din—noise from the arcade, chattery children—was somehow comforting. Then her ears were pricked by a vaguely familiar upbeat tune: "Give me the beat, boys, and free my soul, I want to get lost in your rock and roll and drift away." The lyrics stung like pepper spray. *That's it,* she thought. *I want to get lost in their world, their music. I want to drift away.*

It was like a message sent expressly to her, as if someone understood everything she had been feeling and had created this song from her yearning.

Lily went back to her car. She rested her head on the hood, keys pressed into her palm, the song's words like a feedback loop in her brain. Then she pulled out of the parking spot, got back on the Thruway, and headed north.

Just as it was getting dark, she found an inexpensive roadside motel near the Canadian border. She checked in and dialed home.

"Where are you? I thought you were coming home today."

"I know, I'm sorry." She twisted her ring; it was actually painful on her finger now.

"What's going on?" Stephen asked grimly.

"I'm not really sure. I need a little more time."

"Time for what?"

"Well, the video. I don't have what I need yet. And I'm . . . I'm just confused about a few things."

"Lily, should I be worried?"

"Stephen, I'm really sorry about this. But I don't know the answer to that question."

"That's not any kind of response. What are you saying?"

"I'm saying . . ." *I'm saying I'm out of my mind and I want to stay that way for a little while longer?* That wasn't going to cut it. "I just need a little more time to sort stuff out."

"What stuff? About you? Us? About what, exactly?"

"That's part of what I'm trying to figure out."

"Fuck, Lily, where is all this coming from? Are you telling me you're not sure that you still love me?" His voice cracked, and she felt her heart crack, too, sharp and clear and precise, with the finality and precision of a thin vanilla wafer.

"Not that. No. I very definitely love you."

She heard his breathing through the phone, but he didn't say anything. She waited, tears slipping down her cheeks, not able to speak.

"All right. I'll give you a little more time." His voice sounded tight—angry or afraid. She heard the warning in it, too.

"I promise . . . not too much longer."

He said nothing, and then, into the silence, she heard him replace the receiver.

Her heart began to beat erratically. She got in the shower. She seemed to be spending inordinate amounts of time in water these days, washing the grit and the emotion and the exhaustion away. She was crying again, too. She thought of how she was hurting Stephen, and it was unbearable.

Was it their marriage? Was it coming to an end? Did marriages come to an end in this way, just dissipate, as if they had a shelf life that suddenly ran out?

She bent her head, letting the water run over her. Was the problem that she had thought she was happy and in love, but she wasn't? *No,* she argued, *you were happy, deliriously happy.* That was true. But maybe over time, even if you love and are loved, it's not perfect, because perfection doesn't exist. And so there must be cracks, fissures, perhaps, that go unnoticed. Wants, needs, unfulfilled? Was that it? It just didn't seem to be enough to explain it, this meltdown, to answer the question: Why why why?

She stared at her feet, watched the water bombard them. The drops left her body and made contact with the bathtub floor. She watched their movement downward, the pull of gravity like the pull on her middle-aged breasts. Was it simple physics, then, this pull? Could that explain her seemingly inescapable descent—where? Down the drain like the water? Was her life, her precious, happy life, to be sucked away because of this obsession? Could it really be so strong that she was going to follow it no matter what the consequences turned out to be? Or worse. Would she follow it even if she knew with certainty what the consequences would have to be?

All she knew right now was that she couldn't go home. She simply couldn't.

She got out of the shower, toweled off. Her wedding ring felt tight, and this time, fingers wet and slick from the shower, she was able to yank it from her finger. She stared, shocked, at the red band of raw and inflamed skin.

She bent over, gasping with laughter. The metaphor was just too goddamn awful. She was not going to take it as a sign that she had outgrown her marriage, or that it was unhealthy like the rash. She was not.

She rummaged in her toiletry kit for some antiseptic cream, slathered it on, and crawled into bed. She was, amazingly, exhausted enough to sleep. The song from the rest stop replayed in her mind: *I want to get lost in your rock and roll . . .* She hadn't gotten to hear JJ play his own music for her. What she had asked for and he had promised. What she had longed for most.

◄ ►

By the time Lily had breakfast, gotten sidetracked by a Victoria's Secret store, made the border crossing—luckily she had an enhanced driver's license and didn't need a passport—driven to Montreal, found a hotel, and located the club where JJ and Blaise were due to perform, they were already in the middle of sound check. The manager, so young she looked about Colby's age, let Lily in even though she said no one had mentioned anything about any filming. "Through there," she pointed.

Lily stood in the doorway, watching, not able to step into the room. They were trying out a song she wasn't familiar with and kept stopping to make adjustments. Lily stared at JJ's ragged face, his worn flannel shirt, his legs, slightly bowed, encased in his faded blue jeans. She loved his look of concentration, utter absorption. She had asked him once whether he zoned out when he played, went into some kind of blissed-out trance, and he had looked surprised and said, no, absolutely not, that he was thinking, and thinking hard, all the time.

"Even when you play superfast? I mean, don't you have to be on automatic pilot to pull that off?"

"Just the opposite. You're thinking of the phrasing, of how you want the sound to come out. The whole time you're playing, you're trying to communicate."

Blaise and JJ were stepping down from the stage. Lily suddenly felt dizzy; she could hear herself wheezing slightly. She was actually trembling, as if the expanse of the room were a chasm, and if she moved forward she would fall, and fall irrevocably.

"It's Lily!" Blaise shouted. "JJ, she's here!"

"I decided I couldn't leave you two just yet." Lily avoided looking at JJ.

"We were pissed at you," Blaise said, "but now that you're here, we forgive you. So you cleared it with your company to take the extra time?"

"It was fine," Lily said, although she'd only left a voice mail for Tom and hadn't actually gotten permission.

"Did you book yourself a room?"

"I didn't know where you were staying, so I got one at the Sheraton."

128

"We're at the Hôtel St-Denis. Switch hotels."

"Ready to catch dinner?" JJ rubbed his hands together. "This is a great town; you're gonna love it. There're music venues all over the city. And the food's amazing. If it weren't so fucking cold, I'd think about relocating."

A gust of wind shrieked as they opened the club door as if in answer, slashing Lily's scarf across her face, whipping up from the St. Lawrence like a frenzied poltergeist.

"I'm glad you're back," he whispered, his voice tickling her ear, when Blaise walked to the curb to hail a cab.

"Me, too." Lily hoped he wasn't going to ask her why, exactly, she had returned. She wondered if he would even notice that she was not wearing her wedding ring. She had applied more cream to the angry red band on her finger.

"We made reservations at this French restaurant in the Plateau—that's kind of Montreal's Greenwich Village," Blaise said. It was a tight squeeze in the cab; Lily was surprised to see Blaise rest her head on JJ's shoulder. They seemed in very good spirits. The tension that was usually between them, even when they were more or less getting along, was gone.

"How was today?" Lily asked.

"We explored the city. There's a cool old section down by the riverfront. And last night we got to hear Arcade Fire."

"Do you usually spend your nights off catching other groups?" They hadn't had a night off in the time she'd been traveling with them.

Both heads swiveled to her in surprise. "Of course," Blaise said.

"You don't like to take a break from the music once in a while?"

"It's a thrill to get to hear other people play," Blaise said. "It gives you ideas, you learn, you keep up, you stay fresh."

"Sometimes you get to sit in, too," JJ added.

"Is that fun?"

"Way fun."

"We're blessed," Blaise said. She and JJ exchanged a happy look. Lily felt a fierce twist of envy.

The cab came to a stop on a busy street that, even in the dark and cold, was jammed with people. They sidled through the crowd to the hostess, who seated them under an enormous drooping plant. "Good we made the reservation," Blaise said.

Lily ordered a duck breast in a raspberry cream sauce she knew would take her entire complement of flex points for the week, but she was so nervous she wanted—no, needed—the comfort of comfort food.

Blaise excused herself to go to the ladies' room. JJ and Lily watched in silence until she was beyond earshot. Lily knew there was something she wanted to say, but "How are the scallops?" was all she could manage.

He leaned over and kissed her on the mouth, a kiss as tender and succulent as scallops. His mouth was softer and fuller than she expected.

"I missed you," he said.

From everything he had told her, he had had a far happier day than she had. But that was a given. She knew that whatever it was he felt for her, it would never come close to whatever it was—she would not give it a name—she felt for him. She wasn't going to kid herself on that score.

"I don't really know what I'm doing here."

"Of course you do," he said, giving her his crooked grin. "You came back for me."

Lily felt an explosion of heat, as if she'd bent too close to her broiler. She looked down at the tablecloth. If she could have slid under it, the way her cat used to get under the comforter, she would have.

"You did, didn't you?"

Her head gave a little spasmodic nod.

"Don't be embarrassed. Come on. It's good. It's a good thing."

"Is it?" she said, choking up.

"Lily, have you ever just . . ." He paused, started over. "Have you ever just said, 'Oh, what the fuck,' and done something in the moment because you felt like it, without worrying about what it means or what's going to happen? Like, maybe, when you were a kid and were spontaneous and just lived for the sheer fucking joy of it?"

Lily remembered. She remembered her college days, and going out to bars or parties and getting a little wild, stoned out of her mind and dancing until her bones melted and her hair was soaked. A long, long, long time ago.

"I understand what you're saying, but even so, I don't think I can..." God, this was impossible! "I don't know if I can just, you know, just jump into..."

"I don't want you to do anything you don't want to do."

"Want has nothing to do with it, believe me." Into Lily's vision came the satin camisole sitting in her suitcase. Why had she even gone into the Victoria's Secret store if she weren't planning on sleeping with JJ? She didn't like that store; she had even joined a group of mothers picketing its arrival in her neighborhood. The store had stayed, but at least the thongs weren't on display where children could see them.

She hadn't owned frilly undergarments in decades. Stephen liked her in his oversize cotton shirts. JJ, she guessed, would be more conventional. As she fingered the satiny confections, she had found herself wondering what he would like. A lovely young woman in a tasteful black suit, young enough to be her daughter, approached and asked if she needed help.

"No, thank you, I'm just browsing."

"We have some new arrivals over there." The woman pointed.

Lily went where the woman indicated. She should just leave. Instead she flipped through the rack, lingering over lace and gossamer. She selected a few things and went into a dressing room, praying there were no security cameras.

She stripped and put on a paisley bra-and-panty set with her back to the mirror. When she turned to look, she doubled over laughing, it was that bad. So much for that! She slid back into her cotton Jockey briefs and stretched-out Warner's bra.

But then she temporized by purchasing a shimmery camisole. It was dark blue, with slimming vertical piping.

"Maybe you can't go home until you go to bed with me," JJ said. "Have you thought of that? Maybe it's just something you need to do. At least once?"

Could he be right? Could he be like a stomach virus that she just had to get out of her system?

"Lily, reckless. That's the Lily I'd like to see," he said, as Blaise slid into her seat. "Riding down the avalanche."

"Shawn Colvin." Blaise sipped her wine.

"What?" Lily looked from one to the other.

"'Riding shotgun down the avalanche.' Lyrics. A Shawn Colvin song."

Tonight Blaise and JJ were doing only one set, opening for a young band from Québec City that played loud, Celtic-influenced rock that competed with the din in her brain. Keeping the camera trained on Blaise instead of JJ was tough. And each time she did glance at him, it seemed to her that he was looking directly into her eyes and playing only for her. When he played he was communicating, he had said. Now each note seemed to have a special meaning for her alone, and it seemed to her that what was going on was a conversation, was reciprocal, as if her feelings were ricocheting back to him, and that he was hearing them, even the ones she was trying hard to hide.

After their set, she put away the camera and joined them at a table near the stage. JJ took her hand under the table. The slightly scratchy feel of his calluses on her skin gave her a sensation of intense pleasure. She should pull her hand away. In just a moment, she would. JJ's finger was tracing the inside of her wrist now; her pulse twitched in response. The fiddler stepped up to the mic, feet clogging to her frenetic bowing, mimicking the pounding of Lily's heart.

What to do, what to do? Well, she knew what she wanted. If, God forgive her, she separated Stephen from the equation—only for the sake of clarity, only to see this thing clearly—how, exactly, could anything work? If she accepted that she wanted JJ—not just for sex but also for something more elusive, to somehow be a part of his world—well, a life with a touring musician was no kind of life. She would not want to be back in Boulder, keeping his home fires burning. And traveling with him, following him around like an overeager hound, would make her miserable, too.

The crowd broke out in applause. So what was the point? Her mind wrapped itself around the reality that there was absolutely no long-term viability to anything with JJ, Stephen or no Stephen.

She should pull her arm away, this second. She was risking her life with Stephen, risking her future, risking even her sanity. JJ's fingers were tracing a line from her wrist to the crook of her elbow now, caressing the tender skin at the crease. Lily closed her eyes, swallowed. Unless, of course, JJ was right. She could forget everything else and simply follow the time-honored tradition, the easy way around para-doxes and ambivalences. Just like what her cousin Renée's husband had done that had so shocked and appalled her. An affair.

She felt her breath cut off. If she brought herself to disregard her values and her love for Stephen, well, then she could have JJ, his music, and his world—all of it—for a little while. Like the young maidens in the fairy tale who vanished at night to the ball in a subterranean kingdom but had to return by dawn, Lily could dance her dream with the prince—for a little while.

Eight

The concert was over. Lily detached her arm from JJ. Blaise was eyeing the bass player in the rock group, a stocky guy with unruly curls and a soul patch.

"I'm going back," Lily said. "I'm wiped from the drive."

"Me too," JJ said. He turned to Blaise. "I'll get a cab and drop Lily at her hotel."

Blaise shrugged. "See you tomorrow." She slung her guitar case over her shoulder and headed over to the other band.

Outside, the air was so cold Lily could taste the fillings in her teeth. A cab pulled right up to the club, and someone got out.

JJ held open the door. "I only said that about dropping you for Blaise's sake. You'll let me come up, won't you?"

"Why don't you want Blaise to know?"

"Wouldn't you care?"

"I just wonder what you think her reaction would be."

"Since we're all traveling together right now, it would upset the balance to have us involved. I mean, she's power hungry and has to be in charge, so she'd feel ganged up on and betrayed. . . ."

Betrayed. Who wouldn't Lily be betraying? "We can't do this. It would be abusing her trust. It would be . . . false pretenses or something."

"That's nuts. You're doing the video for free—you're not her

135

employee. She has no rights over your private life. Just because she feels she owns you and everyone else doesn't mean she does."

The cab came to a stop in front of her hotel. "Let's just talk some more," JJ said, getting out after her. "All you New Yorkers like to talk." They took the elevator to her room in silence.

She put the card into the door slot, not looking at him. The click was like a shot ringing out. She opened the door. "Here we are." Her voice sounded shaky.

"Hotel everywhere," he said.

"They must all look the same after a while."

"They *are* all the same." He bounced down on the bed. It was that or the stiff, uncomfortable-looking chair. "Firm," he said. "I like a good, firm bed."

Lily's heart was slamming against her chest. Was she going to start wheezing again? She stood, not knowing what to do with herself. She started to turn down the harsh lights, then abruptly stopped when it occurred to her that it would look too much like an invitation. He was gazing up at her. She plopped down beside him.

"We have to talk."

"Fine. But can we have some wine, too? If you're comfortable with that."

Once the wine came, they settled side by side in bed, facing the mammoth TV opposite, just like an old married couple ready for their favorite weekly series.

"So, what do you want to say?"

"I don't know. I guess none of it needs to be said, really. You know what I'm afraid of."

"You're stuck, that's all," he kicked her lightly with his toe. "That's what they call it, the shrinks. You can't go backward, you can't go forward. You're stuck."

"So what do you do to get unstuck?"

"You're asking me? I usually just wait around for an act of God, because I never seem able to make those hard choices. We've already talked about that."

136

"An act of God?"

"In this case," JJ said, setting down his wineglass on the fake oak of the nightstand and rolling toward her, "I think I'm gonna have to be the act of God."

You are, Lily thought. *Exactly.*

"I'm just going to kiss you, so don't get too freaked. It doesn't commit you to anything." He cradled her face and lightly touched her lips with his. She found her mouth opening, and she gave over. *This is all I'll do,* she thought, pulling his head closer, *just this.* The kiss went on and on and on. His mouth was yielding, his tongue leisurely. Lily finally pulled away.

JJ flopped over on his stomach. She was overcome with remorse, as if she were actually hurting him. "Are you all right?"

"Ugh," he mumbled to the pillow.

"I'm sorry," she said.

He rolled back over. "Come here."

She moved into his embrace. "Just hold me, all right?" He burrowed into her almost the way a small creature might—a dog, maybe, or a calf searching for milk—insistent, needy, and secure in the knowledge of his place in her heart.

Lily stroked his back, his hair, listened to the sound of his breath. It seemed to be all that she could do.

The 2:00 AM hallway lighting threw discolored shadows over JJ's face. He looked as worn out as Lily felt. His shoulders were hunched, his hair a Rasta tangle. He gave her a final, sleepy embrace as they sagged against the doorway. His arms around her felt lifeless. As she watched him walk to the elevator, she could hear the hum and then the sudden clatter of the ice machine down the corridor. They had started to make love innumerable times, and she had pulled back each time, JJ gentle with her ambivalence.

As soon as the elevator doors closed, she stumbled back to the bed, a pain like an ice pick in her heart. Was there really a difference between kissing, touching, and actually . . . doing it? She was dividing up the sex act into permissible and impermissible, the way she had as a teenager. If going all the way was a mortal sin, then French kissing couldn't be. But in Stephen's mind, or in hers if the situation were reversed, would there be a difference? She curled in a ball, covered herself completely with the blanket. How could she do this? How could she continue down this path?

But how could she not? For tomorrow night, JJ was going to play for her, her own private concert.

"Do you remember you promised you'd play your music for me?" she'd asked.

"I remember." He reached over to tuck a stray strand of hair behind her ear.

"Will you?"

"Ah, so that's it," he grinned, showing his slightly crooked bottom teeth. "You're gonna make me sing for my supper."

"JJ, that's horrible!"

"I'm just teasing. I'll play for you tomorrow night if you like. No strings attached."

She picked up her little paperweight, rested it on the palm of her hand, and stared at the wispy guitar. He would play, and his notes would fill the room, would surround her and fill her until she exploded into a thousand pieces of joy.

In the morning, she packed and moved to the hotel where JJ and Blaise were staying, then bundled up for a walk. Outside it was a cold, damp, dismal day. The sky was low and wet, a ceiling of soggy insulation coming down on her head as the wind moaned. She walked to a nearby museum showing Inuit art. When she left, the sculptures having barely registered, she was attacked by hailstones the size of salt crystals. She returned to the hotel. What could she do with herself? What did people do before committing an unforgivable act? She should try and work. She was just opening her binder, where she had been keeping notes for the film, when the hotel phone rang.

"Lily, I got you!" The voice was familiar, but Lily couldn't place it. Somehow, though, it penetrated that this was someone who would expect to be recognized.

"Hello? Who's this?"

"It's Diana. Can't you hear me?"

Lily wanted to smack the phone down and pretend the connection had failed. But even now, when she was about to become a sinner, this was not something her kind of person could do. "Diana, great to hear from you! How did you find me?"

"Stephen called me. I tried your cell with no luck."

Lily sat heavily. "He asked you to call me?"

"No, I'll explain. But first, tell me how you are."

How was she? Blissed out? Psychotic? Both? "I'm . . . I'm . . . I guess I can't really explain," she said.

"That bad?"

Lily hesitated. "I think so."

There was silence at the end of the line. Then Diana finally said, in a low voice, "Have you . . . are you running away with someone?"

"Of course not," Lily burst out, a hysterical tinge to her voice. "I'm doing a performance video for the singer Blaise Raleigh. Didn't Tom explain?"

"Yeah, but he wasn't too clear about it. He wasn't sure when you'd be back."

"Why did Stephen call you?" Lily could barely get the words out. The pattern on the red-and-green plaid bedspread was beginning to shimmy.

"It was sort of awful, Lily. He asked me questions about the weekend we went away. Then afterward, when I thought about it—it was a strange conversation, and he didn't sound like himself at all—well, I realized that he was fishing to see if you had lied and I had covered for you. But don't worry. He finally seemed to believe me that we were together the entire time. All I could figure is that he must have started worrying that you had been having an affair with someone. Ridiculous, I know."

A pulse beat in her throat so hard it could have been a frog thumping to get out.

"You aren't, are you? Not that guitarist? Are you telling me—"

"No, please, stop. No." It didn't count. It hadn't happened yet. She might fall on the ice and end up in the hospital. She could always be hit by a car.

"Well, what's going on? I know it's not really my business, but Stephen sounded so . . . and you're one of my closest friends. You can talk to me, you know that."

Talk? She couldn't talk to anyone.

"I'm just in a funny place, you know? It's hard to explain. It's not about Stephen." Was that true? She waited a second to see if it registered inside her with any conviction, but her internal truth-o-meter was inconclusive. "I just feel really compelled to be here right now and doing this . . . project. Seeing it through."

"OK," Diana said. She sounded skeptical or hurt or confused, or all of those things. Lily waited, holding her breath, hoping she would let it go.

"Will you call me in a couple of days, then? Please?"

"Yes, I promise." She glanced at the clock. Suddenly she felt desperate to shower and dress, to put on makeup and style her hair and iron the velvet paisley top, the one JJ had stroked, his hand on her breast as he lay beside her. *I have to go!* The blood was beating against her temples. But Diana was still talking.

"Let me call Stephen right now," Lily interrupted. "I really appreciate this. Really." She hung up, stared at the phone. She hadn't spoken with Stephen since she'd headed up to Montreal, just two days earlier. Her glance took in her finger, where the skin was flaking off, slightly less red. She'd better call him now, because later . . . But this was despicable. To be calling her husband while she got ready . . . She couldn't even think the words.

Just this one night, she told herself. *Just once.*

Stephen was in a meeting, but his secretary put her through. "What's up?" From his tone she realized there were people nearby, but even so his voice held a wariness and reserve she wasn't used to hearing.

"I just wanted to say hello. Is this a bad time?" Her voice sounded asthmatic. "Should we talk later instead?" There was quiet on the other end of the line.

"That's probably a good idea."

"I'll call tonight if the show doesn't go too late. Otherwise in the morning." She hung up and then bent over double. This was impossible. She couldn't do this. Then she thought of JJ, guitar cradled in his arms, here, playing for her. Her alone.

That night's show was part of a music festival, held in a former brewery in Old Montreal. Lily wanted to get a few shots of the trendy young crowd, a little footage of the other acts for some flavor, and the entirety of Blaise and JJ's thirty-minute set. But she couldn't keep the camera steady.

At last Blaise and JJ came on, their blend of acoustic and R & B a little staid for this crowd. After filming, Lily put away the camera and waited for them to join her. Minutes passed, a half hour, an hour. What was taking so long? She felt as if she were going to pass out. After the last act's encore, when she was about to set fire to something, all the musicians came back on stage for a finale. The sound was deafening, and she felt crushed by people jumping up and down on every side of her. Finally Blaise and JJ joined her at the back of the hall, where other "friends with the band" were waiting.

"We have an early day tomorrow; I'm going back to the hotel," Blaise said.

"Me too," JJ gave an exaggerated yawn. They shared a cab, then parted ways at the elevator. JJ gave Lily a look that said, *Soon.* When Lily got to her room, she saw it was already eleven o'clock. This was crazy. She should call him and say it was too late. She picked up the phone, but her voice asked for room service and a bottle of champagne.

Her face was moist with sweat. The champagne arrived, and she filled the silver bucket with ice. Shouldn't she feel joyous or at least excited? What was the point of having an affair if you felt like this about it?

There was a staccato tapping at the door; a player piano began hammering in her chest. He was standing with his hands resting on his upright guitar case. She flung herself around them both.

He placed his chin on the top of her head, which rested against the guitar case. They stood that way a moment.

"I ordered champagne. Do you want some now or after you play for me?"

"Oh, definitely now."

She untwisted the metal, aimed for the door. The cork flew off with a pop, hit the door, and then rebounded off the wall behind her to fall on the floor at JJ's feet.

"Wow, that's awesome."

"There are a few things I know how to do."

"I'm sure there are a lot of things you know how to do." He raised his glass, said "To Lily," took a quick sip, and then, businesslike, opened his guitar case. "So, fair maiden, what would you have me play?"

The champagne bubbles expanded inside her head. This was it! This was finally it! He settled himself on the edge of the armless wooden chair, lifted out his guitar, and lay it across his lap.

"I want to hear your CD. Start to finish, all 47.33 minutes of it."

He crossed his legs, balanced the guitar, and strummed a few chords. "I'll do my best, but I did some overdubbing, plus I improvised, so it will sound a little different." The pale wood of the guitar gleamed in the low light of the room. She sat on the floor, her back against the bed, her face so close to the guitar she could see the abalone inlay of a tiny seagull near the bridge, smell the woody scent emanating from the sound hole. She suddenly wanted to crawl inside that sound hole and curl up, as if to get closer to the guitar's mystery.

Despite all the times she'd heard JJ play, nothing had prepared her for this. His guitar wasn't amplified, and the sound was soft and intimate. He swept his pick downward, and a shower of notes cascaded over her like a benediction. He glided from chord to chord, building towers of sound, and she held her breath, afraid they would tumble. He picked delicate arpeggios and meandered to strange and unfamiliar places, creating the shimmering soundscapes he had once told her evoked the mountains of his home. She felt herself fill until she thought she couldn't bear another moment.

Nothing, ever, had touched her like this. Nothing, except Colby's birth, had ever been quite this powerful. She closed her eyes. She was dissolving, pooling in the middle of his notes. She felt tears on her face. He put down the guitar and was kneeling in front of her. "That was the most beautiful thing I've ever heard." He held her hands a moment, then lifted her top over her head and slid his hands, those extraordinary hands, over her shivering skin.

The lovemaking was sure and swift, as if once he had her, he wasn't going to go slow and give her a chance to back out again. The music had swelled and softened her; she parted to him quickly. He found her rhythm right away, and they pulsed together fiercely as she gave over to the music of his body. Later he lay sprawled across her. She kept her eyes closed, every nerve exposed and alive, taking stock. Somehow, she was intact. She hadn't exploded into pieces. And as her skin cooled and she came back to herself, she felt, beyond the excruciating joy, surprising relief. She had done it; it was over. It was irrevocable, and it was over. She could get on with her life.

But first she removed the elastic from his ponytail and untangled his hair with her fingers. "Umm, that feels good," he said, so she reached for her brush in the nightstand drawer. She brushed, beginning with the snarly ends and then moving to the top of his head, digging deep into his scalp. The light from the nightstand picked up the blond highlights in the dusky brown.

"How long did it take you to grow all of this?"

"I've had it long since I was a teenager." He reached up, swept her hair from her cheek. "Did you ever have long hair?"

"I did, in my early twenties." He didn't really know much about her at all, did he? He asked her very few questions about herself. Why didn't that bother her? she wondered, pulling apart strands of his hair. She was dying to know everything about him, no matter how trivial—what he kept in his silverware drawer, how many pairs of socks he owned. Lucky for her, he never seemed to mind her questions. But clearly he didn't have much curiosity about her, and she didn't feel much of an urge to reveal herself to him. Why was that? When you were falling in love, you wanted to talk and talk and talk about yourself. So why didn't she? Maybe their spirits communicated so perfectly, there was no need for regular forms of communication.

Oh, please. So maybe she wasn't falling in love but only feared she was.

JJ got up to use the bathroom, walking with confidence even though he was naked. Why were men so comfortable with their bodies? She wouldn't have been able to walk across the room in front of him with such ease. He looked different without his clothes on, thinner and whiter, with little body hair, and the slight bowing of his legs was more pronounced without his jeans. But as she looked at him, her heart caught in her throat, and she felt tenderness and arousal in equal measure.

He stood with his back to her, without closing the door, his tush looking tight and awfully cute. "Cute" probably wasn't a word men liked to have used to describe their butts. She watched him move his hand to his dick and glanced away as the sound of pee hissed against the bowl.

A minute later, he flung himself onto the bed. "I want to devour you head to toe," he said, kissing her along her collarbone.

"I thought you already did that."

"I will feast on you all night." He slid his hand up her leg. "You're so beautiful."

How could he say this and sound credible? "I'm not."

"You are. Women's bodies are a miracle. You're soft and warm and—what's that word? Billowy."

144

Lily laughed. "That's one way to put it." He had probably slept with hundreds of women, all sorts of women, with all types of bodies. He seemed easily pleased. It came to her then that he wasn't a very critical person, except about music—and Blaise.

"No, really. Your skin is so smooth, and the color of apricots. Turn over." After a second's hesitation, she complied. He stroked her back, ran his hand between her buttocks, down her legs. His stroke was rhythmic and slow, languorous, and she began to feel as if she were his music, a slow, dreamy air. Then gradually he was increasing pressure and speed, playing with tension and release, and he swept her up in a crescendo, took her out on a last long, quivering note.

◀ ▶

Lily awoke to the heavy weight of what she had done. She glanced at the clock. It was past eight. She'd told Stephen she would call. She swung out of the bed, planted her feet on the floor, and then doubled over, head to her knees. She dialed their home number and, when he didn't pick up, put down the phone without leaving a message.

Memories of JJ were coming at her like missiles. She was getting strafed, her flesh torn and bleeding, her soul ruined. She had never felt so sick and ashamed, and yet she didn't know if she could stand another minute without seeing him or hearing his voice.

She had scheduled her final interview with Blaise for ten o'clock. She scrambled into the shower, then dialed Blaise's room to see if she wanted to start a little early. If they finished early, maybe there would be time to see JJ.

"Hold on," Blaise said. Lily heard sounds in the background. "Yes?"

"Blaise, can—"

"Sorry, just a sec. JJ, I want to try that again." He was there? He was up already and there with Blaise? "Sorry, what were you saying?"

"I was just wondering about doing the interview earlier. It sounds like you're already working with JJ. How about I film some of that?"

"Stuff's very rough, Lily."

145

"We can always edit it out." When Blaise hesitated, she said breathlessly, "Be right there." She hung up before Blaise could say no.

JJ was on the edge of the bed, guitar in his lap, papers strewn about, a pencil between his teeth. Their eyes locked; he took the pencil from his mouth and gave her a wide grin. He looked fresh, sparkling. She decided the sparkle was all her doing. Suddenly she went all mushy inside—creamy and decadent, like a flan. Why were all her metaphors about food? "Hey," she said.

"Hey."

Blaise frowned, her glance going from one of them to the other. She looked sullen, pale, and too skinny in black velour pants and hoodie.

"Just go back to what you were doing and ignore me," Lily said.

"That might not be so easy," JJ said.

"If it's going to bother you, we'll ask her to leave," Blaise snapped.

"No, it's fine," he said hastily, then winked at Lily behind Blaise's back.

"Where were we?" Blaise asked.

"This chord change." He ran through a series of chords, half singing, half mumbling. "Here. This is how I thought it could go."

Blaise straightened, began to sing. Close up, the quality of Blaise's voice was even more riveting. She stopped abruptly. "I don't like it."

"How about a little syncopation?" He did an intricate picking pattern. Blaise took in a breath, sang a few bars, stopped. "It's not right. Maybe slow it down a little."

They went on like this for a half hour, each variation sounding fine to Lily, although each conveyed a different quality.

"What do you think?" Blaise turned to Lily.

"I'm not sure," Lily said from behind the camera. "I don't have a sense of what you're going for with the song as a whole."

Blaise flung herself on the bed. "I can't decide—that's the whole problem."

"We have a slow ballad and a rockabilly number for the CD so far. Want to try it a little bluesy?" JJ sang a few measures.

"I like that approach," Lily said tentatively.

"Try it," JJ said to Blaise.

Blaise stood, sang it almost through to the end. "It's no good." She flung herself back on the bed, making JJ's papers jump.

"It is," JJ said.

"Stop badgering me!"

"Blaise." JJ sounded patient, but he looked frustrated.

"I said stop."

Lily clicked off the camera. "Why don't we take a break, and I'll come back a little later for the interview?"

"No, no interview. I'm not in the mood." Blaise jumped up from the bed, stomped to the window, flung the curtain aside. "I hate this! Everything is so much of a fucking struggle. Why does it always have to be such a fucking struggle?"

Behind her, JJ rolled his eyes.

"Maybe you're working too hard," Lily said. "Maybe you should take some time off. Go to a movie, or shopping . . ." She sounded so lame.

But Blaise turned around, suddenly cheery. "Could we? Would you come shopping with me? That would take my mind off all of this. It would be fun."

Lily glanced at JJ. He shrugged. She had promised herself just the one night with him, but already she didn't want to let him out of her sight.

"I'll keep working on the arrangement," JJ said to Blaise. "I'll come up with something you like. Don't worry. I always do."

"I'll just take a quick shower," Blaise said to Lily.

As soon as they heard the sound of the water, JJ stood and Lily went into his arms. *I should tell him I can't do this anymore,* Lily thought, but the thought was wispy and vague; somehow it didn't seem so pressing. What was one more day, now that she'd transgressed?

"See what she's like?" JJ said into her hair. "I have to have the patience of a saint."

Lily laughed.

"What's so funny?"

"The thought of you and sainthood in the same sentence."

"Well, with you whisking her away, I'll be able to get some work done," he said, releasing her.

"Do you think you'll be able to come up with something she'll like?"

"Sure. It'll probably be something we've already tried. It's part of the process. She has to hate everything first."

Blaise emerged in jeans, an oversize sweater, and her high-heeled turquoise boots. She took Lily by the arm, blew a kiss good-bye to JJ, and pranced down the hotel hallway. "Let's have lunch somewhere first, somewhere nice."

The desk clerk suggested a restaurant in the old section of town whose specialty was fondue. A scent of cheese baking wafted out as they opened the door.

"Oh, what fun!" Blaise stirred the creamy goo. There was no trace of her earlier crankiness.

"It's back in style again," Lily said. "Strange how that happens."

"With music, too. You go a few years where, say, folk is passé, then some crossover group or artist comes along, like John Mayer, and it's cool again."

"Do you worry about that?" Lily dunked a piece of bread. Warm cheese filled her mouth, and she held it there a moment to savor it.

"What do you mean?" Blaise's eyes, when they narrowed, seemed to get bluer.

"Do you worry that your music will go out of style?"

"No! Do you think it will?" Her voice was a little shrill.

Lily had let the fondue make fondue of her brains. She should know better not to trigger Blaise's insecurities. "Not at all. Absolutely not."

"Do you think we're getting stale? I know we have to keep stretching, but how much?" She was rushing her words. "Your artistry has to come first. You can't worry too much about fads. You can't let them affect you."

"You have a classic sound, and your voice is incredible. You'll never go out of style." Lily tried to sound authoritative. Hers was an uninformed opinion. She had no idea how Blaise's last album had sold, or what the stakes were for the next one.

"Let's go to that mall underground." Blaise slapped her credit card on the table.

In the shops, Lily followed Blaise around, feigning interest in the clothes.

"I know you and JJ were in a band, but I forget how you met," she asked, watching Blaise finger a filmy pastel-pink blouse.

Blaise held the blouse up to her chest, cocked her head to one side, talked to the mirror. "I was playing acoustic and singing in coffee-houses. He was in a rock band. We hit it off, decided to form our own band."

"You were a couple, right?" Lily looked down, not wanting Blaise to read her expression.

"Yeah, for a couple of years, after that off and on. We came to an understanding."

What kind of understanding? Lily wondered, but she didn't see how she could ask. "And it's worked out OK to keep working together?" She knew she was pushing it, but she couldn't seem to stop. If she kept this up, Blaise was going to get suspicious.

"Well, it's up and down. But we're both really committed to the music." Blaise put down the blouse, smoothed it with the back of her hand.

The music came first, it seemed. In fact, both JJ and Blaise seemed subsumed by the music, subjugated to the music, overshadowed by the music.

But then so was she, Lily thought. Maybe more. For it was, of course, quite possibly ruining her life.

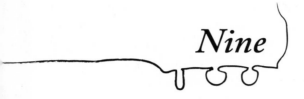

Nine

Over the next few days in Montreal, Lily felt too cold and too hot at the same time: freezer burn. Inside she was warm liquid, like the molten center of one of those amazing chocolate cakes, but outside she was freezing the way Montrealers froze, a bone chill that sent them down into underground tunnels of shops and restaurants where they holed up for the winter. She and JJ holed up in her room. It was shockingly strange touching a body that wasn't Stephen's, experiencing the taste of a different tongue, the feel of a different hand. But little by little, he was becoming familiar. And when she was with him, she was able, sometimes for whole minutes, to be happy, to shut everything else out.

After JJ left to sneak back to his room early each morning, she raced along Montreal's frigid streets in a jog, her eyelashes turning to icicles. Sometimes her feelings were so intense she thought she would dissolve under the weight of them. Apparently, just because she was following her soul or her heart or her libido didn't mean it was easy. Yet desire, longing, need—whatever it was she was giving rein to— trumped everything else: sense, loyalty, principles. To bear that, she had to take it one day at a time, a reverse alcoholic, gradually giving in to her addiction.

With Stephen she did a little mental origami: She folded him up and then folded him up again, until he formed a very tiny shape, a bird perhaps, that she placed in a pocket of her heart. Now and then she called him—she couldn't not call him—but their conversations were so attenuated—"It's me." "I know." "OK, then."—that once she vomited afterward.

"What happened here?" JJ asked her the morning after their third night together, running his finger over the place where her wedding band should have been. Blaise had had an "appointment" with a guy she'd picked up the night before, and so JJ had come to Lily's room, and they had ordered room service and eaten in bed.

"Just a skin allergy." The scaly skin was flaking now. "It's getting better."

"Hmm." If he asked, she was not going to talk about Stephen, she decided, or her marriage. That was off-limits. But he didn't ask.

"Are you OK with all of this?"

"Probably not," she said, "but I don't seem able to not do it."

"Me too," he said. "I mean, I seem not to be able to stay away from you."

"Is it interfering? Are you getting enough time with your guitar?"

JJ laughed. "I really don't work that way," he said. "You don't need to worry."

"You don't practice?"

JJ settled her against him, pulled his arms tighter around her. "Not like a classical guitarist—scales or left-hand exercises." He ran his fingers over her skin as if demonstrating. "On the road I'm playing every day. If we don't have a gig, I just mess around. Sometimes, if I'm lucky, compositions kind of reveal themselves."

Lily stared at his fingers, long and tapered, now tapping out a rhythm on her hip. What a mystery it was, creation. "I can't imagine how it feels to be you, to be able to do what you do." She stroked his arm, riffling the hairs, feeling their silky texture.

"Being with you is inspiring me. I'm full of ideas these days."

"Really?" Her voice was a chipmunk squeak. "Are you working on something new?"

"I am. And it has a title. Stargazer."

"Oh my God."

"Yes," he said, "for you."

"Will you play it for me?"

"Not just yet. Not while it's gestating."

"How do you actually feel when you play?" she asked. "Is it sort of like this?"

"What do you mean—do I feel exhausted?"

"Silly. You know what I mean. Does it feel sexual? Is it totally intoxicating?"

"Sometimes, yeah. Times when it goes really well." He sounded uncomfortable, as if reluctant to reveal what he really felt—he who was usually spewing everything that crossed his mind. "You have to guard against letting it go to your head."

"I guess it can be pretty powerful when everyone's going crazy, and all for you."

"Yeah, you can feel like you own the world. But it's also scary. You have to keep remembering that you're just an ordinary person with just a little bit of ability."

"Not such a little bit." How she loved his modesty.

"People let it mess them up—Blaise, case in point. It skews their perspective and skews their lives, too. They go around thinking the world owes them something—owes them everything—just because they can play or sing." His voice had risen. "Music should be about sharing and making something beautiful, not about your big fucking ego. I mean, if you think you're God, how do you relate to the rest of the world?"

Lily propped herself up on an elbow. "This is on your mind a lot, isn't it?"

"I'm really trying to work on balance, keeping the music in its place. My shrink says I need to develop more of a normal life. But all I really know is music. I've been consumed by it all my life; I don't know how to be or do anything else."

"Is there something else you would want?"

JJ's fingers on her hip stilled. "No. It's probably just I've had enough of Blaise and her moods, sick of playing nursemaid."

153

Blaise had seemed to be doing just fine on her own the last few nights, Lily thought. "So maybe you'll like touring with Ticker-Tape."

"You're like my shrink. You point out my ambivalences."

"I can't tell if you're happy or not in your life."

"You and me both."

"What does your shrink say? What does he think you should do?"

"You know how it works. The shrink never tells you. He says I have to figure it out. I don't know why I bother to go see him at all, except sometimes I just need to blow off steam. I guess I need to do that a lot, don't I?" He blew lightly into her ear.

"You're awfully cute when you're blowing off steam." She began tickling the inside of his thigh.

He grabbed her hands. "I really could get used to having you around."

Lily's breath cut off. But he said nothing more.

He left for an appointment with someone who was interested in buying one of his guitars. Lily made the bed and began to tidy up the room. What would she do if he asked her to go back with him to Colorado? What if he broke from Blaise and went solo—she could manage his career, to which she could apply all her detail-oriented abilities. Maybe they'd find a new place to live. She'd always wanted to see California.

She sat abruptly. How could she be thinking like this! She saw herself walking into her building, the building she'd lived in all the years of her marriage, saying hi to her next-door neighbor as she fitted the key into the lock, twisting it in that particular way because of the funny little catch. As she opened her door, her eyes would fall on the framed photos in the entryway of the places she and Stephen vacationed.

Honor's husband had taken the coward's way out and left a note on the refrigerator. In her mind's eye, Lily saw the silly lobster magnet on her own fridge, a note to Stephen grasped in its claws.

She shuddered. She grabbed the tube of cortisone cream from the nightstand and began slathering it on her finger. JJ would not beg her to stay. He was not the begging kind. Deep down, she suspected, he wasn't the kind to fall deeply in love, either.

She shoved the empty cortisone tube into the wastebasket. What he wanted or didn't want wasn't the point. She needed to concentrate on what *she* wanted, how she felt about her own life.

But not just yet. Because tonight, after the show, there was a big, dressy party for musicians and their guests. JJ wanted to introduce her to a friend from college. It would be thrilling to be perceived as part of a couple with him, even if only fleetingly.

It was only 11:00 AM. She had to work off her excess energy. Outside it was a little less windy, a little warmer, and the wooden ramp over a hole in the sidewalk in front of the hotel didn't squeak from the cold as it usually did. She walked to the summit of Mount Royal Park and took in views of the city, then descended to the western end of Rue Sherbrook, passing hotels and restaurants she hadn't seen before. At one large department store, a flirty print dress on a mannequin caught her eye. She hesitated only a second. Inside, sleek counters were piled with cosmetics, and discreet classical piano music was playing in the background. On the second floor she found the dress. She hurried to the fitting room. It fit—a size 10!—but looked awful. Disappointed, she wandered around, appetite whetted to have something special for the party. On impulse she tried on a gauzy top with ruffles along the deep V neckline. It seemed to slim her round face, and the ruffles made her feel sexy. She walked back to the hotel swinging the thick white shopping bag like a little girl with her first purse. When it was time to get ready, she loaded herself up with bangles and layered some glitter shadow along her eyelids. Why not? Why not live it up? She stood back from the mirror and appraised herself. What would Stephen say if he saw her? She'd always been secure in herself in his eyes. He was generous with compliments, and he seemed to see not the middle-age woman she was but the slender girl with the flowing curls. In this getup, would he think she looked cheap? Ridiculous? She probably resembled a large, black flamingo.

But a sexy flamingo! She began flapping her arms, twirling around the room, singing, "I am the flamingo! I am the flamingo!" to the melody of "I Am the Walrus."

There was a rapping of knuckles. Catching her breath, she flung open the door: "Ta-da!"

But instead of JJ, Lily's sister stood stone-faced before her. The floor tilted; Lily grabbed the doorjamb. "What are you doing here?"

"Nice welcome." Troy's eyes were blazing.

Lily felt her own face flame. "Sorry! Come in."

Troy strode past her and dumped a large duffel on the floor with a thud. Her blond hair was pulled back in a tight bun from which little wisps of hair floated angrily.

"You're staying?" Lily asked ungraciously.

"Not with you, don't worry. I got a room," Troy removed her knee-length white down coat and threw it on a chair. It slid to the floor; she didn't pick it up.

"Why didn't you call me?" Lily asked.

"Why didn't *you* call *me?*" She stood opposite Lily, her tall, lean body rigid.

Lily turned away. "I've been having a hard time." Her voice sounded weak, false.

"That's when people call their sisters—when they're having a hard time."

"It's not the kind of thing I can talk about."

"Bullshit. I knew if I called you'd have told me to stay away."

Troy was right. Troy was always right. It had always been an incredibly annoying thing about her. "OK. So say whatever it is you came here to say." Lily crossed her arms over her chest. Her sister had knocked what joy there was right out of her.

Troy squared her shoulders. "Lily, do you realize what you're doing to Stephen? Colby? You can't just go off in this way and satisfy whatever these urges are!"

Her sister sounded like a pompous know-it-all spewing tired—if true—bromides. Troy had always been a fierce little sister, a bit strict and critical. But seeing the anguish on Troy's face, Lily knew she was genuinely concerned. Not just because of her own moral code, and on behalf of Stephen and Colby, but for her, too. For her sister, Lily.

"Can't you talk to me?" Troy's eyes welled up.

Lily hadn't seen Troy cry since they were children. Troy was the tough one. Lily felt her own eyes fill, and then she was crying, too. "I'm sorry, I'm sorry." She wiped her eyes with the backs of her hands, which came away streaked with mascara. "I'll try to explain, but it will seem completely insane."

They sat side by side on the bed up against the headboard, just as she and JJ had three nights earlier, shoes off, facing the TV. Lily glanced at the clock. She had an hour before sound check. Troy's coming would ruin the evening.

"It's about a man, isn't it?" Troy said. "Stephen wouldn't say, but—"

"Partly," Lily said slowly.

"Are you in love with him?"

Lily hesitated. If she did really love JJ—real, true love of some kind—she wasn't ready to own up. Not to her sister. Not even to herself. "I'm not really sure."

"Sex, then? Is it just sex?"

Could sex ever be "just"? "It's their music. It gets all mixed together."

"You're in love with both of them?" Troy sounded shocked.

Lily laughed. "No, but I'm in love with something."

"You wish you'd pursued your own singing?"

"All I can tell you is that I heard them play, and it was like this tremendous ache, this really deep pain, like loss, that I was feeling. And then I had the chance to do the video. It was like it was preordained, like fate. Or salvation. Something I was meant to do. Even Stephen giving me the camera, and Colby inviting me to the concert where I first heard them. Like something in the cosmos is making me do this."

Troy was silent, her look considering. "Lily, I don't mean to scare you," she said softly, "but I think you seriously need some kind of help."

Of course Troy didn't understand. It was too much to expect. And maybe she was right. Lily probably did need help. "Come with me

157

tonight. There's a concert and a party. You'll see what I mean. You'll get a sense of what I'm talking about."

"I don't know. . . ."

"You're here. Besides, it'll be fun. There will be a lot of musicians there."

"Anyone famous?"

Troy had a weakness for celebrities. Lily pressed her advantage. "Definitely!" Maybe it would be true. "Blaise and JJ know everyone."

"I have nothing to wear," Troy said, and Lily knew she had her.

She began taking off her new blouse. "This'll look great on you."

"Oh, I couldn't."

"I have something else I was about to change into." The only other dressy top Lily had was her velvet paisley, but no way would she let Troy wear the garment JJ's hands had been all over.

Troy preened a little in front of the mirror. "This is really quite nice." Of course it was. On Troy the black ruffles were elegant. Gone, the flamingo.

"Let's drop off your bags in your room," Lily said. "We'll talk more tomorrow, OK? But for tonight, just let me do my work." They were already going to be late.

"I guess," she said, mouth turning down, eyebrows coming together.

Downtown, Lily saw the atmosphere working on her sister almost immediately. Old Montreal was glowing with soft lights, and the sound of laughter and guitar emanated from the club's open doorway. She led her sister upstairs. Blaise and JJ glanced over as they came into the room, looking uncertain when they spotted Troy.

"Blaise Raleigh, Jackson Johnson, I'd like to introduce you to my sister, Troy."

JJ gave Lily a quick eyebrow lift and then hopped down from the stage to shake Troy's hand. "It's great to meet you. Any sister of Lily's is a sister of ours. I hope you're staying for the concert and the party?"

"Yes, thank you, if it's all right?" Troy was almost blushing.

"It's fine," Blaise said. "Pardon us, but we'd better get back to work."

"Oh, I'm so sorry."

"No need," Blaise said. JJ hopped back on stage.

Lily turned to Troy. "Sit here, OK? You won't be in the way of the taping."

"Lionel, please give me a little more guitar in the monitor," Blaise called out. JJ took off on a series of runs. He was showing off, as if he knew Lily wanted him to impress Troy. Blaise sang a few bars, asked for an adjustment, and then said, "Thanks, Lionel, I think we're done."

Blaise placed her guitar in a holder on the stage and swung lithely to the floor. "We usually grab a bite before the show," she said over her shoulder as she strode toward the door. "Come if you want."

"Sure," Lily said, before Troy could say no.

"What brings you to Montreal?" JJ gestured to let Troy precede him.

"I decided to visit Lily," Troy said, her tone a bit challenging.

"Oh? She didn't mention it."

"I made it a surprise." Troy colored. When he didn't respond, she lifted her chin. "I wanted to see what all the fuss was about."

JJ threw his head back, laughing. "Blaise, you hear that? She's just issued us a challenge. We're gonna have to give this lady some show tonight!"

Over dinner, JJ was attentive to Troy, seemingly disarming her; he didn't so much as glance at Lily. Only when Troy excused herself to go to the ladies' room and Blaise was distracted by a fan did he reach for Lily's hand.

"You must have freaked out," JJ said. "Does she know about us?"

"She suspects."

"I'm sorry." He massaged her hand with his thumb, and she felt her eyes well up.

Back at the concert venue, Lily taped only the first set so she could sit with Troy for the second. The crowd was boisterous, one guy calling out, "*Ouais, bébé!*" each time Blaise stepped to the microphone. The rowdiness seemed to ignite rather than annoy her; she did more hair flinging than usual. JJ was a whirlwind of fingers and strings.

"They *are* good," Troy whispered. "I can see why you're mesmerized."

Lily was grateful she didn't add, *But I don't understand why you need to throw away your life.*

Afterward, they squeezed into a cab for the ride to the hotel where the party was being held. Lily had expected snazzy, but she hadn't expected this: a floor-to-ceiling mural of Old Montreal that ran the length of a city block, a bar like an elongated comma cupping an ornate fountain spewing iridescent water. The din made it impossible to have a conversation. People kept coming over to JJ, so she and Troy drifted away. Absent Troy, he would have been introducing Lily to everyone. She accepted a glass of champagne each time a hostess went by, until she lost count. As the night wore on, JJ continued to be surrounded by a never-ending crush of people; there was no salvaging anything of the evening. Finally, Troy retrieved their coats while Lily plunged through the crowd to say good-bye to him, interrupting the slim blonde in a too-tight red dress he was looking at attentively. She leaned in close, whispering, "Call me in the morning." His eyes were momentarily vacant, and then he gave her a quick nod.

Outside, the air was so cold it made her jaw ache. She and Troy walked the few blocks to the hotel. "I really am trying to understand," Troy finally said.

"I know. And thanks for coming tonight—it meant a lot." They took the elevator to Troy's floor, and Lily walked her to her door. She held her breath. Would Troy refuse to leave unless Lily returned with her to New York?

"I guess we can talk in the morning." She gave Lily a hesitant hug. Lily stood a moment after the door closed, registering guilt and relief. Troy had looked downcast, shoulders hunched; she'd looked like someone who had already conceded the fight.

By the time Lily had taken the elevator up three floors and opened her door on her empty, empty room, she was considering going back to the party. She imagined walking into the huge lobby, spotting JJ . . . In her mind's eye, he turned, frowned, not quite as happy to see her as she would like him to be, the blonde in the red dress clinging to his side . . . *Don't do this,* she told herself. But the fantasy hurt so much—sharp

160

as a paper cut, fierce as hot grease splattering the skin—that it was sobering. To be with JJ would be to experience this kind of discomfort regularly, like a dull toothache that might flare at any moment into excruciating pain.

She went to the bathroom and washed off her makeup without turning on the light. She didn't want to see her face. Then she pulled on a T-shirt and slipped under the covers and tucked the blankets around herself in a little cocoon. Troy's presence threatened to strip the gloss from everything. It was as if Lily had been absorbed in a play, and just by her presence, Troy would peel away the artifice and reveal the ordinary props beneath. *Go away,* Lily thought. *Please, please, just go away.*

In the morning she called Troy and asked her to come over for breakfast in her room. Her sister arrived dressed in jeans and a turtleneck, clearly not the business attire that would have signaled she was heading back. Lily wasn't going to be let off the hook.

They made desultory small talk until the food arrived. Lily had ordered French toast, comfort food, but the syrup was too cloying. She pushed her plate aside. "Troy, this is very hard for me to say, so I'm just going to say it. I hope you'll forgive me, but I need to ask you to leave. I really need this time to myself to figure things out."

Troy's eyes bulged, and then she went into a coughing fit. Lily jumped up and began thumping her on the back.

"Enough!" Troy gasped, face red. She grabbed a glass of water, then sat breathing heavily, clearly shaken. By sending her away, was Lily risking what little they had of a relationship? They'd never been that close in the first place. Was this a breach she could never repair?

"I'm sorry, I'm really so sorry." She waited, but Troy didn't say anything. "Can you understand?"

Troy stood up. Her skin looked blanched. "You're sleeping with him, aren't you? You were so upset about Renée, I can't believe you're doing this."

"It wouldn't be the reason. It wouldn't be a choice of one man over another—that's not what this is about."

"It's always that. Or at least that's the consequence, isn't it?"

Lily grabbed Troy's hands. "Don't you see? It's for the magic." They stared at each other. Lily saw the little sister who had looked up at her adoringly as she read *The Lion, the Witch and the Wardrobe* to her in their bedroom. But Troy just shook her head.

"There's no such thing as magic, Lily—you know that."

Lily felt herself falter. She was poised at the edge, ready to sail off, trusting the magic, ready to take the leap.

"Call me if you want to talk." Troy walked to the door, paused with her hand on the doorknob. "Call if you want me to come back. I'll be there for you in any way I can."

Lily buried her head in her hands. She heard the murmurs of the maids making their rounds, the soft swish of their carts on the carpeted passageways, the sound of doors closing, the little click as the plastic key activated the door next to hers, the sound of her radiator kicking on. She couldn't think; she couldn't move. She sat and she sat until she had to pee so badly she was forced from her chair.

He hadn't called. It was already eleven o'clock.

The phone rang; she stared, then dove for it.

"Did you remember we have to drive north for that gig in Val-David?" Blaise barked. "I'll kill Henry for scheduling this today!"

Lily had totally forgotten. "When do we need to leave?"

"An hour. We'll be back here tomorrow, so you don't need your car."

She would ride with JJ. If there had been a blonde with him last night, she was long gone. It was Lily who would be in the car with JJ and Blaise, Lily who was allowed into the inner sanctum. She stood, did a little jig.

"I am the flamingo!"

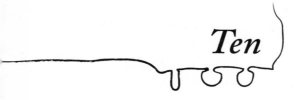

Ten

Approaching the car, Lily could see the back of JJ's watch cap–covered head and the staccato drumming of his fingers on the steering wheel. The blonde in the red dress danced into her mind, and she stumbled. The car door burst open. He bounded out and crushed her in a hug. Her hands slid down his slick jacket; she could barely feel his body underneath the down pillow they made between them. "I missed you," she said, her breath puffing out in the icy air.

"Your sister's gone?" He stroked her hair. It crackled with electricity. She nodded into his chest. He broke from her and put her bag in the trunk. She got into the backseat. Oddly, the moment of intimacy left her disoriented and with a hollow, empty feeling in the pit of her stomach.

JJ went back to drumming on the steering wheel. "Blaise texted she'll be right down. She's in a bitch of a mood. She partied hard, and having to travel this early sucks."

"Can you cancel?"

JJ swiveled his head at her in a parody of shock. "You never, ever cancel a gig. Unless you're, like, in the hospital. It's a cardinal rule. It's the fastest way to career death. You start canceling, it's the beginning of the end."

"Got it," Lily said. Come to think of it, he and Blaise were always prompt for sound checks, and they were gracious to the club managers and sound guys. They never failed to remind the crowd to tip the wait-resses—not exactly the work ethic she would have associated with the freewheeling, self-involved persona of budding stars.

"She's here," JJ said. "Listen. She's always difficult in the car. I've learned to wait and see if she wants quiet or if she wants to talk."

Blaise put her guitar in the trunk and thumped it shut. She slipped into the front seat with a door slam. "JJ, I need coffee, pronto. Do they have Starbucks?"

"I don't know, but there's a coffee place down the street. Latte with an extra shot?" So solicitous, Lily thought; it wasn't toadying—not quite—but it annoyed her.

"Lily." JJ stopped the car. "Anything for you?"

"No, thanks, I'm fine." He left the motor running; Lily sat silent, as instructed.

"It's so fucking cold," Blaise burst out. "How do these people stand it?" She fidgeted with the heat dial. "I've had it with touring. Had it! I just want to go home."

"I guess it really takes a toll."

"It's much harder than it looks."

Lily glanced toward the coffee shop, hoping JJ would be quick. She was tiring of Blaise's neediness. "You probably need rest."

"Putting out, being on. It's so hard."

Lily thought of her the night before, sleek in a tight, gold-spangled sheath that came just inches below her crotch, basking in attention. Who was she kidding? Now, like a maddened stylist, she was grabbing her white-blond hair and scrunching it up.

JJ opened the passenger door and passed Blaise her coffee. How did he put up with her moods?

Blaise fell silent and sipped. They headed north toward the Laurentians. "Scenery or speed?" JJ asked. *Scenery,* Lily voted silently, but Blaise said, "Autoroute."

"We pick up the scenic route in St.-Jérôme, in any case," he added. The land flew past in a white streak, the skies gray and thick.

"It better not snow. We'd better not get stuck up there."

"Canadians know how to deal with snow," JJ said. "The roads will be fine."

"I'm not staying a second longer than I have to."

"We still have the hotel in Montreal—we can drive back tonight if you want," he said soothingly. "Want some music?"

"No." She turned her gaze back to the window. "My head is killing me."

"Aspirin?" Lily offered.

Blaise just guffawed. Lily watched the telephone poles click by. The pale landscape filled her vision. She was just about to drift off when Blaise's cell phone chimed.

"What now!"

"So don't answer it," JJ said. But only her manager and a few select friends and business associates had her private number.

"Blaise here." Her voice was clipped, all traces of the whiny teen-ager vanished. From the way she straightened and said, "Oh, hey, how are you?" Lily could tell the call was welcome.

"Hmm, yeah, sure." Blaise glanced toward JJ and then out the window, lowering her voice. "We're in the car, so why don't we talk later? About three. Yeah, you too. Great." She clicked her phone shut, hummed to herself.

"Henry, scheduling stuff," she said, not looking at JJ. She put her seat back and pulled her jacket over her like a blanket, but it was apparent from her occasional sighs and shifting positions that she was just pretending to sleep. Lily saw JJ's puzzled frown in the rearview mirror. She tried to catch his eye, but he didn't glance back at her.

At St.-Jérôme, Blaise wanted to press on, but JJ said abruptly, "I have to take a piss, and I'm hungry." They found a small café with a sign for, of all things, bagels. All four customers looked up as they walked in.

"Bonjour!" JJ said to the waitress who brought their menus.

"Bonjour, hi. Coffee?"

They ordered the Montreal bagels, which turned out to be smaller and denser than the U.S. variety. "These are fabulous," Lily babbled into the tense silence between JJ and Blaise. "New York is of course famous for its bagels, and personally I think the ones at Absolute Bagels on the Upper West Side are the best—I like that malty, chewy texture, you know? But really, these have something going for them."

Blaise narrowed her eyes at Lily, as if thinking, *Who* are *you?* She turned to JJ. "What time will we be in Val-David?"

JJ pulled the map from his coat pocket and spread it out. "It's not too far. You'll be there in plenty of time for your call."

"Good." She took a huge bite of her bagel. Lily watched JJ watch Blaise. His mouth was grim, his eyes assessing, as if he guessed what was up and was not so much upset as resigned. As soon as they were settled in the motel, Lily would get him to tell her what he thought was going on.

They piled back in the car. Blaise wanted music now. Lily hated the echoey, metallic synthesizer sound of the New Age CD she popped in. JJ and Blaise occasionally made comments to each other about the music, as if everything were fine between them. Lily turned to the scenery; the flat landscape had given way to rolling hills and rounded mountains with folds and hollows like rumpled bedsheets. *Stop thinking about the two of them,* Lily told herself. *Focus on your own problems.* But it was as if they had taken her life hostage.

Val-David was a picturesque resort town of quirky traditional Québecois houses with mansard roofs. "I read that this is a big artsy place," JJ said, as they drove past small galleries and cafés and pulled into a parking lot behind a small inn downtown. Lily intercepted him at the trunk. "Come by, OK?" she whispered just before Blaise was at her elbow, reaching for her guitar.

Lily's room on the fourth floor overlooked the bustling street below. People were hurrying to and fro, calling hellos, dressed in brightly colored wool caps. So many people in the world, so many lives lived far from New York and other centers of power. Did the United States seem like another planet to people in rural Canada—someplace interesting but too far away to think about? Or did it loom like a large office building blocking their sun, causing their houseplants to shrivel?

Where was he? It was already 3:40. She waited ten more minutes, called the desk to ask his room number, and then went down one flight. She knocked. "JJ, it's me."

He opened his door, looking disheveled. "I'm a little freaked." His hair was out of its usual ponytail, and his shirt was only partly tucked in, open to reveal a thermal undershirt. His overnight case and guitars lay unpacked on the bed. "I think Blaise is making a deal with Ticker-Tape Parade."

"Besides the tour? What kind of deal?" Lily stepped inside.

"I don't know, but she's being really secretive. She must be planning to cut me out of it altogether."

"She won't cut you out. Come on, JJ. That's crazy."

"Well, she *is* crazy." He ran his hands through his hair, creating gnarly clumps.

"Can't you just confront her straight out? Tell her what *you* want?"

"She'll do what she wants. She always does whatever the fuck she wants." He sat down, hands clasped between his legs, frowning in concentration at the floor.

"Are you going to be able to play tonight, being so upset?"

"I play happy and I play fucked up and I play sick—you just play." Abruptly he stood. "You're right, I've gotta talk to her, even if it doesn't make any difference. We need to come to some kind of understanding." He pulled a rubber band from his wrist and yanked his hair back into its ponytail, shoved his shirt into his pants. "You'll come tonight? You'll be there?"

"Of course." Where else would she be?

He touched her cheek with his finger. "You're the best." Then, finally, he leaned over and gave her a kiss, a kiss that seemed to remember who she was.

Lily walked slowly back to her room along the dimly lit corridor. The night JJ had sat at her feet and played for her already seemed like weeks, rather than days, ago. Why did everything change? Why did everything you wanted to stay the same change too quickly, and the things you wanted to change were so stubbornly resistant?

She sat by the window, waiting for his call. Outside, beyond the lights of the town, the sky was as dark as sin. Minute after minute passed with no word. Were they yelling at each other, JJ pacing back and forth, the way he did when he was agitated? Finally she gathered her things and went downstairs to wait. The lobby, fusty with frayed and worn patterned carpets, made her sneeze. She sat in a stiff, uncomfortable chair and paged through old magazines whose tattered edges might have been gnawed by mice: *Canadian Rail Journeys. Penguin Eggs Music.* She asked at the desk if there were any messages. Could they have already left, forgotten her?

"No, sorry. Would you like to leave a voice mail?" the clerk asked in heavily accented English.

She suddenly thought to check the parking lot for the car. "Thank you, no." Outside it felt heavy and damp, as if the snow would arrive any second. She turned up her coat collar and hurried behind the inn to the lot. The blue Mazda was there. Just as she started back, she saw JJ and Blaise coming down the street.

"We were having a drink," JJ said when they got closer. He and Blaise didn't make eye contact with each other; Lily couldn't read anything from their expressions. At least they hadn't killed each other.

"Let's get a move on," Blaise said, her tone accusatory, as if Lily had held them up. "It's late."

Lily slipped into the backseat for the ride to an old, rustic building, Théâtre de la Butte, wondering if she could get JJ alone to find out what was going on before he went on stage. But the manager was waiting at the door. He was small and dark, with a bristly mustache, wearing a thick handmade sweater. "Welcome!" he said, clapping his hands together to ward off cold, or with glee, Lily couldn't tell. "Did you know that Québec's first *boîte à chansons* was built here—that is a, how you say, folk-song club. We feature French-Canadian theater here, but for tonight we are fortunate, so fortunate, to have you." He hurried them into the building, talking all the while, not giving Lily a chance to pull JJ aside.

JJ and Blaise went ahead into the performance space, and the director took her on a quick tour. Maybe she should frame the video with tonight's concert, she thought. The atmospheric venue might work well. She adjusted for the lower light and took close-ups of some of the ornate moldings and fixtures, the high ceilings, dark wood.

The association hosting the concert had organized a potluck dinner before the show. People were gathered around long tables, chattering excitedly, many in French. JJ and Blaise were ushered to the head table. Lily put down her camera and asked a group of women if she could join them. Nodding, they sidled over.

"Are you a fan of Blaise Raleigh?" Lily asked an older woman to her right, who was wearing a pink sweater with a poodle appliqué.

"*Je ne parle pas anglais,*" the woman said.

A young woman piped in, "I have all of Blaise's CDs. I'm a huge fan."

"Do they play much in Canada?"

"*Oui,* and the university radio stations play them often. They have a very big following here. I'm in love with Blaise's voice. *Incrôyable.*"

Clearly their manager had known what he was doing by booking this gig, Lily thought, however much Blaise resented squeezing it in. The point was proven after dinner, when Blaise and JJ came out on stage to roaring applause. Blaise was wearing a billowy white blouse with silver threads that shimmered in the light. Lily zoomed in close to capture the gloss. She had a sudden glimpse of how she wanted the film to look, something more impressionistic than the linear approach she had been planning. She caught Blaise hammering her thigh with her fist, JJ hunching his shoulders up slightly the way he did before launching into one of his supercharged runs. She switched her focus rapidly back and forth between them, as if by capturing their interaction she could figure out what was going on between them.

This little town in remote Québec was a bastion of Blaise fans, a die-hard crowd that knew all the material and shouted out for favorites.

Blaise and JJ did four songs in two encores, and if he hadn't broken a string, Lily didn't know if they'd ever have gotten off the stage.

"Fantastic!" Blaise flung open the door to the dressing room. Her face was covered in a patina of sweat. Had JJ played his fingers off to remind her of what she'd lose if she left him out of whatever deal she was cooking up? The two of them were positively phosphorescent; excitement wafted from them like sex, as if the whole tense, miserable day had never happened. Lily, meanwhile, felt ready to collapse.

Blaise had invited the theater's board members to join them for the after-party. Lily, without her own car, had no choice but to slide back into the Mazda. Within minutes, their three carloads pulled up at a local bar, whose patrons looked up in alarm as they trooped in, loud and full of themselves. Blaise ordered tequila, and soon they were doing shots. *What the hell,* Lily thought, and put a piece of lime between her teeth. She threw back her head. "Go, Lily!" Blaise shouted.

The room began to get fuzzy around the edges, and the tension in her neck and back eased. She propped her head against the wall.

"I have an announcement," Blaise said loudly over the din. Everyone stopped talking. Lily looked at JJ. She couldn't read anything from his face.

"We're going to be doing a project with Ticker-Tape Parade. A concept CD."

"What's the concept?" The manager pulled at his mustache.

"Covers of wonderful old Appalachian fiddle tunes and traditional ballads and bluegrass standards. We'll totally transform them. We'll stay true to the original roots music but bring our own sensibilities to bear."

A joint recording project: This went beyond a little tour with Ticker-Tape. But Blaise had said "we," so JJ would be part of it.

"Like Uncle Tupelo?" someone asked.

"No." JJ leaned forward. "They just added in some acoustic instruments. Ticker-Tape already includes pipes, banjo, and Dobro. We're after a complete reimagining."

"More like what Norah Jones does with jazz standards?" a board member asked.

"Yes, but we'll be more adventurous!" Blaise's eyes were wide, her voice louder than it needed to be even over the noise of the bar. She lifted her glass. "Cheers!"

They all raised their glasses. JJ was smiling. Into Lily's mind came an image of the bass player in Ticker-Tape, her eager face and bouncing curls. But then Lucinda Williams was singing in the background: *You left your mark on me, it's permanent, a tattoo . . .* and JJ turned to her, his eyes locking on hers.

It took another hour or so for the evening to wind down. Finally they were driving back to the inn and doing their usual good nights in the elevator.

"Nine AM breakfast," Blaise said. "I want to get back to Montreal early."

"It's almost two now," JJ argued, as the elevator stopped at their floor, one below Lily's. "Let's make it ten."

"All right." She stepped off the elevator. JJ followed her out, mouthing "five minutes" over his shoulder to Lily.

In her room, Lily took off her shoes, brushed her teeth, and lowered the lights. She was exhausted, but no way would she have discouraged him from coming. She settled on the bed and pulled up a blanket while she waited. JJ's knock roused her from a doze. How long had she been asleep? She ran her tongue over her teeth.

"Sorry, I got hung up with Blaise," he said. Lily squinted at the clock: 3:00 AM. "Should I leave?" He held her at arm's length and looked into her face.

"No! I'm fine. I'm dying to know what's going on."

"First, a kiss." He pulled her to him, running his hands down her back, as if ironing her blouse to her body. Everything inside, muscle and bone, collapsed into a warm, mushy soufflé. "Whoa," he said. "I'd better get you back into that bed."

A scented candle on the dresser flickered in the dim light and reflected in the mirror. "I was way off base," JJ said, throwing off his clothes and sliding in next to her under the covers. "My brain is my worst enemy." His hand described small circles on her thigh. "I guess I'm as much of a narcissist as she is—as if all her crap is about me." His hand left her thigh and alighted on her stomach. "Here's what's been going on: She hasn't been writing. She has no new material beyond the three songs for the next CD you've heard us rehearse. She's been in the middle of a block and really freaking out, and didn't want to tell me. It's so funny how fucked up and insecure I am!" He sounded exultant.

"Yeah, really funny," Lily said wryly. "Your insecurity makes me crazy."

"You? You're the sanest person I think I've ever met."

"Ha! If that's true, I feel sorry for you." But the comment brought home how little of her real self she shared with him.

"She puts out a CD every couple of years. She's overdue. So with this project with Ticker-Tape being all covers, she buys herself time to get back to her own music. It's win-win."

"But what about you?"

"It'll be great. I'll have fun with all the musical arrangements."

"But I thought you didn't want to play second fiddle—pun intended."

"It's just this once. I'll still be the lead guitarist. I enjoy playing with other musicians. It'll be something different."

Wasn't this the opposite of everything he'd ever said? But he sounded excited. Maybe she had misread what he wanted—maybe he didn't really want to break away from Blaise and go out on his own, or with another singer. Maybe his unhappiness was because he didn't feel secure with Blaise, and now that he was reassured, the complaints and considerations fell away. As for Blaise, well, her moodiness made more sense. Lily would hate to be in her position, unable to find the vein of creativity that had always been there. How frightening to fear it would never return. Teaming up with another band was probably a shrewd move. "When will you start work on the album?"

"As soon as we're back from Europe, Ticker-Tape will come out to Colorado."

In her mind's eye she saw a cluster of instruments and Ticker-Tape band members crowded around Blaise's living room, some on the peach leather couch she and Blaise had seen in the Plattsburgh showroom. She could never be a part of that. She imagined herself at the door, watching, listening to the banter. On the outside.

But the outside of the inside—watching music in the making, seeing creativity at its source. Would that be enough?

She waited. Did JJ even think about the fact that the day after tomorrow they would be flying to Europe and she would be driving home?

As if in answer to her unspoken question, he slid his hand down her leg, turned her toward him, and smothered her mouth with his own.

◀ ▶

Something was confusing, off-kilter. Her face was too warm. Lily struggled to open her eyes. The light was bright, stabbing her from between the slats of the vertical blinds she must have forgotten to close. She turned over, her hand encountering form. She felt herself go dreamy, remembering their slow, gentle lovemaking. JJ had not left as he usually did to go to his own room.

"Hey," she whispered, pressing her lips to his powerful shoulder. Years of guitar had given him these strong muscles, but she knew he also suffered from pain in his neck and arms. He did a stretching routine every day.

"Hmm . . . you look beautiful," he said sleepily.

"Just call me angel of the morning," she sang. Then, glancing at the clock: "Oops, it's already ten. We should hurry."

"Shit!" He sat up abruptly, clipping her jaw with his head.

"Ow." She rubbed her face. He was out of bed, leaping toward the bathroom. "Should I let Blaise know we're going to be late?"

"No, call down to the desk and tell them—"

He was interrupted by pounding at the door.

"Open up this minute!" Blaise shouted.

JJ, standing naked at the bathroom door, looked at Lily in terror.

"Coming!" she called. JJ gathered up clothes and ran back into the bathroom. He made shooing motions as if to say, *Get rid of her.* Lily was annoyed. It might be a little awkward for Blaise to see them together, but what, really, was the big deal?

Blaise pounded some more.

"Christ, give me a minute!" Lily yelled. She waited until the bathroom door was shut behind JJ, then went to admit Blaise. "All right, all right. So I overslept. I'm sorry."

Blaise charged in, breathing heavily. Her eyes were darting, wild, canvassing the room. Then she stiffened and shouted, "You slut!" and whipped Lily across the face.

Lily staggered back, hand to her face, eyes blossoming with tears. "What's gotten into you?"

"Into me? Into me? How fucking dare you? How dare you sleep with him?"

Lily inadvertently glanced toward the bathroom, then the room. JJ's belt lay over a chair; his cowboy boots, black, elaborately designed, were on the floor by the bed.

"You may not especially like it, but I don't really see how it's any of your business." She spoke calmly and firmly, as if to an out-of-control child.

"He's mine!" Blaise spat, teeth bared, her eyes narrowed to dark-blue pinpricks.

"He's yours?" Lily laughed. "What are you talking about? You don't own him."

"I sure fucking do."

Lily felt her mouth drop open like a suddenly released trap door. "You're crazy!"

JJ emerged from the bathroom, his face pale.

"How could you?" Blaise hissed at him.

"We'll talk about this in private." He grabbed his belt. It whipped through the air.

174

"Say something to her," Lily said. "JJ, say something."

JJ shook his head, grabbed his boots, and stomped out without a word. A pulse began beating in Lily's neck.

"You broke my trust." Blaise's pale skin was mottled with fury. "I'm afraid our association has come to an end." She started out the door.

"Hold on just a minute. Why are you so pissed? You've been picking up guys yourself. You and JJ were over long ago."

Blaise turned back, hand on hip, head flung back, her shampoo-commercial pose. "JJ and I will never be over, Lily. I thought you understood that. I'm sure he didn't tell you we were." She narrowed her eyes again, waiting.

"Of course he did," Lily said. He had, hadn't he?

"JJ doesn't lie. You believed what you wanted to believe."

Blaise turned and headed down the corridor, Lily following at her heels. "It isn't fair of you to blame me." Blaise kept walking. Lily grabbed her arm. "Don't dump this on me. You told me yourself you weren't a couple!"

"Who said anything about being a couple?" Blaise yanked Lily's hand off her arm, then squeezed it, her long nails like knifepoints.

"But that's sick!" Feeling a sharp sting, she brought her hand to her mouth; there were pinpricks of blood where Blaise's nails had broken the skin.

"What we do is our business. You should have kept your distance." She gave Lily a little push, knocking her off balance, then turned and continued down the corridor.

"Stop!" Lily came after her. "Stop trying to control him!"

Blaise turned and shoved Lily, hard this time. "You're just the latest of his over-the-hill mamas; you're pathetic."

Lily sank to one knee. Her chest felt as if it were being squeezed in a vise, as if she were going to have an asthma attack.

A door opened, and a man's face appeared. "*Madame, êtes-vous bien?*" His shirt was half out of his pants.

"I'm OK, thank you." Lily straightened.

He ran over and grabbed her by the elbow to hoist her up. "Would you like me to get help?"

"I'm fine, really, thank you." Lily's face was burning. "*Merci.*" The man insisted on helping her back to her room. She closed the door, her heart pounding, her breathing labored. *Over-the-hill mama.* Was Blaise pathologically jealous, or were she and JJ still sleeping together? Like a homing device, Lily's mind went to the chummy way the two had acted toward each other the first night in Montreal, when Lily had returned after she'd fled for home. The vibes must have been there all along, for hadn't she wondered, that first night on the road, after her dinner with JJ in the Mexican restaurant, if they were in bed together, despite JJ's railing against the ties that bound him?

But how could he have walked off without a word, leaving her to Blaise's wrath? How could he have failed to defend her? He must have decided to get Blaise away to calm her down. That was the only explanation. But when the minutes passed with no word or sign from him, she called his cell and then his room. No answer. She tried the front desk.

"I'm sorry, I'm afraid your friends have checked out."

"No, that's not possible." She heard the panic in her voice.

"I'm very sorry, but yes, they left not ten minutes ago."

Lily ran out into the corridor and to the window at the end of the hall that looked out on the parking area in the back. She didn't see the car.

Lily stood staring, not able to move. JJ had left her without a word or a backward glance. He had left her here, hours north of Montreal. Stranded.

Eleven

Lily didn't care that she was still in her nightshirt, in the corridor where anyone could see her. She stared down at the parking lot; the anticipated snow had not come, and the black dirt-and-gravel lot held only six cars: four black, one silver, one taupe. No blue Mazda. She wanted to cry, but shock had hollowed her tear ducts. Her mouth was as raw and dry as a desert gully. She felt she would stare out the window until she turned to dirt and gravel herself.

Suddenly the sky opened up, and she flinched as rain splatted against the window. JJ could not have left her like this. Not after what they had been to one another. Maybe he was capable of sleeping with Blaise, for whatever his reasons, but she couldn't accept that for him, she had been nothing more than his latest easy lay.

He must have tried to call. She raced to her room, but there was no blinking light on the room phone. She upended her purse on the bed. Her cell wasn't there. She saw it in her mind, still plugged into the bathroom outlet in her hotel room in Montreal.

She packed and slunk down to the lobby, her suitcase pulled behind her like a bedraggled stuffed animal. She was sure that Blaise, who had taken care of all her hotel bills until now, hadn't paid this time, and she was right. While the clerk was running Lily's credit card, she asked him if there were any messages.

"No, madame." He smiled sadly. Disgrace must be reeking from her like a noxious scent. When she asked about train schedules and car rentals, the desk clerk was especially solicitous. He insisted on driving her to the rental agency—it was the end of his shift anyhow, he said. She thanked him profusely but couldn't meet his eyes.

The rain turned to hail, then back to torrents of rain, as she struggled to get her camera and suitcase through the rental-agency door and to the car, becoming soaked in the process. She sat a moment to get her bearings, turning up the heat. Yesterday she had been in a romantic comedy, running away with a man; today she was in a horror movie, dropped like a load of garbage at a roadside Dumpster. The thought of Stephen shot through her brain. She hadn't called him in days—not since Troy had come—but she wasn't going to call now just because she was in trouble.

Slowly she pulled out of the parking lot and headed down the narrow rural road. The sky was so dark it was like nightfall. Rain covered the windshield in sheets so heavy she could barely see. She drove with her head thrust forward like a turtle, peering through the windshield. Blaise and JJ had a last gig; they wouldn't leave for Europe until the next day. But beyond confronting JJ, she had no idea what she was going to do.

Suddenly the landscape was less familiar; she was in deep woods, and ahead loomed a large, Gothic-looking building she didn't remember passing. Clearly she'd gone the wrong way. She needed to turn around, but the road was hemmed in on both sides by trees. She continued on until the road widened before a railroad overpass. Just as she began the turn, the ground gave way. Frantic, she gunned the motor, but the car sank deeper. She gave it more gas, and the engine died. "This can't be happening, this really can't be happening!" she wailed. She turned the key, and the car came back on, but the wheels just spun in the mud. Terrified, she shut off the motor.

Did they have AAA here in the middle of nowhere? Then she remembered; no phone. She'd have to walk back to that Gothic building and look for someone.

She opened the door; water poured in. She slammed the door,

shaking. This was like a cosmic bad joke—she had been ditched by a man and now was trapped in a car taking on water?

She turned the key again, and the engine caught. Before she could reconsider, she put the car into reverse and gunned it. Smoke plumed from under the hood. Was she flooding the engine? Wrecking the brakes? She kept her foot down.

The car lurched. She gave it gas and gripped the wheel and shot back in reverse. She began hitting tree branches and tried to slow, but her legs were shaking uncontrollably. The second she felt solid ground, she shoved the car into park and bent over the steering wheel.

I did it, she thought, giddy. *I survived a storm at sea.* She was near hysterical—she actually felt wet. She reached down; there was at least an inch of water inside the car. Her shoes were soaked through.

She backed all the way out to the closest intersection. Then she stretched her wet coat, shoes, and socks next to her on the seat, blasted the heat, and headed back to Montreal.

◄ ►

Her state of hyperattention lasted all the way back, as if she expected land mines to go off in her face, new ditches to appear in her path. Finally, she was navigating city streets to the hotel. Would she return one car and drive the other home? Would she return both cars and fly home? Would she even go home?

Right now she wasn't doing anything until she had tracked down JJ. If she didn't find him before the show, she'd get him in the morning. She'd follow him to the airport if she had to. He wasn't leaving before she spoke with him.

She wandered the hotel parking lot, looking for the blue Mazda. When she found it, she froze. It was true, then. They really had dumped her. They might be inside the hotel right now. Suddenly, she was as terrified as she was furious. She scooted into the lobby and the elevator, not ready to face either of them. In her room she leaned against the door a moment, calming herself. No light flickered on her

179

nightstand phone, and her cell was plugged into the bathroom socket, as she'd left it. No messages. The last shred of hope dissolved like snow on the tongue.

Why did she want to see him anyhow? What did she think it would do for her? What did she want—to make him tell her to her face that he still had sex with Blaise? Yes, but more than that. If it was true, she needed to know why. Mostly, though, she needed to know what she had meant to him, even if she didn't like the answer.

In the corridor on JJ's floor, a boy and girl were running up and down the hall. They looked at her and stopped, as if expecting her to chastise them. Lily felt her own steps slowing. Maybe she should just leave. Why did she need explanations, anyway? It was all over. He had not defended her, and he had left her—that alone was unforgivable. Clearly she had misunderstood everything. Why humiliate herself further?

She walked on. She heard soft strumming sounds coming from JJ's room, and her eyes teared. The children race-walked past her, giggling. Once they turned the corner and she was alone in the corridor, Lily pressed her ear to the door. Silence. Footsteps. The sound of a toilet flushing.

She rapped on the door.

"Be right there."

JJ opened the door without asking who it was. As soon as he saw her, emotions raced across his face in quick succession: surprise, embarrassment, pleasure.

"God, I'm so happy to see you. I feel so bad. I'm glad you got back OK; I didn't remember that you didn't have your own car until we were already on the highway. Then I tried to call, but your phone was off. Blaise—"

"Shut up," Lily said. She took a deep breath. After a second, he moved to hug her, but she brushed past him into the room and then turned to face him.

"Tell me what the *fuck* all this was about." She bit down hard on the curse word.

"What do you mean?" he asked warily. How was it possible that he could look confused, with only a side of sheepishness?

"Well, for starters, have you been screwing Blaise this whole time?"

"Jeez, Lily, what do you take me for? Of course not."

Lily waited to let this settle in her brain. "JJ," she said when she could, "Blaise was way too angry for there to be nothing between you. And you didn't want her to know about us. I should have realized it didn't make any sense."

JJ came closer but stopped before he reached her, as if sensing he might get hurt. "Blaise is a bitch, she's jealous, and she's a control freak. I told you all that. You can see it now for yourself. I am really sorry for how she treated you."

Lily felt the way she had when Colby was little and they'd be deadlocked in an argument, going around in the maddening circles of child logic. She waited for JJ to say more, but, when nothing was forthcoming, she said, "But you didn't stand up for me!"

"I have a hard time with that," he said.

"That's a pathetic excuse." When he didn't answer, she said, "That's not all there is to it, is it?"

"Well, you know we used to be together," he finally said.

"I thought the operative words were 'used to.'" A thought shot through Lily's brain. "How long ago was it . . . that you broke up?"

"Maybe a year." Now he looked a little uncomfortable, his skin mottling.

"So you haven't had sex with her in a year?"

"Well, no, not exactly."

"What are you saying? You broke up but you still have sex sometimes?"

His eyes caught hers and then darted away.

Lily felt like she was interrogating a six-year-old.

"JJ, when did you and Blaise last sleep together?"

"Maybe a month ago?" He couldn't meet her eyes and took a deep, fortifying breath. "OK, so maybe a little more recently. But it was before you and I started."

"No wonder she was pissed! You're telling me that you have sex with each other whenever you feel like it?"

"She gets horny, I get horny, it happens. But we haven't while you and I . . . I wouldn't do that."

"But you didn't want her to know about us because you know she still has feelings for you and you didn't want to piss her off."

"She doesn't have feelings for me; she just likes to own me."

"And you don't have feelings for her?"

"God, no, I've told you that."

"So you're basically servicing her—is that what you're saying?"

JJ's face flooded with color, and Lily felt sick to her stomach. She sat abruptly on the edge of his bed. She had known he was neurotic, maybe passive, but she hadn't realized he was totally spineless.

He stood over her. "I've been telling you all along how complicated it is with her. For me it's just sex. She wants it, it keeps her happy, what's the big deal?"

"That's so totally despicable!"

"Easy for you to say. You have a husband, sex anytime you like. It's not like you and I are a couple."

Lily looked away. "No, we're not." There had never been any talk between them about a future, except the fleeting scenarios she'd played out in her head.

"We all use each other. Don't think I don't know why you've been with me."

Lily's mouth went dry. "What are you saying?"

"You think I don't know that you'd never have slept with me if I didn't play guitar? You would have had no interest in me if I were a mechanic or a bus driver."

"How can you say that? I care about you—you know I do."

"You wanted your guitar hero."

"That's not true!" But she felt her face flush.

"You're here for, what, a couple of weeks? You can't expect me to jeopardize stuff with her. Music comes first. I have to keep working with her."

Lily let this sink in. "What are you going to do when you meet someone you really want to be with?"

"I do want to be with you, Lily."

"Not enough." Not in a way that mattered. Clearly not enough to overcome the sway Blaise had over him. She remembered the night in the bar when Blaise had ordered him to dance with her. She would always call the tune.

"I guess I'll say good-bye."

"It doesn't have to be this way." He took a step toward her. The skin around his eyes was red and raw-looking; she could almost convince herself he was upset.

"I hope you learn to stand up to her someday."

"Maybe if you stayed?" he said tentatively.

Was he serious? Did he actually think she could save him, or give him a backbone?

She knew he liked the adoration she showered on him and found her useful as a soundboard and a buffer between him and Blaise. But how had she not understood how deep it all went? If one part of what he had been for her was Colby, the corollary was that a part of it for him was that she was the mommy, looked to for help in growing up.

He didn't want her, not really. And he didn't know her. Not really.

"Good-bye, JJ," she said. She went to him and kissed him gently. He clung to her. "I love you," she said, surprising them both. "I hope life is good to you."

"Please don't go." He pulled her closer.

"I have to."

"Please?" His arms tightened. She'd always loved his strength, the feel of his powerful arms, but now she felt smothered. "We're good together. You know we are."

"It's not enough. I'm sorry."

Only when she was really forceful did he allow her to pull away.

The drive south from Montreal to Albany gave Lily ample opportunity to shed as many tears as she wanted. She sobbed copiously and sparingly, she cried silently and noisily, she cried with nothing but the car's motor to accompany her, and she cried with every song on the radio. At first she didn't think about what she would do with the rest of her life, or about what everything meant. She just caved in to her feelings and let loose.

It was a strange feeling to realize that her life was in complete shambles. It was amazing that, in the space of just a few weeks, it was possible to wreck something as big as that. It went way beyond having an affair, realizing it was a mistake, and going home to beg for forgiveness. She'd been driven by something else, something she knew she still hadn't confronted. She had to separate that strand, whatever it was, from the strand that was Stephen and her marriage. It had all started with the music, that ache, that overpowering desire for something bigger than herself. "You wanted your guitar hero," JJ had said. His accusation was close to the mark, but not, somehow, the full truth.

She was a mess, and it was eight o'clock. She wasn't ready to face everything. She needed a warm bed and, even more, she needed a friend. She pulled into the next rest area and made the call.

He met her outside his dorm wearing plaid flannel pajama pants and his university sweatshirt, his face showing anxiety and concern.

"Colby." She threw herself at him and began to cry again. The scent of his hair, of Dr. Bronner's peppermint soap, which she'd used on him ever since he was a little boy, stung her nostrils. "I'm sorry, I'll stop in just a moment."

He patted her back. "It's OK, Mom."

She pulled away, wiped her face with her fingers. "I didn't realize how much I've missed you."

"I've missed you, too. Come on upstairs; your hands are really cold. I'll make you some hot chocolate." He took her bag and led her to the second floor and his dorm room. He said he and Ian would crash with friends so Lily could have privacy. "Clean sheets and everything." She could tell from the neat stack of books and papers that he'd tried to tidy up after her call—there was a pile of clothes on the floor in a corner, leaving a chair free. He gently pushed her into it.

He poured water into two cups, heated them in his mini-microwave, and stirred in cocoa mix. He handed her a mug. "This will warm you up."

It felt strange for her to be the one getting mothered. She laced her fingers tightly on the mug, letting the heat transfer to her skin.

"Mom. Please tell me what's wrong. What's going on?"

It would be wrong, worse than wrong, to truly unburden herself to him. Then again, he wasn't a child anymore; she owed it to him to let him in on the turmoil ahead.

"Have you talked with your father?"

"He said you were away on that assignment. Did something happen? I thought making the performance film was supposed to be a good thing?"

"The music was amazing. I haven't done anything on my own like that in . . . well, forever." Lily stirred her cocoa, trying to locate a path into the mess she had made. "But being on the road . . . it's as if I've been under a spell—kidnapped by a sorcerer and taken to a deep, dark forest."

"Mom, really."

"I know," Lily tried to smile, "but it actually felt like that. I wanted to join their merry band in the forest. I . . . . I wasn't sure I wanted to come home."

"What are you saying? You want to leave Dad?" His voice squeaked, like when it was changing. "Are you trying to tell me you're getting a divorce?"

Lily opened her mouth, shut it. Was that what she truly wanted? Was that why she had needed to see him? The anguish in his eyes was so acute that she wanted to deny everything.

"No, no. This doesn't have to do with your father; it has to do with me. I've been going through something even I don't understand. But I need to go home and see your father. I've done something to hurt him, and he's going to be very angry with me."

"Don't tell me." Colby's arms came up, as if he were about to shove her away. "I don't want to know. Dad will forgive you, whatever you've done. He'll take you back."

"I don't know what I want, Colby, that's all I'm saying."

"Don't you love him?" Colby sprang up from his chair.

Lily grabbed his hands and held them tightly. "Yes! Of course I do. But I have to get to the root of what this has been about. I have some things to work out in myself."

"What do you think it was about, then?" He sat back in his chair, a little color coming back into his face.

She touched his cheek lightly. Just like his father, his freckles stood out in stark relief against his pale skin when he was upset. "When you left for college, it wasn't just that I missed you; in a weird way, I missed *me,* too. As if, if I wasn't mainly a mother, then I wasn't anything at all."

"You could never be nothing, Mom!"

Her eyes teared, and she took a quick sip of cocoa. "Do you think it's unhealthy that we—you and I—have always been so close? Maybe it would have been better if I'd been a little less involved?"

"No, it's great we're close, Mom. I don't have any separation issues. But are you saying maybe for you?"

"I think I just got tired of myself. Maybe I stopped growing. And with you going to college . . ." The night of the concert came back vividly; she could smell the damp autumn air, the pungent leaves, recall the yearning she'd felt to throw off her shoes and race across the lawn with abandon. With the affair, she had been swept off-course. Going after that something she couldn't yet define, she'd gotten sidetracked altogether.

There were no tears during this part of the journey; there was just a sobering dryness, as if the vacuum used to suck up the water that had seeped into the Canadian rental car had removed all her tears, too, leaving behind this dull ache. She waited too long to call Stephen to say she was heading home and left a message on their answering machine. She told herself she didn't want to disturb him at work but knew that was cowardice. How would she face him? In her mind came an image of the loathsome, groveling creature Gollum in *The Lord of the Rings*. But given how badly she had transgressed, Stephen deserved much more than even her most abject apology. He deserved to have her wholehearted, total commitment and love, not her confusion and ambivalence. How could she have turned her back on him, on all their history, all the backbone, maturity, and integrity he possessed, to throw herself at JJ, a moral coward and a selfish, self-absorbed child? How was it that she could feel love—some kind of love—for both?

Lily slowed behind the pileup of cars waiting to get over the bridge into Manhattan. The city sprawled in the distance, the waters of the Hudson choppy in the breeze. She drove down the West Side Highway to Midtown and turned in the Opal at Ninth Avenue and Fifty-fourth Street. When she stepped outside the dealership, she felt assaulted by the noise and chaotic energy of honking cars and rushing pedestrians. Yet even at three o'clock on March 1, it was sunny and warm. Spring was only weeks away. The cold of Canada was behind her.

She took the subway back uptown, sweaty with anxiety. Would Stephen be home, having gotten her message? Would he even want to see her? Should she buy food for dinner, cook? How did one behave in such a situation?

"How you doing?" the doorman said, as if he had just seen her. So much had happened, yet she hadn't been away long enough for it to have registered with him—it wasn't as if her mail had had to be held or packages piled near the mailboxes. It wasn't as if the lock had been changed and she couldn't get into the apartment, or as if her things were cartoned and set aside for movers—or tossed out of the window by Stephen in a fit of rage.

Lily began to put her key in the door and then stopped. Did she have a right to march in as if she belonged here? She tapped the buzzer, as much to give Stephen notice as to acknowledge that she knew she couldn't take her welcome for granted. But there was no answering call, no footsteps. She turned the key and let herself in.

There was a stale, quiet air to the apartment. The windows were closed, no springlike breeze making its way in. She put down her things and went into the kitchen. There was no note for her, and when she opened the refrigerator, it was mostly empty: a few blueberry yogurts, a half-empty container of cut-up pineapple. She sniffed the milk—it was fresh, so he wasn't away, or if he was away, it hadn't been for long. The answering machine blinked two messages. One of them might be from her. He might not have gotten it. She pressed the button, stood listening. The first call was from early afternoon, after she had called, so he must have gotten her message and deleted it.

It felt strange to be a stranger in her own home, to feel so out of place and awkward. She roamed from the kitchen to the living room to the bedroom, looking for clues. At Stephen's side of the bed was a book he had left open—the latest by urban planner Jane Jacobs. It had gotten disappointing reviews, Lily remembered. In the bathroom hamper there were three shirts, all white, and some socks and under-wear, and in their tiny study, where their desks were back-to-back, a neat pile of her mail. She sifted it and threw most away. She paced again from kitchen to living room to study to bedroom, not knowing what she felt, what to do with herself. She couldn't stand this.

She grabbed the phone and dialed his work number. When he picked up, she felt surprised, as if part of her feared he had gone and left her, or she really didn't expect him to be at the office when he knew she was arriving home.

"Hi, it's me." She suddenly felt she didn't have the right to be so familiar.

"Hi," he said, with a noticeable lack of enthusiasm.

"I'm home."

"OK."

The silence settled between them like a thick, toxic clot. "I know we need to talk," she said finally. "Are you coming home soon? Should I make dinner?"

He was silent for a long time. "I'll come now," he said finally. "Just go ahead and order something."

"OK." She waited to see if he would say anything more, and when he didn't, she hung up.

Lily was surprisingly shaken. Had she expected him to say, "Wow, it's great to hear your voice; I've missed you so much"? Some part of her must have been hoping that he hadn't realized what she had done, as if she were Dorothy returning from her adventures in Oz to discover time hadn't passed and there were no consequences to her journey. She turned back to the phone and called Honor.

"Hey, how are you? I haven't heard from you in weeks."

"I have a favor to ask," Lily said.

The sick feeling in her stomach got stronger when Stephen walked in the door. He looked wary, sullen, closed, guarded—anything but happy to see her. She had been hoping that at the sight of him everything would suddenly become clear to her—what she wanted, what she had to do now. Instead, the muck she had sunk into seemed, if anything, thicker, more treacherous.

He looked weary, as if he had been working too hard, worrying too hard. All her fault? Of course it was her fault. He put his things down and shrugged out of his jacket while she stood there wondering if he would put his arms around her or kiss her or do nothing at all. Finally he faced her and waited, and she understood that he was looking for a sign from her. Of course.

She darted to him. His smell, clean, slightly spicy, made her heart ache. His body was stiff, inert; then he began to hug her back, but she was already pulling away. She reversed direction, back into his embrace, but now, in an awkward dance, he had withdrawn.

"I opened wine." Why, at a moment like this, was she making such a banal comment? She should be crying or shouting. Something.

He nodded and took a seat on the couch. She poured two glasses and brought them over, handed one to him, and sat at the other end of the couch. She put her glass down without taking a sip, picked at the tweed fabric.

"So," he said.

"I don't know how to do this." She glanced at him and then away. "I know I've treated you horribly, and I'm terribly sorry. I—"

"Just tell me what you want now," Stephen said harshly. His skin was almost bleached of color, throwing his freckles into stark relief. "That's all. If you're leaving me, I don't want any details, any excuses—just go, get out."

Lily sat back, shocked. "Did you think . . . I mean, I'm not . . . I'm not with anyone else." Lily's cheeks burned.

Stephen's eyes briefly closed and opened; some emotion loosened the tension that had made his face seem tight and expressionless, and she realized it was more fear than anger he was feeling.

The doorbell rang, and she started. He went to the door, pulling out his wallet. She felt acutely uncomfortable with his paying. She realized she was noting all her reactions, as if tallying them up would tell her what she needed to know. Did her discomfort at his paying for their meal mean she didn't feel married anymore? Or just that she felt she deserved punishment? She got out the plates and silverware.

"We need to talk before I can eat," Stephen said, bringing the bag into the kitchen. He glanced at her impassively. "You look like you've lost weight."

"Anxiety." She expected him to say she looked good, but he didn't.

"What was all this about?" He pulled out a chair at the table, sat with his arms crossed against his chest. The gesture seemed both hostile and protective. "*Is* all this about."

It would be such a relief to pour it all out, to go on about JJ, about Blaise, about the music. But such self-indulgence would be profoundly unfair to him, even if it was what he was entitled to hear, maybe even wanted to hear. No, she needed to distill it, explain what it all meant in terms of them. But how, when she wasn't yet clear herself?

"If I tell you I'm confused, that's not going to sit right, but it's the truth."

"Lily, don't fuck with me!" He lurched forward as if he were about to shove the table over. "Are you telling me you didn't have an affair with that guitarist? Are you telling me you don't know if you're in love with him?"

His face was so contorted, she had to look away, her heart pierced by a thousand tiny needles.

"I'm not saying that. But it's not the point. It was very, very wrong of me. There's nothing to excuse it. I treated you horribly. I don't know what I can do about that now."

Stephen was staring, mouth open, as if he needed help breathing.

"I'm sorry. I'm sorrier than you can possibly imagine."

His expression cleared slightly, color seeping back into his face. "Thank you," he said, and it struck her that she had failed before this to apologize. "But that's not what I'm asking."

"For whatever it's worth, it's not like I'm unhappy in our life." She started over. "I don't think it has to do with you, or us. I think it has to do with me, my life, and it all needs sorting out . . ." She was suddenly exhausted. How was she to sort it all out?

"Can't you talk to me about that? Don't you think you owe me that much?"

"Of course I owe you that much! At least that much! But it will all sound so . . ." She trailed off. Could she be true to him and at the same time protect him from the unnecessary hurt of the intensity of her feelings for JJ—or what he represented?

"You're shutting me out!" His fist hit the table, and his expression was so ferocious she inadvertently recoiled and covered her head with her hands.

There was a pause, and then a crash. He had flung the chair onto the tile floor. "What?" she quaked.

"You're not wearing your ring!"

Lily felt the blood drain from her body. She had forgotten; she had grown accustomed to not wearing it while her skin healed.

191

"It's not what you think! Please, Stephen. It was just too tight. I got a rash underneath. I have to take it to a jeweler and have it stretched. Look!" The hand she held out was visibly shaking. They both stared at her finger; there was no trace of a rash, no pale skin, even, to mark where the band used to be.

"You are such a piece of work. You're not at all the person I thought you were."

Lily's eyes welled up. Her chest ached down to the cells, the ache radiating out across her back. Losing his positive view of her hurt more than she would have imagined. "No, it's the truth. I'll show you!" She ran into the bedroom, where she had left her suitcase. Her hands were still shaking so much she could hardly undo the clasps, and it took her minutes to unzip the little side pocket where she'd placed the ring.

Stephen was back at the table, chair righted. His eyes were red.

She fanned open her hand, gave him the ring. "Go on, try."

He hesitated. The same memory occurred to both of them. It was too painful to reenact their wedding, him slipping the ring on her finger.

"You do it."

She slid the ring up toward her knuckle, where it stopped. "See?"

He gave a huge sigh. "I'm sorry. That was ridiculous."

"No, it wasn't. I deserve anything and everything you want to throw at me." She sat down. Somehow the tension had eased some.

"Look, Lily." He leaned forward. "For right now, I just want to focus on what's next. I just need to know if you want to be with me. If you do, then we'll try and work this out. But if you don't, just say so. That's the end of it."

"Can you ever be with me after what I've done? Love me again?" She couldn't look at him and stared instead at a faded wine stain on the place mat.

"I still love you," he said grudgingly.

"I don't deserve you."

Stephen took an audible breath. "You said before you didn't think this was about our marriage; what, then?"

"Something about their world, the music . . . I just found it over-whelmingly powerful."

"Christ, when are you going to stop living through other people?"

"What are you talking about?"

"First Colby, now them. You don't deal with yourself—much less with me. I'm not particularly needy, but enough is enough."

"He's my son! Our son!"

"Exactly—and he and I have a great relationship. Yet I still have a life."

Lily was both stung and astonished. It was like a window opening a crack; there was a whiff of something, a sea breeze, but she couldn't see the horizon.

"I was hoping, once he left for school, that you and I . . ." Stephen shrugged, looked away.

"But you're always so busy! You don't make time for me either!"

"You haven't seemed to care."

She was silent. Had that been true?

"I've had time to think, too, while you've been gone." His tone was cautionary.

She put her head in her hands. "This is really going to shake the dust from the rafters now, isn't it?"

"Maybe that's why you did all this. So if you think this is mostly about you, then you're going to have to work on what it is you've been avoiding."

She had been to hell and back to approach the conclusion he'd just put out there so calmly. When she didn't answer, he grabbed her wrist. "Either way—if it's you, us, or a combination of both—we have to go to couples' therapy. I can't stand this otherwise."

She nodded. She felt overcome with exhaustion. "I'll ask Honor for a referral. I arranged to stay with her for a few days."

"You did what?" He rocked back in his seat.

"I thought I shouldn't just presume you'd want me here."

"It sounds more like you don't want to work things out."

"No, that's not it. I just think I need this to be really hard on me."

"You want to stay with Honor to punish yourself? That's ridiculous."

"Right now I feel scummier than the scum of the earth. I don't think you should make me too comfortable." She didn't want to fuck him over any more than she already had. "I don't want to drag this out, either."

He pushed away from the table and stood. "Go, then."

Outside it was dark, windy, and much colder than it should have been after such a warm day. *My dark night of the soul,* Lily thought, heading to Honor's, wheeling her suitcase behind her. One block, two; she felt more leaden and depressed with every step. Did she really need to leave? Did she really want to bunk out on Honor's couch? What a drag all this was going to be.

At the corner, she stopped to listen, as she always did, if the man in the ground-floor apartment was practicing piano when she walked by. She could go back. She could just drop this. It was all over with JJ. Stephen was willing to take her back—why was she overcomplicating things?

She continued on. Along Riverside, a few late-night dog walkers passed, and the wind blew the trash in little eddies, mini-cyclones at her feet. If she stayed, she might end up taking the easy way out and not confront what she needed to confront. But it was scary. What if she learned that she had to leave her marriage? She hoped—at least she thought she hoped—it wouldn't come to that.

Honor lived on the third floor of a fifteen-story just off Riverside Drive. She greeted Lily in a long robe of blue chenille, her face glossy with night cream. Lily had filled Honor in briefly when she called, afraid of her reaction. Honor seemed mostly shocked, maybe a little disappointed, yet sympathetic. Lily felt a wash of affection come over her, and she kissed her friend's slick cheek. "I so appreciate this."

Honor led Lily into the living room, where a cup of tea and the television, tuned to a late-night show, signaled the discouraging fact that she was not ready for bed. Lily wanted nothing more than to make up the couch and pull the covers over her head.

"I figured you'd want to talk—I made you some herbal tea."

Lily wrapped her hands around the cup, glad at least for the warmth. Honor crossed her legs. She was wearing huge pink fuzzy slippers, like floor mops.

"Aren't they a hoot?" She pointed one at Lily. "My nephew gave them to me for Christmas."

Lily, too, could be single again and have funny slippers. She felt even more depressed than before.

"How are you doing?" Honor asked.

"Awful." The tea was too hot to drink. She put it beside her on the coffee table.

"I'm glad you'll go to a therapist. I see a lot of people who have been through all sorts of marital troubles. They do get past it. Especially ones that are solid, like you and Stephen. I'm sure he'll forgive you." She placed her hand on Lily's arm.

"I don't know that I want or deserve to be forgiven," Lily said.

"Lily, really. You made a mistake. Lots of people make mistakes."

"But that's just it, Honor. I don't know that I wouldn't do it again if I had it to do over. I mean, in a way, it wasn't a mistake."

Honor sat back. "Well, then you were temporarily insane. Hormones. Stephen will understand that."

"I knew at every moment just what I was doing, and I chose to do it. I knew it would all end badly, but I went ahead anyhow."

"So even after that musician humiliated you, you're saying that you would still chose to do it again if you had it to do over?"

"What I mean is, part of me doesn't regret the experience." Lily sipped her tea. It scalded the top of her mouth.

"Well, then you were insane. Clearly you were powerless to help yourself."

"I wasn't powerless. I could have helped myself but chose not to. It was a risk I took with my eyes open. So I can't lie to Stephen and say it

195

was all a mistake. Self-destructive, maybe. And I feel terrible to have hurt him. But it's like it was a lesson I had to learn."

"I don't get it. It's like you're willing to destroy your life over a fantasy. It's not like you're going to be with the musician."

"But what if I don't know if I wish I could? It bothers me that I don't know whether I would have stayed with JJ if he'd asked."

"Wait. Are you saying that because you *might* wish that you were with the musician, you shouldn't be with Stephen? How do you know that he wouldn't choose to be with Angelina Jolie if he had the chance? Just imagine yourself with the musician after twenty years, and compare how you would feel about him then with how you feel about Stephen now—I'm sure the musician wouldn't stack up."

Lily tried to project JJ twenty years into the future. Hopeless.

"You told me the musician turned out to be an asshole. So you're saying that if he weren't an asshole, you might have wanted to be with him, and if that had been the case, you might have considered leaving Stephen for him, and so because that possibility exists and you're not 100 percent sure, you shouldn't be with Stephen?"

"Don't you think Stephen deserves for me to want to be with him more than any other man in the world?" Lily's head was spinning. Why wouldn't Honor leave her alone and let her go to sleep?

Honor frowned, momentarily at a loss for words. "If you weren't so fucked up, I'd be pissed at you, but since you clearly are insane, I'm going to have to take pity on you."

Take pity on me. One of Blaise and JJ's songs. Lily turned away.

"Oh, sweetie," Honor said, enfolding Lily in her ample arms.

Twelve

The city had changed; it seemed newly fresh. She was noticing things she rarely had—water towers on tops of buildings, telephone poles harboring baby sparrows, intricate window guards. A fierce, tenacious wind came off the Hudson near Honor's apartment off Riverside Drive. The sun was brighter, shadows stronger. A chorus of birdsong pushed its way into her consciousness each morning as she lay on the couch under the living room window, waking her too early. On warm days, days that shouted renewal, the pain was that much harder to bear.

After work every day, as she avoided going back to Honor's apartment until it was late, Lily got an inkling of how the homeless might feel. She wandered Urban Outfitters, Whole Foods, Harry's Shoes. She rode the subway to impulse locations, walked for hours through parts of the city she hadn't visited in years—the Lower East Side, Wall Street, Washington Heights. She was even rediscovering Riverside Park. She loved its sweep, which ran almost the entire length of the west side, its curving arm of pathway embracing the water on one side, the tall, majestic line of prewar buildings on the other. The park was worn and comfortable: Pathways were cracked, benches old, and the cars on the highway emitted a steady, somehow-lulling roar. New Jersey looked so close across the river, it seemed swimmable.

The community garden in the park was a mess of ugly debris that showed no sign it would soon be vibrant with spring bulbs. On sunny days there were bicycles, balls, babies. She looked into their faces as they slept in their strollers, wondering what the crazy world would seem like to them as they grew up. She hovered by the dog run, mesmerized by the sniffing, racing, bounding behavior, life unleashed, unthinking. Graceful young women ran past, slender and vibrant, their ponytails sashaying left, right, left, right. Squirrels scampered, birds swooped in flocks, chattering. But there were no signs yet of buds on the brittle branches of the tall tall trees, gnarled and stately, lining both sides of the pathway where she walked up and back, up and back, anything to delay her return.

When it was too cold or wet for walking, she took refuge in the Barnes & Noble on Eighty-fourth and Broadway. Grateful for its café and bathroom, she mentally took back every nasty thing she had ever said about how the company had driven all her favorite independent bookstores from the neighborhood. She wanted to be surrounded by books, the comfort of books, but she couldn't focus long enough to read. Except poetry. She craved its secret language, cryptic lines, stunning images. Poetry gave her that sense of remove, that perspective of tapping into something more universal than the sorry state of herself. Music was too painful. More cerebral, poetry gave her the kind of transcendence and escape she could handle. It propelled her just the right distance from her life, gave her the sensation she sometimes had in flying dreams, where she hovered like a giant insect at the level of the treetops.

This morning, as with every morning since her return, she awoke to the awareness that everything had changed except the constancy of pain. Now she sat up, stretched her kinked muscles. The shower was running, Honor already up. Lily went to the kitchen to make her coffee and boil water for Honor's tea. This was her last morning here. She had bought bagels, cream cheese, and lox from Murray's as a good-bye thank-you. The therapist had said a longer separation would be helpful, at least until Colby came home for spring break, by which time things might be stable enough that they needn't let on what the full extent of the breach had been, and Stephen agreed. Lily had been at Honor's long enough. So she had steeled herself to call Troy, who owned a house in Brooklyn. Braced for a lecture, she had been surprised to hear "I'd love it! Please come, and stay as long as you want."

Now, waiting for Honor's tea to steep, Lily stared at a pastel drawing on the kitchen wall of a young girl with her hand resting on a deer. She could almost feel the coarse hairs on its neck. She remembered a music box she'd had as a child, the top painted with a deer peeking from a forest of vibrant green, the tinkling melody of "Für Elise." She was nostalgic for her childhood and her sister—the effect of the therapy, no doubt. The therapist had suggested that everything that had happened might connect to Lily's earlier self, to parts of herself ignored or dormant through the years of motherhood.

But last night at the therapist's office, the session turned to talk far more difficult than the past.

Lily followed Stephen into the room. He waited until she was seated and then placed himself a careful foot or more away. He wouldn't meet her eyes but stared straight ahead, the palms of his hands flat on his thighs, aligned with the sharp crease in his khaki pants. Lily picked up a pillow, pale green silk, with delicate embroidery, and placed it on her lap.

The therapist was thin and angular, with wispy gray hair and penetrating eyes. She leaned forward. "Stephen, I know this will be hard, but do you think you can share your feelings with Lily about how her actions have impacted you?"

Stephen didn't answer. Lily's fingers tightened on the pillow. "I don't know if I can," he said finally. Lily darted a quick glance at him. His hands were tightly clasped, as if holding on to each other for dear life, and he was hunched over. She looked down, plucked at a stray thread.

Then he drew in his breath. "It's obvious how I feel, isn't it? I feel like anyone would in this situation."

"How would anyone feel in this situation?" the therapist asked.

"Betrayed, obviously!"

"In what way do you feel betrayed?"

"I don't even know how to begin," his words now came out in an uncharacteristic rush. "I don't understand any of this—it's totally unfathomable to me. The woman I married, the Lily I thought I knew, could never ever have hurt me like this. I had no idea there was anything wrong, or that Lily was dissatisfied."

"I wasn't, I wasn't dissatisfied with you."

"But then, how?" he burst out, finally turning toward her. "How could you do this to me . . . to us? How could you have done what you did with that man? It's like denying everything we've been. How could I have meant so little to you? It's like you took a grater and just scraped it over my skin."

An image of blood puckering up from raw skin bloomed in front of her eyes. "I'm sorry, I'm so sorry."

But Stephen went on as if he didn't hear. "I'm sorry, too. I'm sorry I can't play a fucking guitar. What is it with women and rock stars? I would never have thought you could be so shallow. I don't buy that this was some little fling that meant nothing. I don't believe you would have jeopardized everything for that. I think he meant more to you than you're letting on."

She froze, unable to say anything, and just shook her head as if to say, *No.*

"All you've given me are rationalizations." His voice now was calmer, but his face was blazing. "You are so fucking full of shit. Do you know how completely inadequate you've made me feel?"

"Please don't feel like that. This had nothing to do with you! I know I don't deserve your forgiveness, but please, can you at least believe me that this wasn't your fault?"

"What, so I was just collateral damage?" At that his eyes welled up, and instantly the skin around them was red and parched. She had only once seen Stephen cry, after his father died. She reached across the space between them and grabbed his hand. He didn't respond, but neither did he push her away.

She held onto his hand. "I was caught up in something, and I wasn't thinking about you. It *was* selfish. I'd give anything not to have hurt you like this!"

"Well, you have." He pulled his hand away, pressed his chambray shirtsleeve to his eyes. "You've ruined absolutely everything! Don't you understand that we can never go back, that it can never be the same? I don't know how to go about trying to forgive you. I don't know who you are anymore."

His words exploded at her, cracked through the surface of her body.

"I can't bear what I've done to you."

"You have to bear it," Stephen said. "There's no other way."

"I know," she whispered.

"Stephen," the therapist interjected, "we can see how much pain you are in. But Lily seems to be saying this isn't about any failures on your part. Remember, she did make the choice to come back. I know this is terribly painful for you both. But that's the work. There's no easy way to build back a relationship, but I think there's a strong enough foundation here. Lily, it will take time for Stephen to regain trust, and it won't be easy for him to understand and forgive. You're going to have to work harder than he does, make more of an effort. And you both have to work on communicating more. For now, I think it would be helpful to schedule a few individual sessions with each of you, and then we'll meet again as a couple. Lily, we'll start with you. Can you make an appointment around one o'clock tomorrow?"

Lily nodded; she felt so heavy she had trouble getting up from the couch.

She ate a power bar on the subway and arrived at the therapist's office a few minutes early. The waiting room was bright with paintings she was sure were there to stimulate associations. *My Tangled Life*, she thought, of the one with white squiggles against a black background. *Enough Self-Pity*, she dubbed the one with a yellow spinning top and bright-green swaths. The therapist's door opened, releasing a young woman with red-rimmed eyes. "Lily?" the therapist said. Lily felt knots in her stomach—nerves, plus the skipped lunch. She settled gingerly opposite the therapist in a cushy tan leather chair. The therapist regarded Lily over steepled hands.

"I thought it might be easier for you to talk about your experience without Stephen present. I sense you've been holding back to protect him. While it's important in our couples' therapy to focus on the issues between you, it might be helpful to unburden yourself about JJ to me, and for me to get a better understanding."

Lily felt as if skeins of old cracked skin slipped from her body to the floor. "You're right . . . but I'm not sure anyone could understand . . ." She stopped herself, hating the whininess.

"Try me."

Lily hesitated, trying to form words. "I know it probably seems like it was a midlife crisis, or that I was bored, or that it had to do with Stephen. But it didn't feel that way. JJ was only part of it. I felt literally compelled. Driven. As if by a force outside of myself."

"What kind of force?"

"Like a greater truth, sort of."

"What greater truth?"

"That's just it—I can't say. I admit it sounds nuts."

"Why don't you try."

"What I had, what I got to touch with the music, with being on the road—it was like touching gold. It became too important to me not to touch."

The therapist nodded. "I see. Like getting a glimpse of paradise."

"Yes," Lily said, surprised.

"Soldiers who come back from a war feel something like that, too, in the sense that the intensity of their experience doesn't communicate to others easily, and they have a very hard time reintegrating into their lives. I would very much like it if you would tell me about it—how you felt, what it all meant or seemed to mean, as you were going through it. Don't worry about how crazy you think it sounds."

This was what she had longed to do, Lily realized. She had been desperate to pour it all out to somebody.

The therapist leaned back in her chair.

Lily began with the concert, the moment of imaginary impact, the Cupid's bow, the poison dart. Occasionally the therapist murmured or asked a question, but she mostly said nothing. Yet somehow Lily felt as if she got it.

"You're describing something of an archetypal journey. Fairy tales are built on this model, too, right? A classic quest in which you endure frustration, sleep deprivation, food deprivation, humiliation, to reach the goal."

"But what was the goal?"

"Ah . . . good question. Here's what I want you to do. I want you to view everything you filmed."

"Won't that just make it worse? Make me feel it all too much?" Lily had avoided even looking at her tapes. She had stashed them in a bag deep in a cabinet at work.

"See what it brings up. Let's schedule another session for Monday, and then I'll see you and Stephen together."

Lily left feeling drained and weak, yet somehow lighthearted. Outside, the streets were thronged. It was sunny and warm after days of wet drizzle, and children were skipping down the street, their parents loaded down with abruptly shed jackets. Joggers raced into Central Park, the soles of their sneakered feet like white pompoms hitting the pavement. Even the traffic, roaring downtown, sounded upbeat, musical.

The next day, Friday, she waited until everyone had left the office. Then she microwaved a frozen dinner and sat in front of the screening TV in the conference room and dimmed the lights. She had over twenty hours of footage; she would stay until midnight watching as much as she could. She'd bought a big box of tissues.

In a small notebook she had annotated the performances after each session, but she found she remembered almost everything without needing to refer to it. At the first concert, her camera was on Blaise almost all the time—there were only quick, almost furtive, shots of JJ. She recalled her shaking hands and tumbling stomach, the fever pitch of excitement that was more misery than joy. But as she watched, she found herself laughing at Blaise's jokes, tapping her foot to the music, feeling her throat ache with the sad melodies, her head shake with amazement at JJ's prowess, as if she hadn't experienced it dozens of times before. When Blaise's voice cracked on a high note, Lily felt it deep within her, even though she had heard her voice crack on that same note in the same way so many times before. God, they were good.

Lily gave over to watching, to accepting whatever flotsam and jetsam wanted to surface. Hours went by. The music flooded her to her marrow. She cried and stopped and cried some more. She cried because the music was so moving, and she cried for her memories and what they had meant and what they hadn't really meant, and she cried for what she had loved and lost forever.

What was it that had captured her? If it was an illusion that she had gambled on, what was the illusion of, exactly? The music was real—real notes, real melodies, real passion, real skill. *Give me the beat, boys, and free my soul* . . . She had wanted to feel that, to feel her soul free. And when an audience jelled, when everyone was breathing like one organism, when they were enthralled by the performer who could transport them that way and give them a taste of the sublime, well, was that an illusion? Pure feeling, pure beauty—was it just a fantasy? Wasn't beauty truth—and wasn't truth supposed to trump everything?

Lily took out the tape and put in the last one, the one she had taken the day before everything had come crashing down. How desperately she had wanted that transport. She had been hooked on it. Hooked, by extension, on JJ. Bewitched. She remembered an illustration of the Pied Piper leading his column of children out of town, away from their parents, to a mountain in the distance that sparkled with promise. As a child, she had stared at the picture so hard she could hear the jaunty tune coming from the light-footed piper, a tune so entrancing even the leaves fled the trees to follow.

Lily fell asleep in the conference room. She woke up to the sound of the cleaning man's key in the door. She went to the ladies' room and washed up, stopped in a nearby café for breakfast, and then, instead of going to Troy's, went back upstairs to watch some of the tapes again. Afterward, she took a break, walked around the block, bought a candy bar and some milk, and came back to the office to watch again.

She didn't return to her sister's until late Sunday evening, after Troy and Peter were in bed. When they came downstairs, she had a cheese-and-veggie quiche warming in the oven, fresh-squeezed juice, and a fruit salad waiting for them.

"Lily, this is really very sweet," Troy said. How cute she looked, Lily thought, with her mussed morning hair and rosy cheeks.

"Fantastic!" Peter said, taking a huge bite of quiche. After breakfast, he kissed each woman on both cheeks and left them to talk.

"I really, really appreciate your letting me stay here, you know."

Troy waved her hand dismissively. "You've thanked me ten times already."

"But I haven't thanked you for coming to Montreal. Or apologized for how I treated you. It really meant a lot that you cared enough to come."

"I know you were going through a difficult time," Troy said. "I know I came down on you like a sledgehammer. I think I was just threatened by the thought of you and Stephen breaking up."

"Oh—I see. Well, I know I'd feel the same if it were you and Peter."

"How are you doing now?" Troy looked at Lily over her juice glass and then quickly away.

"It's hard. But the therapist we're seeing is great."

"What does she say?" Troy refolded her napkin.

"She's having us talk about our marriage, naturally, but she's mostly focused on me. She's had me talk about my childhood and my dreams about what I wanted when I was young and what happened along the way—you know, work, motherhood."

Troy brought her knees to her chin, gaze on the floor. "When I got back, Peter and I had a long talk. It was good; things we needed to say.

So I guess I'm grateful to you. I think it's easy to get caught up in daily life and take each other for granted sometimes."

"I'm glad something good's come of it, then," Lily said. But no matter how painful the process, no matter how guilty she felt over how she had hurt Stephen and, by extension, Colby, there was a part of her that could not reject what she had experienced. But she would keep that realization to herself.

"I'm just happy you came back."

"Me too."

They both hesitated, and then they embraced. On impulse, Lily stood and kissed the top of her sister's head. It smelled of ginger and vanilla.

"I love you, you know."

"Me too," Troy mumbled into her shoulder.

"Well, we'd both better get ready for work."

On the train from Brooklyn to Manhattan, Lily closed her eyes, trying to get clear in her mind what the tapes had told her before she met with the therapist. She had noticed so much she had missed at the time—the vulnerability behind Blaise's tough posture, JJ's passivity. Mixed in were ideas about how to edit the tapes, a way to intercut the shows with the interviews, but she kept trying to shoo those thoughts away and focus instead on what would be relevant in the session.

"So?" the therapist said, when they sat opposite each other again.

Lily sipped from a coffee she had picked up on the way. "It was a good exercise—very good, though I don't quite know why."

"You seem surer about something. What do you think that might be?"

Lily hesitated. "Well, I'm clear that whatever's been going on for me wasn't just some kind of delayed adolescence, or my life being stale. I know it was real. I know—" She stopped herself.

"What is it you know?"

"That it was really, really important."

The therapist nodded. "I agree," she said, surprising Lily.

"You do?"

"Something was essential. I don't think you would have taken such extreme action otherwise."

"I remember once, in thinking about Blaise and JJ, I thought in terms of God—or of some eternal mystery. That I had an equation in my mind between music and power. But I don't think I'm on a search for God."

"Maybe not God, per se, but transcendence of some kind? Some deeper meaning in your life? Tell me, what did you think of your work?"

"Come again?"

"How did you find the tapes—from an artistic point of view?"

"Oh. Well, I was actually kind of surprised. They were much better than I thought they'd be. I mean"—she leaned forward—"they need a ton of editing, but . . ." She sat back.

"Why did you just stop yourself?"

Lily felt herself flush. "I shouldn't be . . . I don't know."

"Enjoying them? Do you know this is the most excited I've seen you? What do you think that means?"

Lily squirmed.

"Lily, I want to posit something. I think you're right that this occurred because you needed to burst out of yourself, not your marriage. JJ, his music, became the means. Your task now is to find a way to bring this new awareness, and eventually this new self, into sync with the parts of your old self, your old life, that are still vital and that you want to retain. To synthesize them. In some cases, when one partner goes through changes like this, the marriage ends, because the other partner can't be open to those changes. But I don't think Stephen will be an obstacle. Working in music may be one path for you."

"I don't understand. You mean, do concert films?"

"Would that be so crazy? It would seem from the evidence that music has a very profound importance for you. Give it a little thought, and we'll talk about it when I see you both tonight."

Lily raced down the three flights of stairs to the street and headed back to her office. She felt tingly, and twice she had to stop and press her hand to her chest to calm her heart. It seemed what the therapist was saying was that it wasn't a choice between one world or the other, but a way through to a new one, a more authentic self.

She made it back to her office barely aware of how she got there. She stood waiting for the elevator, bouncing on the soles of her feet. That musician from Ticker-Tape who wanted to make a teaching video—what she had done with his card?

Suddenly she felt herself deflate, like an air mattress run over by a camper. What was she thinking? She had a job. She couldn't be running around doing music videos.

The elevator doors opened. Three young women followed her on, snazzily dressed and expertly made-up. Auditions on the eighth floor, Lily assumed. The elevator moved slowly, creaking. The girls were glowing with nervous anticipation—they were risk takers, holding fast to their dreams. It sure looked a lot more attractive to be going out on a limb than to be sitting in the nest, bored but safe.

Lily walked into Tom's office and closed the door. "I have a proposal."

"What's this about?" Tom smiled, but his smile was a little wary.

Her palms were sweating, and she surreptitiously wiped them on her slacks.

"First, I want to thank you again for giving me the time off."

"You took it without pay, so—" his hand made a dismissive curlicue in the air.

"When I was on the road, I was approached by another musician, and it gave me an idea. This could be something MTK does. I wondered how you'd feel about releasing me from other duties to pursue the concert-video business for the company?"

Tom didn't even pause to think about it. "Oh, I'm afraid not, Lily. We're really not in a position to take on any more risk. In fact . . ." he hesitated, "in fact, it seems like you've already got one foot out the door, and quite frankly, if you wanted to quit and go out on your own, you'd make things easier on us."

Lily felt her mouth drop open.

"Sorry, I didn't mean how that sounded. I just mean that we've been considering layoffs, and if you did want to leave, we wouldn't have to face that, at least not just yet." When Lily just stared at him, he added, "we'd really, really miss you, of course."

Lily said a quick, "OK, thanks, I thought it was worth a shot, I'll think about it," and hurried out, finding refuge in the ladies room. Her chest was tight, and she felt lightheaded. She reflexively reached for her inhaler, then put it back in her pocket, and instead took several deep breaths to calm herself. She wasn't being let go, not quite, but clearly, in staying away so long, she had not just pushed against the boundary of what was permissible, but breached it.

Well, I guess I've really done it, she thought. Breaching her life in every possible way seemed to have been what she'd wanted.

So what now?

She sat in the nursing chair, where women did their pumping, and let the silence settle around her. She closed her eyes. She tried to recapture her sense of elation after the therapy session, the fleeting moment of awareness of how much she wanted the chance to do music videos.

She sat up. She was done pumping breast milk, actual or metaphorical. She was going to do Blaise's film, the version that had been gradually taking shape in her mind, and it would be so terrific that Blaise's lingering animosity would not prevent her from using it. A month from now, maybe two, she would visit Blaise's website and see the video there, and she'd feel pride like she'd never known before.

Lily left work a few minutes early so she had time to get her thoughts in order. She and Stephen were to meet at the Joan of Arc monument on Ninety-first and Riverside Park and walk over to the therapist's office together.

The sun was setting later now; it stayed light till well after six. It was March 21, officially spring. Lily felt a pang: six months to the day. It had all begun on September 21—the concert with Colby. She sat down on a bench overlooking the Hudson watching light flash on water.

She glanced at her watch. Ten more minutes. How would Stephen react to her idea? To go out on her own, to be an independent videographer at a fairly professional level, she'd need at least $10,000 just for the HD camera, steady cam rig, and motion-graphics-editing software, plus maybe six months' income before any money came in. Would Stephen see her branching out on her own as a positive outcome of her transgression—or a constant and painful reminder of it?

Lily glanced at her watch again. Five minutes. She began to walk out of the park, passing in-line skaters and children playing baseball on hard-packed dirt. Stephen would be prompt, as always. He would be anxious, as always, that she—as always—would be slightly late. But she wouldn't. She'd be exactly on time. In such small ways and larger ones, she would regain his trust, though it might never, ever be complete.

She passed the dog run, admiring the sleek dog bodies, the eager panting tongues, the grace and beauty. Beauty—art, music, language, whatever form it took—was for her a necessity. That was key to what she had been discovering. And if she went ahead with her plan, she was no longer going to be just appreciating it, she would be making it.

Something thrummed through her, upsetting her delicate equilibrium, and she was tearing up. There, under a tree, was a boy with shoulder-length blond hair and blue jeans, cradling a guitar. He was humming to himself and strumming. The guitar was barely audible, and yet the sound had traveled through space, beaten its way through all those molecules, to find and devastate her.

And then Lily knew something else. Something completely improbable: Right from the first, she had fallen in love with JJ. It was that simple: In the second she had connected with his music, she had fallen in love with him. Thought of that way, her obsession made sense—consistent with the flush of falling in love. Impossible, yes. But maybe love was always inexplicable. One just accepted it.

JJ was unworthy of her love, but love him she did. And now she had to carry that love, and the pain it had brought her, with her forever. It would remain inside her, like a stillborn child, even in the midst of the love—deeper? better? more mature?—she felt for Stephen.

Lily realized she had stopped in the middle of the pathway. She moved quickly uphill, heading for the monument, streams of parents and children passing her, calling to mind the day she and Stephen had dropped Colby at college and stood surrounded by parents and children. She had watched Colby walking away and thought she knew everything there was to know about sorrow.

Stephen was waiting by a streetlight. He didn't see her, and she stood a moment, absorbing the sight of him. His face was tilted up to the sun, his pale auburn hair lifting slightly in the spring breeze.

Acknowledgments

Thanks and love to Janna Rademacher for being my personal Sherpa through the hills and dales of the publishing landscape. I am also deeply grateful to my agent, Barbara Braun, for her belief in this novel, and to Brooke Warner for championing women writers. Much appreciation as well to the rest of the awesome team at She Writes Press, especially Crystal Patriarche, Cait Levin, and Annie Tucker. Warm thanks to Lily and Mike Schenkler and Jody Winer for their insightful advice, to the many musicians I've interviewed for *Acoustic Guitar* and other magazines for sharing their experiences, and to my family and friends for their encouragement, support, and inspiration.

Discussion Group Guide

1. *Play for Me* begins with Lily dropping off her only son for his first year of college. How much, if at all, do you think this departure has to do with the events to follow? Her husband is steady and calm about it, as he is with many things. Do you think it is harder for women to have an empty nest? Why?

2. When attending the concert at her son's school during a weekend trip, Lily has the realization that she is much older than everyone else: "The auditorium was packed, loud, buzzing, working up a head of steam. Lily was suddenly aware of how much older she was than most of the audience. Not that anyone noticed or cared; she was clearly invisible." Is aging different for men and women? If yes, in what ways?

3. During the concert, Lily is shaken to the core by JJ's playing. In her words, the "notes of the guitar had pierced, as if they had done permanent damage, shifted her very DNA." Discuss how Lily thinks of this moment as "damaging" and inevitable, beyond her control.

4. How is Lily altered by the sound of Blaise and JJ's music in that moment? Is it JJ or the music that throws Lily off balance? Are the two inseparable?

5. After the concert, Lily's daily routine becomes almost unbearable: "She, somewhere along a line she could no longer remember, had become a creature of order, even stasis." Does this realization drive her to escape and sneak away to watch Blaise and JJ perform? What do you think may be missing from Lily's life?

6. Lily thinks to herself, of the asthma caused by her pregnancy, that "she had lost her voice and gained a son; it was a trade she never regretted." Do you think Lily's view changes over the course of the novel? Is the loss of a son or loss of her "voice" more at the heart of what Lily is searching for?

7. Lily finds a way to be on tour with the band by offering to do a video for free. What is the significance of Lily shifting from audience member to watching the concerts behind the lens of her camera?

8. Discuss JJ and Blaise's relationship. How do they help and/or hinder each other? How does the dynamic shift when Lily joins them on tour? What do JJ and Blaise each need from Lily?

9. Lily becomes increasingly destabilized by her preoccupation with music. She finds herself thinking "Maybe reactionaries were right, and music *was* subversive." Discuss the power of music.

10. Is it possible to have a second chance or to reinvent yourself once your life is settled? In which ways might this need—desire—be awakened? Is Lily compelled to follow JJ and the music? Does she consciously choose this spontaneous choice to follow the band; does she consciously choose betrayal?

11. Is Lily stronger upon her return home? Have her actions gotten her closer or further from her growth as a person?

12. Does Stephen react the way you expected him to upon Lily's return? How do you feel about his reaction and how he chooses to move forward?

13. Were you angry or shocked by Lily's behavior? If so, do you think you would have felt the same if a male character had behaved similarly?

14. What do you think of Blaise—is she vulnerable, disturbed, manipulative, egotistical?

15. What do you think JJ feels for Lily—true romantic love, or something else? When he says to her that he isn't about being a "star" but just wants to play music, do you believe him?

16. What do you think is at the heart of fandom, and hero worship?

17. Lily struggles throughout the novel with her weight—does her weight loss represent something on a deep level, and if so, what?

18. Lily goes on tour throughout the northeast, but she takes an irrevocable step only when she crosses the border into Canada, into the cold wintertime of Montreal. How is the author using this setting to intensify the action in this part of the novel?

19. What do you think is the importance of art, music, literature, etc. in human lives? Do you see the arts more as an enhancement or more as a necessity?

20. Do you think everyone has the capacity or need for creative fulfillment, whether realized or not?

About the Author

© Alexa Brandenberg Photography

Céline Keating is a writer, editor, and music reviewer. She is an active board member of the environmental organization The Concerned Citizens of Montauk, as well as of the New York chapter of the National Women's Book Association. Her short fiction has been published in many literary magazines, including *Prairie Schooner, North Stone Review, Santa Clara Review,* and *Emry's Journal.* Her nonfiction has appeared in *Acoustic Guitar,* minor7th.com, *Coastal Living, Guitar World,* and *Poets & Writers.* She lives in New York City and Montauk, Long Island. *Play for Me* is her second novel.

For more information about Céline and to subscribe to her newsletter, please go to: www.celinekeating.com

Selected Titles from She Writes Press

The Geometry of Love by Jessica Levine
$16.95, 978-1-938314-62-9
Torn between her need for stability and her desire for independence, an aspiring poets grapples with questions of artistic inspiration, erotic love, and infidelity.

Wishful Thinking by Kamy Wicoff
$16.95, 978-1-63152-976-4
A divorced mother of two gets an app on her phone that lets her be in more than one place at the same time, and quickly goes from zero to hero in her personal and professional life—but at what cost?

Shelter Us by Laura Diamond
$16.95, 978-1-63152-970-2
Lawyer-turned-stay-at-home-mom Sarah Shaw is still struggling to find a steady happiness after the death of her infant daughter when she meets a young homeless mother and toddler she can't get out of her mind—and becomes determined to rescue them.

Warming Up by Mary Hutchings Reed
$16.95, 978-1-938314-05-6
Unemployed and depressed former musical actress Cecilia Morrison decides to start therapy, hoping it will get her out of her slump—but ultimately it's a teen who cons her out of sixty bucks, not her analyst, who changes her life.

Duck Pond Epiphany by Tracey Barnes Priestley
$16.95, 978-1-938314-24-7
When a mother of four delivers her last child to college, she has to decide what to do next—and her life takes a surprising turn.

Stella Rose by Tammy Flanders Hetrick
$16.95, 978-1-63152-921-4
When her dying best friend asks her to take care of her sixteen-year-old daughter, Abby says yes—but as she grapples with raising a grieving teenager, she realizes she didn't know her best friend as well as she thought she did.